MURDER, JUST BECAUSE

The Return of the Snowman
5th Novel in the Detective Quaid Series

Yolanda Renée

Copyright

MURDER, JUST BECAUSE
The Return of the Snowman
5th Book in the Detective Quaid Series

www.yolandarenee.com

Email: yolandarenee@hotmail.com

ISBN: 9780985820633
Imprint: Yolanda Renee
YR Publishing

Dedication

In memory of Steven Ray Musgrove.

Forward

Please note this story has explicit sex, violence, and language and is not recommended for anyone under the age of 18.

I hope you enjoy the story, but also understand that the issue of rape and sexual abuse is a real one and happens daily in the United States.

Please, if this is an issue for you or someone you know, please contact the. National Sexual Violence Resource Center - http://www.nsvrc.org/

National Sexual Violence Resource Center
123 North Enola Drive
Enola, PA 17025
717.909.0710 Phone
717.909.0714 FAX
717.909.0715 TTY
877.739.3895 Toll-Free

Table of Contents

v

CHAPTER ONE

Mother's Day

May 13th

The wedding decorations included a light snowfall, made even more beautiful by the tiny white lights twinkling in the surrounding trees. Luminaires lit the walkway, and at the top of the steps beside the church entrance, a guitarist strummed and sang softly.

Clad in a bright red choir robe, Fern Jenkins slipped through the double doors and scurried upstairs to the balcony. While the other choir members sang, she focused on the action below.

Finally, there he was…the groom.

With a smile, she pulled a .38 special from her pocket, aimed at his forehead, and squeezed the trigger.

A loud crack jolted her awake.

Breathing hard in the darkened room, Fern struggled to get her bearings while savoring the lingering remnants of her dream. The same recurring fantasy she'd enjoyed ever since she'd first read about that pig, Steven Quaid, and his wedding plans. How she hated that man! Every day of happiness for that half-breed detective meant another one of misery for her beloved son Stowy.

Fully awake now, she shivered. What the hell? The last thing she remembered was drinking wine in the living room, but now she was in her bedroom, lying naked on her stomach, her hands and feet shackled to the bed.

Another crack sounded, and she felt the cruel sting of a whip striking her bare back. "Oh, my God!" she shouted, pulling at her restraints and twisting her head in a vain attempt to see her attacker.

"I thought that might wake you," a gravelly voice said. Zeke snapped the whip again, and its twisted leather branded the tender skin of her buttocks. "I understand you enjoy whipping,"

She groaned. "I only enjoy giving them."

Wielding the whip like an angry god, he lashed her back again. "I don't remember asking a question, bitch!" Then, without mercy, he struck again and again.

"Please, no more," Fern cried. Maybe if she played his game, he'd treat her better. "I'll do anything you want. Anything. Just please stop."

Instead, his hits grew fiercer. "Oh, you'll do what I want, because you have no other choice. Tell me, Momma. Stowy claimed that you loved giving pain. Do you enjoy receiving it as much?"

"Stowy? You know, my boy?"

Her assailant paused, panting. She could practically hear the grin in his voice. "Know him? I conquered his ass, then taught him all I knew. Your little Stowy shared many a story about how you loved to beat him, then reward him with sex. This is directly from him. He called it repayment for all the sacrifices you've made on his behalf."

The quick break was over, and the stranger continued beating her with renewed enthusiasm. She pressed her body deep into the mattress, a desperate attempt to escape his blows. When he finally stopped, a trickle of blood flowed across her tortured flesh, providing a peculiar kind of perverted pain relief.

"I don't understand," she gasped. "Stowy sent you?"

Chuckling, her torturer untied her feet. "Gift wrapped. I'm determined to fulfill my promise to your offspring, but enough talk. Get on your knees!"

He wrenched her mouth open, shoved his dirty fingers inside, and probed her gums. "Good start. Dentures are out. If you want to live, you'd better prove you're as talented as Stowy says you are. He says you can suck ten years of paint off a pole in seconds. Better than any woman he's ever known. Show me. Pretend I'm your precious little boy and give me your best." He plunged his rock-hard cock into her mouth. "Suck my Popsicle, you selfish bitch. Pretend it's root beer-flavored, like the ones you never shared with poor little Stowy." When she hesitated, he wrapped his fingers around her throat. "Or would you prefer this?" He tightened his grip.

She shook her head vigorously and then did his bidding just as enthusiastically, slurping and sucking until his seed exploded down her throat. She swallowed and, eyes closed, leaned back onto her knees. "Now what?"

"Don't sound so grateful." He laughed, climbed onto the bed behind her, and squeezed her ass. "Our boy Stowy told me you'd enjoy a good fuck, and I'm more than willing to give you one." He pressed the bulbous head of his cock against her clenched ass hole. "Relax, bitch. It'll only hurt for a minute."

"No!" Fern cried, trying to escape his grasp. "Please. Don't…at least use lubricant."

"Shut up!" he snarled. "I didn't use any lube Stowy's first time." He spat on his hand and rubbed it on the head of his cock. "Just a little spit is all it takes. Your boy wants you to know what his first day in prison was like." Zeke Savon, Stowy's former cellmate, rammed his cock into her. Ignoring her screams, he kept thrusting until his seed filled her with a second hot load.

She was a crumpled heap when he left the room, and she was still whimpering when he returned several hours later. "So, sweet Momma, how do you want to end this?" he asked, a shit-eating grin on his scruffy face.

"I have money. It's all yours. Just please let me go," Fern cried.

"Stowy said you'd try to negotiate, but he never mentioned money. So how much are we talking about?"

Without waiting for an answer, he shoved his cock back into her mouth. "Doesn't matter. A blow job is more valuable than gold. Ahh…that's it, Momma, show me how much you want to live."

"Stowy was right. It's been a real pleasure," he said after he finished pounding her ass for the second time. "When I arrived in town, I couldn't think of anyone I wanted to rip into more than you. Prison life sucks, and the touch of a good woman was all I wanted. Well, that and a good steak." He laughed and slapped her bloody ass. "What can I say, Fern? Your son wanted you to have this experience, and I was more than happy to give it to you. Now, it's time to give him the proof of our fun."

Several brief flashes of light perforated the darkness. "For the past ten years, your little Stowy was my number one bitch, but now, the honor's all yours. Smile so he can see how much you're enjoying your new position. Let's see what he thinks of these pictures."

A few minutes later, Zeke said, "Sonny boy wants to talk to you." He pressed the phone to her ear.

"Stowy!" she gasped.

"Hi, Mommy. Did you enjoy your Mother's Day gift?"

~~*~~

CHAPTER TWO

Hawaiian Honeymoon

June 5th

A light mist swirled across the dunes, but Sarah knew the rising sun would deliver a quick burn-off and begin another picture-perfect day. She watched the sun's slow ascent from the window of her romantic honeymoon hideaway, but as the sky lightened, her mood grew darker. The breathtaking sight usually filled her with joy, but this morning, she couldn't shake the uneasy feeling in the pit of her stomach. It didn't help that a phantom had haunted her dreams. She continued preparing for her morning run, but while she stretched, she searched the horizon, scanning for some unknown threat.

Next to her, still in bed, Steven threw off the blankets and sat up. "Where do you think you're going?"

"I'm meeting Brent for a run on the beach. You know that thing I do every morning while you're still dreaming," she teased.

He shook his head and rubbed the sleep from his eyes. "Dammit. I miss the cabin."

"Oh?" She finished fastening her hair into a ponytail and faced him, eyebrows furrowed. "Hawaii was your idea, mister. Cabin fever, if I remember correctly. At least that's what you told Frank."

"I was wrong. At the cabin, we cuddled every morning, but here, you leave me alone in a cold bed so you can run with another man. I swear, since we've gotten here, you've spent more time with Brent than you have with me. Just last night, I had to wait for hours while you partied the night away."

Sarah sat beside him. "And whose fault is that?" she asked quietly. "You were supposed to be with me last night, but you stood me up because of your case. You're the one who made the commitment for us to go to that luau, and when you bailed, Brent had no choice but to fill in for you." She frowned. "You waited for hours? If you finished work that early, why didn't you join me?"

He shrugged. "I kept thinking you'd be back any minute," he confessed. "I didn't expect you to stay very long or to enjoy it." He winked. "Not without me."

She leaned over and whispered, "You're the one who brought me here. I know you're working on a case, but you told me we'd be spending most of our time together. You also said you wanted me to get healthy, and I'm doing all I can to make that happen, which, by the way, includes running with Brent." She glared at him. "So, make up your mind. What do you want?"

"I want a honeymoon." He kissed her neck and gently pulled her back onto the bed.

Smiling, she stroked his cheek. "Good choice. Let me call Brent to let him know I won't be meeting him this

morning." She grinned. "Honeymoon aerobics are much more fun than a run."

Steven cursed under his breath and sat up. "Sorry to be such a jerk, but I just noticed the time. You might as well go for your run because I have to get to the office to wrap up this case. I'm sorry, but I promise I'll make it up to you. After this, it'll be nothing but a honeymoon and all the aerobics you can handle." He leaned in for another kiss.

Sarah pushed him away and sighed. "Promises, promises. You get me all hot and bothered, and then you send me out in the cold." She grinned at him, shaking her head and getting to her feet. "Okay, it's not exactly cold, but still…"

He stood and tried to take her into his arms, but she backed away. "I'm not kidding! This is your last chance. I'm losing patience. Finish with the job today, or the honeymoon is over. Don't let Frank bully you this time."

"You've got it!" he declared with a salute. "Today, I wrap up the case. Then, it's honeymoon haven. You have my word." He spread his arms wide, hoping she'd join him for a final hug.

"You'd better!" Smiling, she threw a pillow at his head before going outside. "No more hugs or kisses until you fulfill your promise!"

"You'll see!" Steven yelled at the closed door as he pulled on a pair of jeans. He finished dressing, grabbed a cup of coffee, and went to the patio to monitor Sarah's run. Despite what she thought, Steven never slept through her early morning excursions. He couldn't. Even though her bodyguard Brent was always at her side, Steven still felt compelled to look out for her. He continually scanned the horizon, the dunes, and the rocks dotting the beach.

He finished his coffee and spotted Sarah and Brent. That was quick. Maybe he still had time to jump in that shower with her. Frank could wait a few more minutes.

His phone rang, and when he answered, Frank yelled, "Where's Sarah?"

"Out for a run." His entire body chilled. "Why?"

"Get her in the house! I'm seconds away."

Steven heard the roar of a helicopter in the background, and before he even asked the question, he had a bad feeling about what the answer was going to be. "What the hell's going on, Frank?"

"The killer's after her."

Steven dropped the phone, grabbed his gun, and took off running. He made it to the beach five seconds after the sniper took aim.

CHAPTER THREE

Plane Crash

June 5th

"Control tower, this is medevac flight UC-294, requesting permission for take-off."

"UC-294, please stand by."

The pilot dried his hands on his pants and glanced over his shoulder into the cabin behind him. "Just between you and me, I can't wait to dump the son of a bitch we're hauling today. I know none of the maximum-security cons are upstanding citizens, but from what I've heard about this guy, he's one of the worst. This asshole kills for fun."

The co-pilot laughed. "Must be your first prison evac. Listen, I've been on plenty of these flights, and there's nothing to worry about, believe me. They've got that asshole strapped down good and doped up even better, so he won't be causing any trouble. It'll be just like any other run."

"Thanks for the pep talk. If you're right, I'll buy you a beer."

After a short burst of static, the flight controller's voice filled the cockpit. "All right, flight UC-294, you are now cleared for take-off. Ascend to forty-one thousand feet and hold steady. Enjoy an uneventful trip, boys."

"Roger Wilco," the pilot said. "Out."

The take-off was satin-smooth, and the pilot quickly ascended to the assigned altitude and then switched to autopilot. "So far, so good," he said.

"Like I told you, just like any other run," the co-pilot said. "And how about if we make that beer a bourbon?"

The pilot laughed. "Sure, we can do that. Hell, if everything goes well, I might even treat you to a steak."

A deafening explosion shook the airplane. "What the hell?" the pilot yelled, turning off the autopilot while struggling to get the jerking plane back under control.

The co-pilot craned his neck to look out the window.

"Smoke," he said in a shaky voice. "And flames." He swallowed. "Engine number two's toast."

As soon as paramedic Larry Beach heard the explosion and saw the smoke and flames outside the window, he neutralized the guards and unstrapped his patient. Then he gave the patient a shot to counteract the sedative and shook him violently by the shoulders. "Dammit, Stowy! Wake up! Now's our chance!"

Stowy woke up swinging. "Get off of me!" he snarled. "What, dammit? What is it?"

"Whoa! Easy, man. Something went wrong," Larry said, shoving a parachute into Stowy's hands. "I think an engine exploded. We're going to have to jump now."

Instantly alert, Stowy jumped up from the gurney. "Pants! I need pants! I can't jump in a damned hospital gown."

He ran his fingers through his hair. "And winter gear…we'll need that, too."

Larry clapped him on the back. "I've got it covered, buddy. We've got everything we need right here. I even took the guard's clothes for you, but we have to hurry. If we don't get out now, we could go down with the plane."

Stowy tossed the hospital gown aside and pulled on a pair of pants. "Are you sure it's going down? They seem to have it under control."

"You really want to hang around to find out?"

The plane banked hard left, and both men flailed their arms in a mad scramble to stay on their feet. Then the flight abruptly evened out again before banking in the opposite direction.

"Maybe you're right," Stowy said. "I think this crate's going down, and we need them to think we went with it. Put some blood on your lab coat and twist it around the gurney. And leave your dad's watch, too. I'll leave my dentures and the handcuffs, along with a little skin and blood. That should keep them busy for a little while."

"But what if the plane doesn't explode? What if they manage to land?" Larry asked. "Then what?"

"No time to worry about that now. I've got people to see

and places to be. First, we stay alive. Then we'll deal with the results."

"Mayday! Mayday! Mayday! This is flight UC-294. Our last known location is just south of Moose Pass. We've lost one engine, and all instruments are failing. We are going down. I repeat we are going down. We have six on board."

Stowy gave Larry a shove. "Hear that? Let's get the hell out of here!"

After they muscled the door open, they pushed the two naked guards out. Then they double-checked their chutes and jumped into the cold Alaskan air. Seconds later, the other engine exploded, and as the airplane plunged toward the ground, it lit their way like a fiery comet.

CHAPTER FOUR

Disbelief

June 5th

The setting sun was creating a breathtaking kaleidoscope of colors, but Steven was oblivious to the beauty. He didn't give a shit what the sky looked like. He didn't give a shit what anything looked like. The only thing that mattered right now was getting to Sarah.

His head and heart pounded in sync with the manic FWOP-FWOP-FWOP of the chopper blades. While his empty stomach churned, its queasiness worsened by the overpowering scent of burnt oil. He swallowed the sour taste in his mouth and leaned forward, as though willing the helicopter to fly faster.

As soon as the hospital came into sight, he tensed like a mountain lion prepared to pounce, and before the chopper's skids touched the ground, he unstrapped, pushed the door open, and jumped. With a muttered curse, he quickly regained his balance and took off for the hospital at a dead run.

Panting, he burst through the doors, sweat trickling down his face, and scanned the immediate area. No sign of Sarah or Brent, so he trotted to the admission desk and elbowed his way to the front of the line.

The nurse frowned at him. "Sir, you'll have to go to the end of the line."

He flashed his badge. "Sorry, ma'am. Official business. I'm looking for the man and woman who were just delivered by helicopter. Couldn't have been more than fifteen minutes ago."

She nodded and pointed. "Through those double doors."

Adrenaline flooded his system when he pushed through the doors, and his heart did a series of cartwheels. Halfway down the corridor, there stood Sarah beside a gurney, and she looked just fine. On her own two feet. Not shot.

Seeing her was one thing, but he wouldn't believe she was okay until he wrapped his arms around her and felt her warm body next to his. He made short work of the distance between them, and when he was only a few quick steps away, she leaned over and kissed the man lying on the gurney. Brent. Not on the cheek, either. Right on the lips.

"I'll be right here. I promise," Sarah said to the semi-conscious man. Then she bowed her head as though in prayer as Brent was wheeled into the operating room. She never even glanced in Steven's direction.

A nurse touched Sarah's arm and said, "He's in good hands, Mrs. Summers. Please, come with me, and I'll make sure you get a change of clothes." Then she led Sarah away.

Steven stared after them helplessly. Mrs. Summers! What the hell? He tried to follow, but Frank and two other agents joined him. "Steven, you need to go with these men and give them a statement."

"I need to see Sarah."

"Not until I talk with her first. You couldn't tell me what happened. She can." Frank nodded to the officers. One placed his hand on Steven's shoulder. Steven flinched, but Frank held up his hand. "I'll make sure she's all right. Like I told you, Sarah took control of the situation after we landed, and she's the reason Brent made it here alive."

Steven's shoulders dropped, but he nodded. "Let's get this over with," he said to the other two officers.

Sarah slumped tiredly in the waiting room, her hand pressed to her left side. Her white tee shirt and shorts were splattered with blood, as was Frank's jacket, which he'd draped around her shoulders right before she got into the helicopter. She shivered, pulled the coat tighter, and closed her eyes.

"Mrs. Summers?" the nurse said. "Sorry to keep you waiting, but I finally found you something to wear."

Sarah opened her eyes and smiled weakly. "Thank you."

"They're just scrubs, but they'll be more comfortable than what you're wearing. You can shower, too. There's a room just down the hall. A nice hot shower will make you feel better." She handed the scrubs to Sarah. "Take your time. The surgery will take a while."

Frank plopped into the seat next to Sarah. "That's a wonderful idea," he told the nurse. "Thank you."

After the nurse left, he said, "I'll need those clothes as evidence."

Sarah nodded. "Of course."

"How's Brent?"

She shrugged. "They just took him into surgery. Holding his own, I pray." She looked around the room. "Where's Steven? Didn't he fly in with you?"

"He did, and he was in the hospital before I even got out of the helicopter. But I needed him to give his side of the equation while you give me yours. Don't worry. I know he'll join us soon."

She nodded. "I see." She shivered again and stood. "Please, excuse me for a few minutes. I need to get out of these clothes."

Frank grabbed her arm.

She winced and sat back down. "Ouch."

He furrowed his eyebrows. "Are you injured?"

"Just a bruised rib. Sorry, don't mean to be a wimp, but now that the adrenaline's worn off, I'm really feeling it."

"You should've been checked out, too."

"Later. Right now, all I want is a shower, clean clothes, and for Brent to be all right. By the way, I said I was his wife, so they'd let me help take care of him. You'll see to that, won't you? I know Steven won't mind. After all, Brent saved my life. We have to make sure he...he has to live." Her voice faded away, and she bit her lip.

Frank squeezed her hand. "Don't you worry. I'll take care of everything, but before you shower, I need you to tell me exactly what happened today."

Sarah took a deep breath, winced, and leaned back. "Brent and I run every morning. We have ever since I first met him during my art tour. He's remarkable, and the reason I survived captivity." She stopped suddenly. "Sorry, Frank. Extraneous information."

"It's all right. Go on."

"Brent always ran in protective mode, shielding me from a possible attack. He had his attention on the area ahead. I always felt safe with him." She lowered her head and sighed. "This morning was different."

"How so?"

"I don't know exactly. Something just felt off, something I felt before I left the house. I wasn't into the run to start with, and then Steven said something that rubbed me the wrong way. To top it off, Brent and I got into an argument, but despite all that, we still went running. We were both determined to rid ourselves of the stress."

"If you don't mind me asking, what did Steven say?"

Sarah smiled. "Only that he wasn't happy about my morning runs, and that our time together didn't feel like a honeymoon. I know he's right. Being here changed everything. To tell the truth, it's probably not fair to blame him for my stress, because I had a bad feeling before he ever said a word."

She pulled the jacket around her shoulders and looked at Frank. "I should and do hold you responsible, but Steven's attitude certainly didn't help. You and your damned serial killer cases." She wrinkled her nose at him. "Then Brent told me that he's blaming this job for his broken engagement. Let's just say it was a bad morning, all around."

"And I thought everyone loved Hawaii," Frank said, his disbelief carved in a deep frown.

Sarah shook her head. "Not this time. Sorry."

Frank shrugged. "Can't win them all. Please, go on."

"Despite all that, we ran out five miles. Then I decided to make it interesting."

Frank noticed that Steven had just entered the waiting room. He signaled for him to hold back until he finished his questioning. "Interesting? How so?"

"A race. The winner had to make breakfast. I was trying to lift Brent's spirits, and mine too." She smiled, and then a shadow passed over her face. "That man can run circles around me. I've never beaten him in a real race, not once, but as soon as I mentioned pineapple hotcakes and maple syrup? He was determined to let me win."

Before continuing, she took a slow deep breath and grimaced in pain but brushed it off. "A quarter-mile from the house, I thought I saw the glint of a gun sight…then I spotted the man behind it. I yelled, 'Gun!' Everything happened so fast after that. When I stopped to retrieve my gun, Brent must've been in the zone, because he ran right past me. Almost without thinking, I took the shot, and when Brent turned around to look at me, that's when the sniper pulled the trigger. It was only a matter of seconds between the two rounds, but because of me, Brent was in the line of fire." She closed her eyes and shook her head. "The bullet hit him. It was meant for me, wasn't it?"

She looked at Frank. He nodded.

"I stopped running, and now he's fighting for his life. It's all my fault. I knew something was wrong. The clues were there, but I didn't listen." When she opened her eyes, they were glassy with unshed tears.

Frank handed her his handkerchief. "Brent won't see it that way. He was doing his job and protecting you. I'm just glad we got there when we did. Getting him to the hospital so quickly will make all the difference. Anyway, Annie Oakley, you got the sniper. Put a bullet right between his eyes."

"Good!" Steven said as he joined them. "The bastard is dead?"

Frank nodded.

His face lined with worry and his muscles taut, Steven knelt in front of Sarah and clasped her elbow. "Thank God you're all right, Mrs. Summers." Hiding the rage that was roiling inside of him, he winked and gently touched her hand.

She clung to his fingers. "I am."

"But you're the one who took the shot? Did Brent even pull his weapon?" To counter the undertone of anger in his voice, he smiled, moved a stray tendril of hair from her face, and caressed her cheek. Her very pale cheek.

Sarah covered her face with trembling hands. "I saw the shooter first, so I did what Brent taught me." She shook her head. "God forgive me, I killed a man," she whispered.

"It's all right. You did the only thing you could," Steven assured her while looking around the room for a nurse. "Come on. Let's get you out of here. There's got to be someplace you can rest."

She shook her head again, barely suppressing a sob. "No! I can't leave. I have to wait for word on Brent." She suddenly sat up straight, eyes wide. With a slight wince, she turned her attention to Frank. "Why did that man want me dead? Who was he?"

"Yes, Frank," Steven said as he rose from the floor and sat next to Sarah, his arm cradling her arm, their fingers entwined. "That's a good question. Who was he, and why the warning call? What aren't you telling us?"

Frank cleared his throat. "Maybe I should check on Brent's condition." He stood.

Steven jumped to his feet, towering over Frank and wordlessly persuading him to retake his seat. "Tell me what the hell's going on, Frank. Who was it?"

Frank sighed. "Pierre Slade, Jarod Bardot's half-brother."

"Oh my God," Sarah said, her shoulders collapsing. "Bardot's brother...I thought...you said there was no family. There was no one to pick up the contract."

Steven's eyes flashed. "Yes, Frank. Remember? We had that discussion right before I agreed to bring Sarah here to work your serial killer case. Your offer was a free opportunity to honeymoon in Hawaii. You swore there was no threat to Sarah's life and that her safety would be your number one priority. Your words exactly." His hand balled into a fist.

"I'm sorry, but I didn't know. We just found out Bardot's father had a son by another woman the same year he married Bardot's mother. Bardot and Slade met in prison, figured out their lineage, and became close friends. Very few people knew they were related. Fortunately, Slade's ex knew, and when she got busted for robbery, she ratted him out."

Sarah stood, and all the color drained from her face. As though mesmerized, she held out her trembling palm and stared at the fresh blood dripping through her fingers. "I thought all that blood was Brent's..."

Her eyes rolled back, and with a shudder, she collapsed.

~~*~~

CHAPTER FIVE

Mosquitoes

June 6th

Mosquitoes swarmed around the two men, buzzing maddeningly around their ears, peppering their sweaty skin, and feasting non-stop on their blood. Swatting and cursing brought no relief. Neither did a covering of mud from the lake.

Larry crushed another one on his neck, leaving a bloody smear behind. "We have to get to higher ground, Stowy. These little bastards are driving me nuts. It should be cooler up there, and they hate the cold." He waved his hand around his ear to shoo the swarm, which scattered and then immediately returned. He blew out his breath and scratched his neck. "God, I'm exhausted."

Stowy glared at him. "Screw you and your exhaustion. It's your fault we're in this mosquito shithole. Some getaway plane."

"It's not my fault the damned thing blew! What about your friend Zeke? He's the one who was responsible for the plane, not me, and I wouldn't be surprised if he's the one who sabotaged it. Why wouldn't he want you dead? You stole his position as alpha the day you arrived. Sure, he became a loyal friend because he knew you'd kill him if he didn't. Between him and your mother, the one you said was selling your trophies, you have enemies, my friend, a passel load of haters."

"Shut the fuck up!" Stowy yelled. "It's your damned fault we're lost. You said you know these mountains, but obviously, that was a lie. We've been wandering for hours." He shook his head. "Even a moron knows we'd be sitting ducks for the searchers if we move to higher ground. Our best bet is to stay low." He shoved Larry and kept walking. "And for the record, Zeke never was and never will be my friend. Like Mother, he's a user and only out for what he can get. Mom's no mother, but don't you worry. I'll take care of them. You can count on it."

"Humph!" Larry stood and straightened his clothes. "At least I got us out of that plane alive. That was all me," he muttered, but his voice was drowned out by the sound of helicopters.

Both men looked up.

"Shit! I thought we'd have more time, but somebody must've seen the explosion," Stowy said, sprinting for cover. "Come on! Stay under the trees. We're going to have to step it up, lardass."

Larry ran to catch up, and after panting a few deep breaths, smiled, and said, "Do you smell that?" He sniffed the air again. "Fish! By God, somebody's cooking fish."

Stowy grinned. "Now that's more like it. What do you say we invite ourselves to dinner?"

~***~

Fern giggled like a schoolgirl after the cork exploded from the champagne bottle and ricocheted off the refrigerator and kitchen cupboards. She held out her glass, and Zeke obliged by filling it with the bubbly drink. "I can't believe we pulled it off, can you?" he said.

"I never doubted." Fern stood on tiptoes to kiss him. "Your connections and my money." She held up her glass for a toast. "To my baby boy, may he rot in hell with his good-for-nothing father."

They clinked glasses. "Here, here," he said before downing the glassful. "Shall we eat?" He pulled out a chair for Fern at the kitchen table. "There's nothing better than home cooking, and you, my love, you know what I like."

"Well, I do appreciate a man with an appetite." She winked. "And you have exactly what I want." Her hand slowly caressed his inner thigh, then gently massaged his cock through his jeans.

Zeke adjusted in his seat. "Keep that up, and I'll never get through this hunk of meat."

"I can't help myself," Fern said, giving him a flirty smile. Zeke kept eating. Still, she persisted. Irritated that she wouldn't allow him to enjoy the meal, he grabbed her by the collar.

"I'm sorry. Really. I was just flirting," Fern insisted.

"Too late! My appetite's been raised." Zeke forced her to her hands and knees while pushing his chair back from the table. "Prove you're not just a tease. No hands allowed," he said as he undid his belt. "If you fail, I'll use this on you for dessert."

Shaking, Fern did as he ordered and expertly undid his zipper with her mouth. She even popped the snap at his waist and released his cock from captivity. Starting at the head, she licked, then sucked down his shaft until his entire member was in her mouth.

"Oh God, I swear I have died and gone to Heaven," Zeke said around a mouthful of steak as Fern continued to pleasure him. He spread his legs to give her easier access and kept eating. After he swallowed his last bite of food, he lifted Fern from the floor, bent her over the end of the table, and ripped off her panties. Then he grabbed a handful of butter and, after slathering her ass with it, slid his cock into her.

"That's it, baby. So good. So tight." He slapped her ass. "You ready for a wild ride?"

Fern didn't answer. Zeke grabbed her hair and pulled her head back, then slapped her ass hard. "I asked you a question, bitch."

"Sorry, master. I'm more than ready Give it to me hard."

Pleased, Zeke smacked her ass again. "Good girl. What is it that you want from your master?"

"I want you to fuck me so hard I scream your name," Fern said dully.

With a frown, he grabbed his belt, then impaled her ass, again and again, thrusting harder and harder, his balls slapping her ass as he beat her with his belt. "I want to hear more enthusiasm from you, dammit! Isn't this what you were asking for?"

"Yes, master, yes," she moaned. "Yes, yes! Fuck me, fuck me hard!" she screamed.

Zeke's orgasmic roar sounded like a bear. "Now, that's what I call a great meal," he said. "From now on, that's how I want all my meals served." He sat down and pushed Fern toward the bathroom. "Go clean yourself up. But first, give Poppa a big kiss."

While Fern was in the bathroom, Zeke finished her meal. She returned to the table with coffee, a chocolate cake, and a smile on her face. "When do we leave for New Freeport to build that cabin you want?" she asked.

"First, we have to get rid of the rest of Stowy's souvenirs and find a buyer for this place. There's no rush, is there?"

"Not really. It's just that I want to start a new chapter with you. Since you've come into my life, I feel like a new woman."

"And you make me feel like a man. By the way, how old are you?"

"Old enough to know better but nowhere near old enough to be your mother. And how dare you insinuate that I am?" She laughed.

"Baby, it doesn't matter how old you are. I've never felt this way about any woman. You make me feel like I'm a teenager again. Love feels good, really good."

"Oh, Zeke," Fern cooed. "I've never been happier."

Several hours later, they lay wrapped in each other's arms. "When should I file the insurance claim?" Fern asked. "One million dollars. It's just so hard to believe that a serial killer dies, and we get a million dollars. Double Indemnity is such a lovely idea."

"You're going to have to wait for a while. You don't want anyone to think you're impatient to benefit from your son's death, do you? Besides, you're going to need a death certificate, and you won't be able to get that until they finish with their investigation."

"I never thought of that. Although there's no real hurry, is there? I can't believe how easily you tamed that boy. I tried for years, but he was just too high-spirited, and quite honestly, I was afraid of him."

Zeke laughed. "After fifteen years in prison, I learned how to bend a man to my will in a very short time. Your son gave me less trouble than most. It was as though he was looking for someone to show him the way."

"I'm not surprised. Stowy's father had no clue. He needs a man's influence." She smiled. "Just like me."

With those words, Zeke handcuffed her to the bed. "Then, let me demonstrate a few of my best techniques."

~~*~~

CHAPTER SIX

Blame & Rage

June 6th

Pacing in tight circles like a caged bear, Steven rechecked his watch and frowned. Dammit, shouldn't the surgery be over by now? If anything happens to Sarah...

Frank burst into the waiting room. Steven glanced at him, clenched his jaw, and then stared his friend down. "What the hell do you want?"

Frank held up his hand. "Whoa. Take it easy. I'm concerned about Sarah. Waiting for word, just like you." He cleared his throat. "I heard that Brent is holding his own."

"For now."

"You're blaming him?"

Steven narrowed his eyes. "No, Frank. The credit's all yours."

"You've got to understand—"

"The hell I do! You promised me Sarah was in no danger. Swore that keeping her safe was our number one priority. And where is she now? In surgery! Goddamned surgery with a bullet in her lung!"

Frank studied his shoes. "I know, and you have a right to be upset, but what you don't understand is that Pierre Slade was our serial killer, and he killed all those people to bait you and gain access to Sarah." He looked Steven in the eye. "We played right into his hands, but hindsight is twenty-twenty. We simply didn't know at the time. If I had any idea, I never would've told you about the case. I'm sorry, but—"

Steven glared at him with laser beam intensity. "You damned well should've known! The one request I made was an investigation into Jarod Bardot, specifically to make sure no one was waiting in the wings. Do you remember what you said? Do you remember the file you handed me?"

"It was based on the best information we had."

"Yeah, well, it wasn't good enough, Frank. You failed. You failed me, but most of all, you failed Sarah." He ran his hand through his hair wearily. "I've got to get out of here. The air is stale, and I can't stand to be around you right now."

As Steven walked, he considered the events of the day. Thinking about what happened to Sarah filled him with blind rage, so maybe he didn't see things clearly. It was easy enough to blame Frank, but was it fair? Sure, Frank told him about the case, but nobody forced him to get involved. That was all on him. He's the one who wanted in. He could've…he should've…been focused on what was best for Sarah, but her health issues and a honeymoon in Hawaii came in a distant second and third to the heady attraction of catching another psycho. So, whether he wanted to admit it or not, all of this was his fault, not Frank's. The only one he had to blame was himself.

When he walked back into the hospital, Frank was nowhere to be seen, so he went looking for someone who could give him an update. Instead, he saw Sarah being moved from the recovery center. Her eyes were closed, her skin pale, and she seemed smaller than usual. Innocent and completely defenseless. In a world where I keep putting her in contact with evil. Why can't I protect the one I love the most? His heart hurt at the self-realization, and his rage turned inward. They wheeled her into a private room, and he tried to follow, but a guard stopped him.

"I'm sorry, sir. No visitors allowed."

"I'm no damned visitor. I'm her husband!"

The guard placed a beefy hand on Steven's shoulder and steered him away from the door. "Not possible. The lady's husband's already in there, so if your wife's in the hospital, she's in some other room." He pointed to the nurses' desk. "Go talk to them. They should be able to clear things up for you."

"But you don't understand—"

"Sir, if you don't leave, I'll have to call security."

Steven held up his hands. "Fine. I'm going, but can you at least tell me where your boss, Frank Stover, is?"

"Afraid not. I have no idea where the boss is."

Steven opened his mouth to say something else and then thought better of it. He nodded curtly and walked to the nurses' desk.

The nurse gave him a bright smile. "Can I help you?"

"I was hoping to get some information about a patient. Sarah…"

"Oh, yes, Mrs. Summers."

"That's right," Steven said through gritted teeth. He didn't know how much more of this pretend bullshit he could take. It was one thing to go along with Sarah posing as Brent's wife so she could look after him, but now she needed care, too. Dammit. He should be the one caring for her, instead of being stuck on the outside. Not even allowed into her damned hospital room.

Another nurse looked over and smiled. "I'm sorry, sir, but we can't give out any information on that patient. You'll have to contact this gentleman." She handed him Frank Stover's business card.

"You've got to be kidding me!"

~***~

An hour later, Frank escorted him to the door of Brent and Sarah's room. "Mr. Quaid has full access to this room," he told the guard.

Steven entered without waiting for confirmation and raced to Sarah's side. "What are you doing out of bed?" Instead of being in her bed where she belonged, she was struggling to get to Brent. Steven picked her up and carried her to her bed. "What the hell?" he growled. "You just had surgery."

"But…"

"How can you get well if you're up playing nursemaid to—"

Doctor Westgate yanked the door open. "What's going on? I could hear the yelling halfway down the hall."

Frowning at the distress he saw on Sarah's face, the doctor pointed at Steven. "That's enough! You need to leave," he said, grabbing Steven's arm and dragging him from the room. In the hallway, Westgate glared at him sternly. "Mr. and Mrs. Summers don't need that kind of agitation. I don't know what you think you were doing in there, but it isn't helping either one of my patients. I don't want you anywhere near either one of them. Understood?"

He turned to the guard and said, "See this man? He isn't to be allowed in that room again without my permission."

The guard looked at Steven and nodded. "We met earlier. No problem, doctor. I'll see to it personally."

Steven looked from one man to the other. "But my...but I—"

"Move along," the doctor said with a wave of his hand. Then he turned and went back into the room, leaving Steven staring after him like a kicked puppy.

"I'm sorry about that, Mrs. Summers, but that man won't be disturbing you again. He was right about one thing, though. You need to take care of you. Your husband is doing fine." He buzzed for a nurse.

While holding her left side, Sarah gingerly lay down. "Please don't keep him away, doctor. He wasn't disturbing me. That's just the way he is, and he's, well, he's a very dear friend. To both of us."

"There's no good reason for you to be dealing with that kind of disruptive behavior right now, Mrs. Summers. You just had surgery, and you need to stay quiet. Give yourself time to heal." He inspected her bandages and hit the nurse's buzzer again. "This is what happens when you don't follow your doctor's orders. It looks like you may have torn your stitches." He gently lifted an edge of the adhesive tape. "I understand your concern for your husband, but you have to take care of yourself, too. You do realize we took a bullet from your lung and rebuilt a rib, don't you?" He pulled at the tape again, and Sarah grimaced. "Sorry. The nurse usually does this." He hit the buzzer again. "The bottom line is, if you want to heal properly, you're going to have to stay in bed. At least for a few days."

"I know all that, doctor, but you don't understand! It looked like Brent was bleeding, so I rang for the nurse, but nobody came. What was I supposed to do? Somebody had to check on him."

"I see," the doctor said. "I'd better have a look-see." He bent over Brent's bed and quickly stopped the bleeding and reinserted the catheter. "Good catch, Mrs. Summers. His IV came loose." He shook his head. "I'm sorry. This never should've happened. A nurse should've answered your call immediately. Something tells me your call button may need some surgery of its own." He pushed the call button on Brent's bed and returned to her side.

"Now, where were we?" He finished removing her bandages and, while preparing to redo some of the stitches, said, "Your husband's doing as well as can be expected. The bullet entered his right side, collapsed a lung, broke his collarbone, and exited out his left shoulder. So, it did a lot of damage to his body before it went into you. He's lost a lot of blood, and I'm not going to lie to you. His condition is still critical." The doctor finished with the stitching and took her hand. "Just talk to him. Reassure him. Let him know you're here. He'll hear you, and right now, your voice has more healing power than I do." He winked at her. "Just promise me you'll do it from your own bed."

Sarah smiled. "I promise. Thank you, doctor. I appreciate all you've done for both of us, but would you mind doing me a favor? I really need to speak with Frank Stover."

The doctor nodded. "I'll have him sent in. As long as you promise not to get out of that bed again."

"I promise."

"Good. I'll be back in a few minutes, just as soon as I find a nurse and a call button that works."

~***~

Hunched over with his hands stuffed in his pockets, Steven wandered the corridor and mumbled to himself. "I can't even yell at my own wife. Goddamned stupid doctor. What gives him the right?"

He rounded a corner too quickly and nearly ran over a pretty nurse. "Oops!" she chirped. "Can I help you?"

"No. Sorry about that, miss. Just feeling sorry for myself."

"Oh, I'm sorry. Have you lost someone?"

"No. At least I hope not. Maybe you can help me understand something. Why do women insist on taking such dangerous chances?"

She smiled. "Why not? You only live once. So, I take it your girl is here because she did something dangerous?"

He nodded.

"Would you love her as much if she weren't exactly the way she is?" She stepped back and gave him a once-over. "You look like a man who faces life head-on."

"No. probably not. You're right. She's perfect just the way she is." He smiled. "Thanks."

Her smile brightened. "She'll be fine. You'll see."

Steven left the hospital to walk the streets of Honolulu, with one burning question filling his mind: Would their lives ever be sane?

~~*~~

CHAPTER SEVEN

Bug Off

June 6th

"Look at all this gear! A tent, sleeping bags, candy bars. Oh, my God! Bug Off! We're saved!" Larry stopped rifling through the campers' supplies and sprayed himself from head to toes with so much repellent, his skin glistened with it. "Out-fucking-standing!"

Stowy grunted. "You damned well better not use it all." He finished hog-tying the two campers, and then dragged and dropped them into the tall grass near the water. "I truly appreciate your hospitality, boys. Not to mention your donations. Especially this handgun and hunting knife," he said, carefully testing the sharpness of the blade with his finger. "This here's some quality stuff."

With the speed of a jaguar, he smashed one of the men over the head with the gun. Then he removed the other man's gag and waved the gun at him. "Now it's your turn. You can end up like your buddy there, or you can tell me how far we have to travel to get out of here. Cooperate, and you're free. It shouldn't take a couple smart guys like you long to get out of those ropes after we leave."

The camper gaped at the blood gushing from his unconscious buddy's head and quickly nodded. "Seward Highway is ten miles to the east of us, but you'll have to climb the bluff to get to it." He motioned toward the cliff on his left. "At the top, there's a four-wheeler. From there, follow the logging road to the end, and that's where you'll find my pickup. The keys are in my right-hand pocket. You're welcome to take them and go, but if you'd like, I could show you the way." His voice was shrill and shaky, but he managed to meet Stowy's penetrating stare with a hopeful half-smile. "It'd be no problem. You guys will be long gone before my friend, and I make it halfway back to civilization."

Stowy smiled. "No doubt, but I have a much better idea." He admired the hunting knife's gleaming blade for a moment, and then, with one powerful slash, nearly severed the man's wide-eyed still-smiling head. After a quick nod of approval, Stowy gave the other man the same treatment, then cleaned the blood from the knife. He retrieved the truck keys, reclaimed the ropes, and headed back to the campfire. As he walked away, a swarm of hungry mosquitoes descended on the bodies.

Larry looked up as he approached. "It's about time. Let's eat this fish while it's still warm." He grinned. "What were you doing? I thought I was going to have to eat without you."

Stowy dropped to the ground and reached for one of the fresh graylings. "If you did, that would've been the last thought you ever had." He held up a set of keys. "I was arranging our transportation home."

Larry laughed and snagged another fish. "Just kidding. That's awesome. You know I wouldn't let you starve. I even left the bigger ones for you."

Except for a few unintelligible grunts and some appreciative lip-smacking, they ate the campers' meal in silence. After he finished, Stowy licked his fingers and stretched. "That was mighty fine, but we'd better get moving. Pack up what you want, and let's get out of here."

Stowy stuffed the gun into his waistband. "I really hate guns, but this might come in handy if we meet a bear or two."

"You talking the animal or the cop?"

"Both." Stowy smiled as he admired the hunting knife. Huffing out a hot breath, he cleaned off a speck of blood, still clinging to the blade before putting it into its sheath and hooking it carefully to his belt. "Beautiful," he whispered, patting it gently. "C' mon, Larry. We need to go. All that fresh blood will attract predators."

Larry stared at him, open-mouthed.

"What are you waiting for? Don't just stand there. I told you we have to go!"

Larry didn't move. "Bloody hell, you killed them?"

"What'd you think I'd do? Leave them here so they could tell the searchers which way we went?"

"I…I guess not, but murder? I've never killed anyone."

"Is that so? And what do you think happened to those two guards you pushed out of that plane without parachutes?"

"I…I never thought about it."

Stowy snorted. "What? You think they sprouted wings on the way down? You dumb shit, your ass is on the line as much as mine. If we're caught, you're going down with me…so now do you think you might be ready to MOVE?"

CHAPTER EIGHT

Headlines

June 8th

The Queen's Medical Center waiting room was decorated with colorful furniture, tropical plants, and ceiling-to-floor windows that afforded breathtaking views of the city and ocean. Still, Steven was too busy pacing and cursing under his breath to notice any of it. There was no excuse for the way that nurse treated him, dammit. Westgate was in charge, and he gave Steven the green light to visit, so what the hell right did she have to throw him out? Not his damned fault, Brent overreacted.

"It's good to see you with your eyes open. How do you feel?" Steven asked Brent as he entered the room, but he stopped short when he noticed that Sarah was missing. "Where's Sarah? What happened? Where'd they take her? Is she all right?"

"Calm down, boss. She's fine." Brent grimaced as he tried to sit up.

The nurse added a pillow behind his back. "They took her to x-ray to make sure that rib is healing right. She's been experiencing too much pain," she said.

"Damn, woman won't quit fussing over me," Brent added with a grin.

Rubbing the back of his neck, Steven stomped to the window. "Show some gratitude, asshole! She's barely left your side."

"Just as any dutiful wife of mine would do. I'm one lucky man, but I can't believe you went along with this charade." Brent's chortle was cut short by a stab of pain, but his grin lingered.

Steven's fist clenched, and he was at Brent's bedside in two steps. "Ungrateful bastard! You're alive because of her." He cast a sidewise glance at the nurse while Brent's grin faded to a ghost of a smile. "There's nothing funny about any of this. Sarah wouldn't even be here if you'd been doing your job! Pineapple pancakes? What the hell's the matter with you? Is that all it takes to distract you from your work?"

Steven ran his hand over his face. In retrospect, maybe he shouldn't have unloaded on Brent like that. Not yet, anyway. Still, just because the guy's heartbeat went screwy for a few minutes was no reason for the nurse to kick him out. All he was trying to do was see his wife, for heaven's sake.

He stopped pacing and collapsed into a chair with his head in his hands. Jesus, he needed to get himself under control, and soon. Carrying around this much rage wasn't doing anybody any good. Least of all, Sarah.

But why the hell wouldn't she talk to him about what happened? She had to be torn up over the killing, but she was acting like it never happened. Instead of letting him in and expressing her feelings to him, she was showering all her words and attention on Brent. Was he jealous? Damned straight, but mostly he was mad at himself because he didn't get to the beach fast enough to save her from this misery.

"Is there a Steven Quaid here?"

Steven looked up. "I'm Quaid."

The messenger handed him a manila envelope. "Please sign here."

Steven immediately realized it was from Captain Reed in Anchorage, so he quickly ripped it open. Inside was a copy of the Anchorage newspaper. In bold letters, its front-page headline screamed **The Snowman, Stowy Jenkins, DEAD**!

According to the article, Jenkins died when the Medevac plane carrying him to the Anchorage hospital went down in the mountains near Moose Pass. Authorities say the recent copycat murders might be a feeble attempt to resurrect the man—

He walked over by the windows, and with his back to the room, punched Captain Reed's number into his phone. "Captain? I got your message. Do you have proof?"

"Dental records confirm it, but to be honest, there's not much else to test. The plane exploded, so the remains are in bad shape. We'll run DNA on whatever we can scrape up, but at this stage, I'd say the man is history."

"And the copycat murders?"

"They began about a month ago — a poor imitation of the Snowman. There've been so many mistakes, they shouldn't even be called copycat killings."

Steven blew out his breath. "Good to know. I'll try to relax. Thanks, Captain."

"How are Brent and Sarah?" Reed asked, but he was talking to an empty line.

~***~

When walking for what felt like hours gave him no peace, Steven slipped into a bar to drown his sorrows in a bottle of whiskey. That much he remembered when he awoke the next morning, but what happened after that was beyond him. He rubbed his pounding head and threw his legs over the side of the bed. How'd I get here? What the fuck happened.?

Listening, he heard someone rattling around in the kitchen, not even trying to be quiet. Sarah? Was Sarah cooking breakfast for him? He smiled. How the hell long had he been sleeping, anyway?

"Good morning," Frank said. "It's about time you got up."

"You. Figures. I was hoping…never mind. What happened?"

Frank laughed. "Look in the mirror."

After checking his appearance, Steven shuffled back into the kitchen and collapsed onto a stool at the breakfast bar

"Is this shiner your handiwork?"

"Nope. You took on a whole damned bar full of men. I have no idea which one of them gave it to you, but I do know that you sent three of them to the hospital. If the bartender hadn't said you were acting in self-defense, you would've been carted off to jail. Instead, they let me come in and pick up the pieces." Frank handed him a cup of coffee. "Drink this. It looks like you need it."

"Shit." Steven rubbed his head and took a sip of coffee. "It's coming back to me. Honestly, I think I was looking for a fight."

Frank chuckled. "You think? Did it help? I know you're mad at me, but a bar fight. What's bugging you? Are you still blaming Brent, or is it Sarah this time?" He turned back to the stove to flip the flapjacks.

"I don't…okay, yes, maybe there's a hint of jealousy, but mostly, it's self-directed." He took a long swallow of coffee. "The truth is, it's my fault. I'm supposed to protect her, but all I do is put her in danger."

"So, you're to blame?"

Steven shrugged. "Sometimes, I think marrying her was the worst thing I could've done to her."

"Bullshit! The two of you belong together like pancakes and syrup. Speaking of which—" He handed Steven a plate of food.

Steven looked at the pancakes dubiously before taking a bite. "Not bad. Good coffee, too. You're hired."

Frank laughed as he sat on the next stool with his plate. "Got the recipe from Sarah," he said, smiling. "Couldn't get the thought of them out of my head after she told me about them. And you'll be pleased to know Westgate had Sarah moved to another room. Says his next step will be to tie her to the bed."

Steven almost choked on a mouthful of flapjacks. "Now that's good news. And it just changed my whole opinion of the man." Steven put another forkful into his mouth. "Did you hear about Jenkins?"

"Heard he was dead."

Steven laughed humorlessly. "I wouldn't count on it."

~~*~~

CHAPTER NINE

Homecomings

June 10th

It was dusk by the time Stowy finally made it out of the wilderness. The truck he stole had just enough gas to get him to Anchorage. He left it in the mall's parking lot and caught the bus to his neighborhood. By now, he figured the animals were ripping the last bits of flesh from Larry's bones, and it was the asshole's own damned fault. Sure, the guy did him a solid by helping with the escape, but that sure as hell didn't earn him a free pass to whine non-stop like a snot-nosed little girl. Nobody could've put up with his whiney shit a second longer. Nobody. Matter of fact, the way Stowy saw it, he did the whole world a solid when he slit the yapper's throat.

He got off the bus just a block from his house, rubbed the back of his neck, and stepped up the pace. Without that fat fucker slowing him down, he should be at his mother's house in no time, and if she knew what was good for her, she'd damned well better have some steak in her freezer. High dollar stuff with plenty of marbling, not that leathery shit they tried to pass off as meat in the joint. He was going to take a long steamy shower—for as long as he'd like, and by his own damned self. There'd be no stiffies going up anybody's ass while he was trying to wash—with soap that didn't smell like cleaning solvent. No sirree. It'd just be him and all the hot water he wanted. Hell, he might even take a bubble bath. He smiled. It was going to be a memorable homecoming.

Stowy dragged his weary body into his mother's yard and frowned at the empty driveway. Where the hell was she? Muttering under his breath, he crept around back to retrieve the key he'd hidden ten years earlier. In just a few minutes, he opened the door and walked into his mother's kitchen. Everything was as immaculate as ever, but it wouldn't be for long.

He made a beeline for the freezer, and with a grin, pulled out two ribeyes and set them on the counter. Then he headed for the bathroom, stripping off his clothes as he walked. The hot shower felt as good as he expected, but the steaks were calling to him so loudly, he had to cut the bubble bath short.

Just as he swallowed his last mouthful of steak and eggs, he heard his mother's inept doorknob-jiggling and key- fumbling at the door. She'd never been able to unlock that door worth a shit. He leaned back in his chair and, with a slight smile lifting his mouth, waited for her to walk through the living room to the kitchen.

She smelled the odor of cooked steak and exclaimed. "Is that you, Zeke? I'm starved." She shrieked and dropped her shopping bags to the floor. "Oh, my God! You're alive!" Her hands flew to her face, and she stared at him, open-mouthed.

"Sorry to disappoint you, Mother, but yes, I'm very much alive."

She shook her head without taking her eyes from his face. "They said your plane went down. Everyone said you were dead."

"And in your grief, you just had to go shopping. Have you already cashed in my life insurance?"

She laughed nervously and went over to his chair to hug him.

"Oh, Stowy, my Stowy. It's nothing like that. You know shopping has always been my therapy." She kissed the top of his head. "But, well…tell me. How did you do it?"

He pushed her away. "I'm tired. I need to rest. Where's that no good-for-nothing Zeke Savon? I have a bone to pick with him."

She shrugged, picked up Stowy's plate, and carried it to the sink. "He left a week ago. Said he was going to the prison to see you. Didn't you see him before your flight?"

Stowy grunted. "Right. And you've heard nothing from him? Didn't I just hear you utter his name? I thought you two were planning a wedding."

She gave a little snort of laughter as she wiped the grease from her stove. "That pig? Over my dead body. Sure, we had an understanding, but marriage? No way!"

"Is that so? That's not the way Zeke tells it." He stood and walked toward his mother, stopping right behind her, close enough for his hot breath to ruffle her hair. "He sent me nothing but glowing texts about your loving relationship and your upcoming nuptials."

She took a step backward and rubbed his body with her behind. "I played the game. It was either that or lose my life. You know how cruel he can be."

Stowy wrapped his hand around her throat. "Cruel? You call his love for you, cruel? You called it adoration when you taught me your version of love!"

"Stop, Stowy! You're hurting me, baby!"

With a self-satisfied smile, he tightened his grip.

Coughing and gagging, she clawed at his arm while he dragged her to the bedroom, but he didn't release her until he threw her onto the bed. With barely contained rage, he glared at her while she gasped for breath. "I learned a lot while I was in prison, Mother," he said. "Now, I know what a sick, controlling bitch you are, but your tricks will never work on me again." He spat on her. "As far as I'm concerned, you're already dead."

He put her hands into the cuffs that were already attached to her bed and then gave them a good yank to make sure they were secure. "I'll sleep better knowing you're incommunicado."

"Stowy, please. I'd never turn you in. Surely you know that! You're my boy, my son, my reason for living. I'd do anything for you." A couple of stray tears drizzled down her cheeks, and she smiled at him. "Didn't I do what you asked? Zeke and I got you out of that hellhole, didn't we?"

"Yeah, in a plane that turned into a bomb. I was never supposed to survive that ride, was I? My guess is somebody rigged the engines. Somebody named Zeke, and I bet it was your fucking idea."

"Oh, Stowy, you're wrong. So, so wrong. I could never ever—"

With an exasperated snarl, he slammed a ballcock into her mouth so hard, her crocodile tears gave way to real ones.

"Shut up, Mother! I've heard enough of your lies." After relishing her helplessness for a minute, he smiled. "I'm glad to see you still like your toys. I'm exhausted, but I'll be back after a good night's sleep. You'd better hope it's a good one, or you'll never get out of this bed."

But he couldn't sleep. Not yet. First, he had some work to do. He went to the basement to get the deadbolts he'd removed from the door's years ago. His stupid mother told him to get rid of them after he changed the locks, but he knew they'd come in handy someday. Today was that day. After putting them back on the doors, he nailed the first-floor windows shut. There weren't any windows in his basement bedroom, but he paid particular attention to securing the door down there. When it was sealed tighter than a bank vault, he finally crawled into his old bed. With a sigh, he closed his eyes.

When he awoke twelve hours later, he went straight to his mother's room, crawled into bed beside her, and nuzzled her neck. "It's so good to be home."

"Undo my hands, and I'll really make you feel at home," she whispered after he removed the ballcock from her mouth.

"Promise?"

"Your wish is my command. You know I'm the only one who can give you what you need."

Stowy released her, and after a bathroom visit, she returned to the bed naked. "Now come to Momma's arms. I'll make you forget all about that nasty prison. Nobody can make you feel as good as I can."

Then she proved it.

CHAPTER TEN

Coming Home

June 25th

In awe of the stunning duality of beauty and destruction, Sarah snapped countless photographs of the fiery flows of lava, blackened countryside, billowing smoke, and rising steam. Even though she suspected Steven had arranged the volcano tour to get her out of the hospital and away from Brent, she'd jumped at the opportunity to see Kilauea's eruption in person.

Once Sarah had all the pictures she wanted, the helicopter flew them back to Honolulu, where Steven shared another surprise. In the limo, Steven held his wife close. It felt good to have her all to himself, and to complete the day, he shared another surprise. "Now that the doctor's going to release Brent, and we can all get out of here, I arranged something very special for him." Steven paused for so long, Sarah sat up to look at him.

"What?"

He gave her a shit-eating grin. "Guess who's going to meet our plane and take over his care?"

Sarah gasped. "You didn't! Oh, my God…Helen? Really? She's really going to be there for him?" She grinned at his nodding head. "That's awesome! Those two definitely belong together, but how'd you manage it?"

He laughed. "Guilt trip. I told Helen what a great decision she'd made in breaking up with the big baby. And how pissed I was that you'd foregone our honeymoon to get him back on his feet. I also told her I'd fired him because of what happened. In other words, I pointed out what an idiot he was and how she deserved so much better."

Sarah smacked his shoulder. "That's awful!"

"What can I say? Reverse psychology works." He laughed and pulled her back into his arms "So, what do you say? Are you ready to go home?"

She gave him a weak smile. "Thanks, today was just what I needed, but yes, I'm ready for home, sweet home." She cuddled against his shoulder. "I've missed you."

Steven sighed and tightened his hold. "I've missed you, too. It took a punch in the eye to make me understand, but I finally figured out that taking care of Brent was something you had to do. It was your way of coming to terms with what happened. You turned into Clara Barton, and I turned into Rocky Balboa. We dealt with the stress individually, but the important thing is we're back together again. Right?"

"You're not sure?" Sarah sat up and looked at him, concern wrinkling her brow.

He shrugged. "I'm still dealing with my failure. I hate letting you down, and I'd understand if you're disappointed in me. It seems like no matter what I do, I can't keep you safe."

"Then quit taking responsibility for things you can't possibly control. I don't blame you. I don't blame anyone. Life happens the way it happens. It just is."

"Easier said than done. It's in my DNA to want to protect you." He pulled her in for a kiss. "And I'll keep doing it until my dying breath."

"And I'll never go down without a fight. You can count on that."

~***~

Twenty-four hours later, Sarah was curled up on their couch in Anchorage with Dancer and Bear asleep in her lap. Puffy smudges of exhaustion underscored her eyes, but she continued to gaze into the fireplace, as though mesmerized by the flickering flames.

Steven nudged her gently. "Okay, you might think you're hiding it, but I saw that yawn. Let's go. It's time for bed. This will all still be here tomorrow."

"Is that an invitation or an order?" She frowned. "Can we talk first?"

He nodded. "Sure. What's up?" He sat down behind her and put his arms around her.

"That's what I want to know. Why all the added security?"

"I'm just taking a few precautions."

"A few?" She twisted in her seat to face him. "For God's sake, there's even a guard on the deck. I can see him from here."

"And you will, at least for a while." He rubbed the back of his neck, took a deep breath, and blew it out slowly. "Listen, the papers said Jenkins died in that plane crash, but I'm not ready to accept it as fact just yet. Until somebody proves to me that he's dead and until Frank's absolutely positive there aren't any more Bardot relatives gunning for you. We're going to have to be extra careful. Better too much security than not enough. Sorry, angel, but I just got married, and the last thing I want to be is a widower."

She smiled. "But just think how much more attractive you'd be to all your admirers."

Steven stood grimacing. "Funny." He kissed her forehead. "Come on. It's bedtime, and I want company." He picked her up and cradled her in his arms. "Ready?"

"Ready," she said, hugging his neck.

The next morning, while enjoying a fresh cup of coffee, Steven said, "I've been thinking. Since our trip to Paris is off, how about a new destination?"

Sarah took a sip of her coffee and smiled. "I'm listening."

"What would you say to a move north? We could spend the summer at Granddad's cabin while we redo the one Uncle Sky gave us as a wedding gift. It'll take a lot of work and some major redecorating, but we can turn it into a getaway. Our home away from home."

"I think it's a wonderful idea!" She moved to his lap and smiled as she ran her fingers through his hair. "We can continue our honeymoon in the wilderness, just like we planned." She lowered her mouth to his, and with a soft groan, he unbuttoned the top button of her blouse. Their kiss deepened, and he stroked her neck before sliding his hand lower toward the next button.

Emma cleared her throat before setting two plates on the table. "Breakfast is ready."

Steven laughed. "Thanks, Em. Sorry about the PDA, but we're still honeymooning."

Emma chuckled. "Don't mind me."

As she turned to leave, Steven grabbed her hand and grinned. "After breakfast, I want you to pack whatever you'll need for an extended stay at the cabin. We're moving this honeymoon to the mountains!"

She looked from his face to Sarah's and then back again. "And you're taking me?"

Steven nodded. "It's the only way I can assure that she," he pointed at Sarah, "will continue to get healthy and not overdo it. I've just hired her to redecorate my uncle's cabin.

We'll need you to keep us both on track."

Yes, sir," she said with a smile. "I can do that."

Sensing excitement in the air, Bear, and Dancer barked their approval.

CHAPTER ELEVEN

Plans

July 4th

Stowy lolled in his basement bedroom in his underwear, lazily browsing the Internet in a half-hearted attempt to catch up on the local news. Most of it was boring, boring, boring, but one tidbit caught his attention. The corners of his mouth curved upward, and then he laughed out loud.

"So, Quaid's on his honeymoon and won't be back to work until after the new year, huh? Oh, we'll just see about that. I've got some mighty fine surprises in store for you, Mr. Big Shot. For you and your bride."

"Stowy, breakfast is ready!" his mother yelled down the steps.

With a growl, he jumped up and raced upstairs. "Dammit! How many times do I have to tell you not to yell my name? What if a neighbor hears you?" He knocked her sideways with a sharp slap. "Don't do it again!"

"I'm sorry," she said, gently rubbing her cheek. "I forgot. Having you here is like old times. I'm just so happy."

Stowy hugged her. "It's all right, Mother. I know you mean well, but I can't have you slipping up like that. I'll be out of your hair soon. The furniture's being delivered to my new place today, so I should be able to move in soon. The cops are convinced I'm dead, or they'd have searched the house by now."

"Captain Reed visited the day the plane went down. He seemed happy to inform me of your death, but he did walk through the house, as though he wasn't sure. Or, I don't know, maybe he's just a busybody. At any rate, they haven't been back, so I'm sure you've convinced them."

"I haven't seen them watching the house, either. Maybe all's well that ends well."

"I think you're right. It's so good to have you back, truly wonderful." She kissed the top of his head and set a plate of eggs and bacon in front of him.

"I love being free. And the new place you found for me is perfect. I'll be able to conduct all my business from there with no problem."

"You can thank Zeke for that. He purchased it under that false name, so it's not tied to either of us."

"I would thank Zeke, but he's disappeared. You haven't heard from him, have you?"

"Me? Shit, no! Bastard ran out on me, too."

"Wonder why. All Zeke talked about was how well you two were getting along."

"That man's a bald-faced liar! And so cruel. There's no one more brutal. No one! I just did what I had to do to survive."

Stowy observed her. "You're right about that, Mother. No one." He put a piece of bacon into his mouth and licked his fingers. "Just so you know, I'll be moving the last of my things out tonight, and then you'll be rid of me."

"Oh, Stowy, I don't ever want to be rid of you." She kissed his cheek and poured him a cup of coffee. "What's your first move?"

"I've got some remodeling and decorating to do. A murder plan to finalize. And since my beard is now fully realized, with some of your makeup magic, I'll spend some time getting the lay of the land. It feels good to be able to move more freely now."

"Have you considered going back to West Virginia?"

"That's what I'll do eventually, but not until I make Quaid pay for what he did to me. I spent ten long years dreaming about it. You understand, don't you, Mother?" He pulled her onto his lap. "They wronged your little boy, so they need to pay. I deserve this, don't I?"

She hugged him tightly. "Yes, you certainly do, and I'll help any way I can."

"I'm counting on you, Mommy. I've always counted on you." He kissed her soundly, and when she stood, he slapped her butt. "Getting a little broad in the ass, aren't you? Got any

of those cupcakes left. After that long stint in the pokey, I've got a lot of bulking up to do."

~~*~~

CHAPTER TWELVE

Honeymoon Bliss

July 15th

Although the sun was shining and temperatures were in the seventies, a storm was brewing inside of Emma. Muttering under her breath, she snapped the lid onto the container of brownies. She looked up and glared daggers at Steven when he came into the room, which he chose to ignore.

"Are the goodies ready to pack?" he asked.

She handed him the brownies and frowned as she watched him add them to his backpack. "Forty miles. You're going to make her trek forty miles through the wilderness. Are you crazy? Why not take the helicopter? There's no reason for you to make such a dangerous trip on foot."

"This will be more fun," he said with a grin.

"Huh!" she snorted. "Some fun. Sleeping in the woods with bears and who knows what other wild animals. Dangerous is what it is, and she's just now healed."

Steven double-checked the stash of ammo for his 30.6 and HK 45. "Stop worrying, Em. Sarah's doing great, and she's looking forward to the trip as much as I am. As far as the animals go, you know I'll protect her. And don't forget her trusty sidekicks. Dancer and Bear will look after her, too."

Emma huffed. "You better take care of her, or you'll answer to me. And the scar that bear gave you will look like nothing compared to the one I'll give you if you don't keep her safe this time."

He laughed and gave her a big hug. "I promise. She'll be well protected. Please stop worrying."

Sarah bounced into the room with a big grin on her face. "All ready? Help me with my pack, and we can hit the road."

Emma shook her head. "You two are gonna give me gray hair and ulcers."

Sarah hugged her tightly. "Oh, Em, we'll be fine. Steven grew up in these mountains. There's not a thing for you to worry about."

"Fine. Enjoy your grand adventure, but you'd better call or text me regularly, so I know you're okay," Emma said gruffly. Then she sighed. "If I were twenty years younger, I might even join you." She ruffled Sarah's hair fondly and then turned to Steven. "I almost forgot. Elliott said to tell you he'll be bringing the last of the supplies up in about a week. Said something went wrong with the order, so he had to find a new supplier. I hope you know what he was talking about because that's all he told me."

Steven nodded. "I do. Thanks, Em." He finished securing Sarah's backpack and patted her on the butt.

"Ready?"

"You bet!" She smiled at him and blew Emma a kiss.

"See you back in Anchorage, Em. Love you!"

Then, with Dancer and Bear on their heels, they went outside, joined hands, and headed north. Emma watched from the door until she could no longer see them. "Be safe," she whispered.

Once they reached the trail, Sarah stepped up the pace.

"We're not going the full forty miles today. Why the big rush?" Steven asked.

"I want to get to Gabby's place early enough to visit with her and the girls before bed."

"Relax! We'll get there with time to spare."

"Okay, fine, I'll slow down just for you, old man." She poked him in the side before relaxing her pace. "I wish Gabby would let us do more for her."

"I do, too, but she's a proud woman. We'll do what we can, but she wants to stand on her own two feet and handle things her way. I admire that, but I sure as hell wish she didn't have to go it alone now. His family should be helping her. It infuriates me that they've turned their backs on Gabby and the girls just because she's Inuit."

"I know. It makes me mad, too. Gregg gave his life fighting for freedom, so I guess his parents think they're free to be as racist as they want to be."

Moving at a steady pace, they arrived at Gabriella Sunne's cabin in the early evening. Sarah sniffed the air appreciatively as they approached. "Do you smell that?' she asked.

"Hmmm. Smells like Gabby's baking bread." Steven patted his growling stomach. "Tell you what. Why don't you go ahead, visit with Gabby and the girls, and I'll go catch some fish to go with it."

"Great idea." Sarah turned toward the cabin, and Steven went toward the creek. "Have fun, but be sure to catch plenty. I'm so hungry, I could eat a moose."

Steven laughed. "As you wish." Sarah continued down the path.

It was only minutes later that the screen door slammed, and two little girls came running through the yard. "Miss Sarah! Miss Sarah! You came! You came!" Myra squealed. Right behind her, eighteen-month-old Moya's short chubby legs were working overtime in a valiant effort to keep up with her big sister.

Sarah dropped to her knees and wrapped her arms around both girls. "Of course, I did. And I have presents, too!"

"Art supplies, so we can paint like you?" Myra asked.

"Girls, please! Let her breathe," Gabby said with a laugh, wiping her hands on a towel before giving Sarah a quick hug. "It's good to see you looking well again. Where's that husband of yours?" She looked past Sarah down the path.

"He's getting dinner."

"He didn't have to do that, but fish for dinner is what I was planning. The girls and I were just about to go fishing. But instead, let's enjoy a glass of tea on the porch while we wait. Give me a minute, and I'll fetch the pitcher."

"Sounds lovely, "Sarah said as she took a seat on the porch, her backpack at her feet. "Emma sent some goodies, too," she said as she removed the food container from her pack.

"Cookies and brownies…mmm," both girls said.

"We'll save the brownies for dessert and have a few cookies with our tea." Sarah let them choose two treats apiece.

Gabby returned with a tray, poured the tea, and sat down opposite Sarah. "So, you're finally going to see your cabin."

"Yes. It's time to make it our own. I hope you and the girls will come up for a visit when it's finished."

"Just let me know when, and we'll be there with bells on. Wait until you see it! It has an amazing view of the valley."

Sarah grinned. "That's what I heard, and I'm looking forward to painting it. Steven's told me so many stories about the place. It almost sounds too good to be true."

"It's true, every word of it. I've heard the same stories from Sky, and that man doesn't know how to lie."

Sarah laughed. "Now, I'm even more intrigued."

They enjoyed an hour visiting before Steven strode proudly toward them, carrying a stringer of fish. The girls ran out to meet him and danced around his legs as he walked to the porch. Gabby took the fish from him while the girls looked on in awe.

"Hello, Gabby." He kissed her on the cheek. "We hope to get to the cabin in another twenty-four hours or so, but would it be all right if we set up camp here tonight?"

"Absolutely. Make yourselves at home. I'd invite you to stay in the cabin, but I think as honeymooners, you might be more comfortable under the stars. Have a glass of tea, and I'll set these in the sink and be right back."

"Under the stars is perfect," Steven said before he downed the glass of tea Sarah handed him.

"A sleepover, and Hawk's staying, too!" Myra squealed, as both girls giggled.

Steven picked them up, and they showered him with giggly kisses. "So, how are my cute little angels?"

"Are you going to read us a story tonight?"

"You bet. I've got just the one."

"Is it about a princess?" Myra asked.

Steven shook his head. "Nope. It's about two princesses."

Gabby rejoined them. "Dinner's in the oven. It'll be ready soon."

"That was fast! Thanks. I'm starved. Sarah was so anxious to get here; we didn't even stop for lunch." He laughed, and Sarah punched his shoulder. "How are you, Gabby?"

"I'm well, considering all that's happened."

"Have you figured out your plan of action?"

"I have, and I can't stay here. Not alone. With Gregg, it would've been a great adventure, but I can't do it without him. I'm going to take the girls back to Anchorage. I'll get a job, and the girls can attend school. My friend Hazel's already offered me one of her rental houses, and she said she put in a good word with her boss."

"What about your cabin?"

"I want to hold onto it for the girls, but in the meantime, I'm going to rent it out to hunters. A neighbor has already agreed to keep an eye on it for me, and he'll make sure it stays properly stocked and clean." She smiled. "I think I have it pretty well figured out."

"Sounds that way. If there's anything we can do, let us know." He carefully set the girls down on the porch.

"You've done more than enough already. Elliott dropped by with the supplies, and we had a wonderful visit. He's a lovely man," Gabby said with a slight blush. "Girls go wash up for dinner and set the table. We have guests!" Turning to Steven and Sarah, she said, "Come in. Dinner will be on the table in no time."

"You two go ahead. I'll be in as soon as I set up the tent."

After a good night's rest and a pancake breakfast, the ascent took most of the day, and when they got there, the view and cabin were even better than Sarah expected.

"This place is beautiful just the way it is," she said as she explored their cave-like domicile. Which Uncle Sky and Aunt Doreen had divvied into two bedrooms, a storage area, a large living area with a fireplace, and a small kitchen. "Except for the dust," she added, wrinkling her nose. "We've got some cleaning to do. Tonight."

It was one in the morning when they finally lay entwined on the bed Sky had built so many years ago. "I'm glad you suggested the new mattress and blankets," Steven said. "They feel like heaven after a tiring day like today." He held a finger up and grinned. "Not that I'm complaining about all the hellish cleaning. The place looks and smells terrific."

Sarah smiled. "Yes, it does. Much better. Speaking of which, I'm thrilled Elliott was able to fly that tub out before we arrived. He did a beautiful job installing it, too. Not that we needed a bath or anything, but we did smell like a couple of mountain goats." She propped herself on one elbow and looked at him with one eyebrow cocked. "So exactly how much other work got done before you brought me up here? Besides the bathroom, I mean."

"Okay, you caught me. While you were recuperating, I had the water system and generator put in, along with the tub. I didn't want you to live in a construction site. Summer's just too short, so Elliott and I worked it out. That man has talents!" Steven said with a satisfied smile.

"He fashioned that bathroom… or should I say spa… from an old storage room. Amazing!" Sarah said.

"Yeah. What can I say? It's true. Happy wife, happy life. The more comfortable you are, the happier I am. Are you upset that I had those things done without you?"

She swung her leg over his body, sat up, and smiled down at him. "Not at all! I'm thrilled with what you've done. This place is sheer magic! Not only did you add some creature comforts, but you kept the original footprint, too. It's perfect. Thank you!" Still straddling him, she leaned down, allowing her hair to brush, whisper-soft, against his naked skin like silky feathers. "This has to be the best wedding present ever," she said. "Remind me to thank your uncle."

"What about me?" he asked huskily.

She nibbled his ear and planted a trail of gentle kisses down his chest. "I may have an idea or two on that subject." She lifted her head and gazed into his eyes, lips parted. Then without losing eye contact, she moved toward him with tantalizing slowness. "Honeymoons are heavenly. Don't you agree?" she whispered.

Without answering, he pulled her close. "Come here, woman. I'll show you heavenly."

CHAPTER THIRTEEN

The Need to Kill

July 20th

Stowy's new home, an A-frame chalet reminiscent of houses on an alpine slope, was replete with lovely exposed beams, a distinctive wiggle board treatment, and fanciful railings on the deck. Its expansive picture windows provided breathtaking panoramic views of the picturesque valley. Its open floor plan could've easily sprung from the glossy pages of a modern design magazine. But that was all for show. Nothing more than selling points to make any realtor swoon. Stowy didn't care about any of those things, because his real living area was underground. In the basement. Away from prying eyes.

And now that he was situated in his new base of operations, Stowy wasn't going to wait any longer. He'd been fighting his natural urges ever since the escape, but no more. He had to do it. Had to. He needed it. Like a junkie without a fix, his skin was crawling with need.

He had to kill.

He felt safe. Cocky, even. Thanks to those Snowman-like murders Zeke committed, any blood Stowy shed now would just be chalked up to the copycat. That is, if he were sloppy enough. Who else would the idiots blame? After all, the whole world believed the real Snowman died in the explosion.

"Time to feed the beast," he crowed as he loaded his kill bag. His close-cropped hair, neatly trimmed goatee, and mustache were dyed dark mahogany. To complete the image, he was wearing dress pants, a starched shirt, and a professorial-looking sweater vest.

Confident that no one would recognize him. Stowy whistled tunelessly as he put on his sunglasses, tossed his bag into his new dark gray pickup, and climbed in. When he revved the engine, anticipation surged through his body, and his pulse quickened.

It was time to visit his favorite hunting grounds—Fourth Avenue.

He wore a self-satisfied smile as he trolled the notorious neighborhood. Ten years may have passed, but everything on the avenue looked precisely the same as he remembered. Finding a willing victim should be just as easy now as it was the last time he was here. The stupid bitches always thought they were safe.

He zeroed in on a tiny blonde, who was sashaying down the avenue in long self-confident strides. Her tight pink shorts barely covered her ass. Which swayed from side to side like a metronome, and the white blouse tied beneath her perky breasts bared a tantalizing expanse of smooth, taut skin that made his mouth water. She was just what he needed.

He slowed his truck to a crawl beside her. "Hey, sweetheart," he yelled out the window. "You lookin' for a party?"

She stopped walking, and with hands on her hips, cocked her head and smiled at him. "That all depends. Are you willing to pay for the entertainment?"

Stowy flashed a wad of hundred-dollar bills. "Does this answer your question?"

"Sure does!" She opened his door and hopped in. "So, where is this party, and what kind of entertainment do you want?"

"It's in the Wellington neighborhood, and what we're looking for is a nice striptease dance. Can you do that?"

She grinned. "Mister, with the right music, I'll blow your socks off!"

When Stowy cruised down his new street, she looked from one large house to another, wide-eyed. "Wow! You weren't kidding, were you? This has got to be the ritziest neighborhood in Anchorage. Are we going to a bachelor party? Somebody getting married?"

"No, but it is a celebration." He winked. "You'll find out what we're celebrating when we get inside."

He showed her in through the garage. And for a change of pace, he even let her walk in on her own two feet. He might as well save the caveman approach for his next party. It'd give him something to look forward to.

When they entered the house, her head swiveled from side to side as she ogled the modern décor. "This place is awesome! Is it yours?"

He smiled. "It is, and I paid cash for it. Would you like to see party central?"

"Not just yet." She smiled coyly, sat on the buttery soft leather couch, and ran her tongue slowly around her lips. "How about if I do you right here first? Then we can join the others."

Stowy slid his zipper down as he walked across the room to her. "I believe that could be arranged. This beast has been bursting to let loose."

"Oooh! Impressive," she said appreciatively. "Bring that big boy over here."

He stood in front of her, his swollen penis pointing at the ceiling. She trailed her fingernails lightly down its length, and a responding chill of anticipation ran down his spine. With gentle barely-there touches, she stroked and teased him, and he groaned. Impatient for her to get on with it, he plunged both of his hands into her hair and urged her head forward. In one rapid movement, she took all of him into her mouth and down her throat. He closed his eyes, threw his head back, and groaned loudly. His legs shook, and his groan turned into a triumphant howl as she sucked him dry in record time.

He opened his eyes. "Nicely done. I see you didn't waste a single drop, and I appreciate that, but I think it's time for the real fun to begin."

He helped her up and led her to the basement door. As he unlocked it, he said, "I don't want my party life to interfere with my real life. I worked too hard for all of this."

"I don't blame you! This place is exceptional."

She followed him down the steps into the darkness. "Careful!" he said. "I wouldn't want you to fall." He grabbed her hand, flipped on the first light switch, and quickly turned to see her reaction.

She stopped walking and gasped. "Oh, my God! Oh, no, no, no!" She shook her head, and with a primal groan, frantically tried to pull away from his grasp.

He smiled enigmatically, tightened his grip on her hand, and dragged her behind him as he turned on the rest of the lights, gradually illuminating his full array of torture tools. Her groan quieted to a guttural animal-like whimper, and her body shook uncontrollably as she stared at the shiny new autopsy table sitting in the middle of the room. A large bed with a plush cover sat in the corner of the room, but she was blind to its presence because she couldn't rip her tear-filled eyes away from the cold metallic surface of that table.

She struggled even harder against his iron grip and swatted at him with her free hand. He chuckled and captured that one, too. "Now, now, now. You're wasting your time. This may not be the party you expected, but I assure you, it's the only celebration I care for, and you're my main attraction."

She doubled her efforts to escape, but Stowy just laughed, picked her up, and carried her to the table. After dumping her there, he immediately strapped her down with leather belts and yanked on them to make sure they were tight enough. Then, whistling while he worked, he sliced through her blouse's tie.

Tears streamed down her cheeks as she rolled her head from side to side. "Please, mister. Please don't do this. I'm only twenty-two. I don't want to die."

He stopped whistling and smiled at her. "What makes you so sure you're going to die?"

She sniffled and regarded him hopefully. "You mean you aren't going to kill me?"

He shrugged. "I'm not sure yet. You did such a lovely job upstairs, I may decide to let you live. If I did, what would you do for me?"

Desperation, mingled with hope, shone from her eyes. "I'll be your slave. Whatever kind of sex act you want me to do, I'll do. I can cook, too. And clean. Anything! I'll do anything you want. Just please, please let me live."

Stowy nodded and unbuckled her ankle restraints. "You know what? I like the sound of that. You've got it, sweetheart! From now on, I own you." He finished removing the rest of the straps and poked her in the chest with a finger. "You're my slave, and you have no rights whatsoever. Got it? No matter what I ask you to do, you'll do it, and you'll do it immediately, without whining or complaining. Deal?"

Shakily, she sat at the end of the table. "Deal," she said solemnly. She sat up straighter and wiped the tears from her eyes. "Tell me what you desire, master. Your slave wishes to please you."

"I believe you promised me a dance." He walked over to the counter and turned on his favorite country music. "Show me."

She closed her eyes and internalized the music, allowing it to fill her senses. Then, swaying sensuously, she flipped her hair, caressed her body, and slowly removed her clothing.

Stowy applauded and walked across the room toward her. "Well done, slave. My cock's ready to explode. Get on your knees!"

Even though her blow job was as howl worthy as the first time, he wasn't satisfied. Having a slave empty his balls was fun, but it wasn't enough. No matter how pleasurable an orgasm was, that pleasure was fleeting, and he needed something more. What he wanted…what he still needed…was to kill.

Several hours later, his nameless slave was dead. Bathed in her blood, Stowy jerked himself off with blood-soaked hands, while glorious memories of her screams fed his fantasy.

CHAPTER FOURTEEN

Interrupted Again

September 1st

In the early morning light, the mountains glowed in luminous shades of blue, white, and pink. The night before had brought the first snowfall of the season. As much as he hated the thought, Steven knew they were going to have to leave their little piece of heaven and move back to the cabin on the Koyukuk before winter hit.

From the door of his uncle's cabin, now his and Sarah's cozy retreat, his brow was furrowed as he gazed at the valley below and sipped his coffee. The anniversary of the day he'd flown to Paris, proposed, and then married the woman of his dreams was fast approaching. Their first year sure as hell hadn't been as rosy and stress-free as they'd hoped…as he'd promised. He had to make amends for all the things that went wrong. What could he possibly do to make this anniversary special for Sarah? How could he convince her it was all worth it? That he was worth it.

A pair of excited yips caught his attention, and he smiled at Dancer and Bear as they ran past, flinging snow and mud in every direction. The way they were chasing each other, rolling around, and playfully nipping, reminded him of the fun times he'd spent here as a child. His Uncle Sky was determined to turn him into a warrior, and thanks to him, Steven honed his skills in these mountains, even if the two of them sometimes butted heads in the process. No matter how much they nipped at each other's heels, they'd always been close, and he knew no man finer.

He grinned and shook his head at the puppies, whose thick white coats were now mottled a distinctive muddy brown. They were having fun now, but he had a feeling there'd be hell to pay when Sarah saw them. Then again…maybe not. She'd been spoiling them since the first day she started training them to be her companions, so she was bound to cut them some slack. Their bond was stronger than a little bit of mud. Sarah loved those dogs, and they loved her.

They'd lay down their lives for her, and he feared she'd do the same for them.

For the umpteenth time, the same maddening thoughts taunted him: what if Dancer and Bear had been with her in Hawaii? Could they have protected her? Taken the shooter out? Maybe a different outcome would've been possible.

He sighed and shook it off. Not much point torturing himself because he couldn't change a damned thing now. Time to let the what-ifs go. As he knew all too well, there were always mountains of them after any tragedy.

The FWOP-FWOP-FWOP of an approaching helicopter drew his attention skyward. He frowned, set his mug down, and with Dancer and Bear right behind him, jogged toward the landing area on the hill behind the cabin.

Frank waved and hopped out of the chopper.

"What do you want?" Steven asked flatly.

Frank's smile disappeared. "Whoa, buddy. Is that any way to greet an old friend? All these months later, and you're still pissed?"

Remnants of his frown remained, but Steven shook his head and chased it with a smile. "Not really." He stepped forward hand outstretched. "I just wasn't ready to let such a peaceful morning go, especially with such a rude interruption. Hatchet's buried. How's it going, Frank?"

"I'm fine," Frank said, accepting Steven's handshake. "Downright dandy, now that we're on the ground. Those winds had me wondering for a while there. It would've been your fault, too, because you turned your damned cell phone off."

Steven laughed. "It's not off. I blocked your number."

Frank shook his head and chuckled. "That possibility never occurred to me." He ran his hand over his face. "Well, you look good. The wilderness agrees with you."

"You flew out here to check on my health? How touching."

"No, I came to let you know the Bardot brothers are officially out of business, and Lucifer's vendetta is kaput. We helped the French authorities round up the entire gang, and they're all in jail now. It's over."

"You're positive?"

"I am. Trust me. It's over, Steven."

"How many times have I heard the words trust me from you?"

"We can only do so much. The world is full of crazies, but you know what? That doesn't make it okay for you to disappear."

"Doesn't it?"

"Well, maybe for the short term, especially since it's your honeymoon. No one can blame you for that."

"Well, that's mighty big of you, old man," Steven said with a chuckle. "How about a cup of coffee?" he asked the pilot.

'No, thanks," the pilot said, holding up a thermos. "I'm covered."

Steven nodded and turned to Frank. "Come on. Let's head back to the house, and you can tell me what you're really doing here. You could've emailed that information about the Bardot's, so I know there's something more."

"You're right. There is. First, I wanted to deliver this care package from Emma." He handed over a large picnic basket. "And second," he said, clearing his throat, "I want to convince you to come back to work."

"Dammit, Frank! We've already had this discussion, and my answer hasn't changed. No! I'm not coming back, at least not until my honeymoon is officially over."

"Listen, I understand. I do, but something's happened that might change your mind."

Steven stopped walking. "Something's always happening. Dammit! What? What is it this time?"

Frank grimaced. "There's no easy way to say this. We think Jenkins is alive."

"Son of a bitch! I knew it!" Steven dropped the picnic basket and walked in a tight circle, shaking his head. "What happened? How'd he do it this time?"

"A witness came forward a few days ago. He says two chutes came down before the plane exploded. The dentures we found in the wreckage were Jenkins, but that would've been an easy enough plant. We've put a rush on the rest of the DNA testing, but I don't need it, because my gut's already telling me the bastard's alive."

"Of course, he is. Shit! That bastard has nine lives!" Steven retrieved the basket and trudged angrily to the cabin.

"Well?" Frank said as they reached the deck. "Are you coming back? Will you help us nail him again?"

Steven chewed on his lip before answering. "Has he killed anyone yet?"

"We don't think so. So far, the only similar M.O. has been from the copycat. And before you ask, Reed visited his mother, and said he saw no signs of Jenkins being there."

Steven pointed to a deck chair. With a nod, Frank sat, and Steven moved to the rail and looked out over the valley. Dammit, he thought he was done dealing with Jenkins. His mind flashed back to their last encounter, and to the loathsome threats that bastard made. In his gut, he knew what he had to do, but could he ask Sarah to forego the honeymoon once again? They had several more months, and yet, here he was, once again thinking about putting his job ahead of her.

The door opened, and Sarah came out with a tray holding three mugs of coffee and a plate of fresh cinnamon buns. "Hi, Frank," she said, handing him one of the cups. "You're looking well."

He stood and kissed her cheek. "So are you. Matter of fact, you look incredible. I can see why Steven doesn't want to come back to civilization. Living up here seems to agree with both of you."

"I love it here." She set the tray down and leaned on the railing next to Steven. "It's okay. Stop trying to protect me. I know Frank wouldn't be here if it weren't important, and I know you miss the challenge."

At the sound of her voice, the puppies came running, and as soon as she spotted them, she laughed. "Oh, my goodness, look at you two monkeys! I've seen cleaner pigs!

And you still think you should get a treat, don't you?" She scratched their mud-encrusted heads and pulled a couple of dog treats out of her pocket. Then she turned back to Steven. "You're awfully quiet. You do want to help, don't you?"

"Not at the expense of our honeymoon."

Sarah smiled. "All you have to do is promise me that when you finish your cases, the honeymoon will continue. I want all my time with you to be honeymoon-like." She brushed his hair back from his shoulder. "I know you have to do this. I know it's important. It's who you are."

He put his arm around her. "Are you sure?"

"Positive. Frank wouldn't have come if he didn't need you, and I do miss Leeann. I know Emma wants me home, too. All she talks about are the bears."

"You don't have to come up with any more reasons. I know what you're doing, and I love you for it." He pulled her close and held her as if his life depended on it.

Frank cleared his throat. Ignoring him, Steven held her close and said, "I'll do what I need to do for you. And when it's over, the honeymoon will definitely be back on. This time we'll go to Paris." He searched her eyes.

She smiled for him and lightly nodded. "I'll hold you to that."

"I expect you to. Thank you." Steven kissed her hand and held it to his cheek. "Okay, Frank, when do we start?"

~***~

Steven sang along to the music playing softly in the background. Emma's picnic basket held Sarah's favorite French dish, perfect for an impromptu anniversary celebration. It was a little early, but he was unexpectedly reporting back to work tomorrow, and there was no telling what they'd be doing on the actual date. September 16th was still a couple of weeks away, but the beef bourguignon, cheesecake, and romantic music were here now. Steven set the table while he waited for Sarah to finish luxuriating in the scented bubble bath, he'd prepared for her.

Impatient for her to join him, he went to the bedroom.

Standing in the doorway, he watched Sarah run the comb through her hair. Every move was graceful. Sensuous. Reflections from the firelight danced in her hair and gave a shimmering glow to her naked body, making her even more irresistible than usual. He cleared his throat, and she turned to him. With a smile, she strolled to his side.

"I love looking at you," he said huskily, running his fingers through her hair and down her back. He pulled her closer, and all thoughts about dinner vanished.

"I love the way you look at me," she said, undoing his shirt, belt, and zipper. "Happy almost anniversary, husband."

He picked her up, cradling her luscious body close to him. She threw her arms around his neck, and he looked into her eyes before claiming her mouth with his own. Without breaking the kiss, he carried her to the bed and laid her gently against the pillow.

While he kissed, explored, and teased, she managed to remove his clothes. Before consummating the last night of their honeymoon, he looked deeply into her eyes. "Angel, thank you for blessing my life."

CHAPTER FIFTEEN

Another Maggie Dies

September 1st

Snow already covered the foothills surrounding Anchorage, triggering the annual southern migration of visitors and residents. Glad to be rid of the infestation of tourists, Stowy took a break from putting his latest supply of killing materials away to have a bite of lunch and read the newspaper. He stopped chewing when he spotted the kick-in-the-gut headline: Quaid to Track the Snowman's Escape.

He dropped his fork, spit out his food, and with a clenched jaw, started reading the article. Evidence that the Snowman didn't die in the plane crash in June has made its way to Anchorage, and Detective Steven Quaid has cut his honeymoon short to find the monster—

"FUCK!" He balled up the paper and threw it across the room. Then he punched the table and stood, absentmindedly rubbing his throbbing fist. So much for working in the background and letting that asshole Zeke take the blame. Son of a bitch.

He studied the young girl sitting quietly on the bed, her finger moving beneath the words and her lips moving as she read a True Confessions magazine article. His latest slave had already been here for twenty-four hours, the longest he'd let one live so far. She was probably dreaming about how much money she'd make selling her how I survived story to the magazine after he released her.

Stupid bitch. As if he'd ever let her go. He rubbed his chin, considering. Maybe he should do her now and be done with it. The only problem was his freezer. It was already packed with bodies, and he wasn't sure she'd fit. Dammit, he should've bought a bigger freezer.

"Hey, you!" he said. "Get over here."

She immediately dropped her magazine, scurried to his side, and fell to her knees. With eyes cast downward, she reached for his zipper.

Stowy grunted his approval. "Good thing, you know your place. It's the only thing keeping you alive." He smiled as she took him into her mouth. For now, that is.

After she sucked the stress from his body, he pushed her away, and she returned to the bed, spitting and wiping her mouth on the back of her hand. He considered slapping her for being so disrespectful but decided to let it go. Might as well let her have that moment. Her moments would be running out soon enough.

His phone signaled an incoming message from Zeke, and he grinned as he read it. Well, well, well. Talk about an invitation he was happy to accept. It looked like his lucky bitch slave wouldn't be dying so soon, after all. She was going to have to wait for her turn. Zeke already had another whore primed for the kill, and he was willing to share the fun.

After securing his slave, Stowy sent Zeke a quick on-my-way response and headed for the condemned warehouse. It took him twenty minutes to get there, but before entering what was left of the abandoned building, he looked around. Seeing nothing suspicious, he pulled the heavy door open and slipped inside.

An overpowering stench greeted him in the pitch-black darkness. Gagging, he switched on his flashlight app and wiped his burning, watery eyes. Then, drawn by the sound of screams, he made his way to the basement.

The girl was lying on a table. Naked and bound, she was bleeding profusely, and Stowy's heart rate accelerated when he looked at her more closely. She reminded him of one of his first blood art victims. He smiled.

"Lovely, Maggie. Sweet Maggie. Long dead, Maggie." He nodded a curt greeting at Zeke. "You've cut her too deeply. She'll be dead soon."

"Sorry, I didn't wait for you, but I followed your instructions!" Zeke said, stuffing a rag in the girl's mouth and holding the knife out towards Stowy. "You want to finish the job?"

Stowy accepted the knife. "I thought you'd never ask." With a sick smile contorting his mouth, he hid the knife at his side as he approached the girl. After removing the gag, he basked in the foolish glimmer of hope reflected in her eyes. "It's all right, my love," he crooned, caressing her cheek. "You're going to be just fine."

"Are you the police?" she asked weakly.

He held up the knife and smiled. "Not exactly."

Her ear-splitting scream echoed in the room, and Stowy smiled at her again. "That's it, my pretty. Scream. Scream. SCREAM!"

Relishing the sounds of her terror, he slowly slid the sharp tip of the knife along her cheeks and then delicately sliced her breast into paper-thin pieces. Like the maestro he was, he wielded the blade masterfully, deliberately enhancing her terror to feed her screams and his ego, but in a matter of minutes, she didn't even have the strength to whimper. With a frown, Stowy finished her off by slicing her throat.

Zeke breathed a sigh of relief and removed his hands from his ears. "I love watching the life leave their eyes, but damn! How do you stand the screaming?"

"It feeds me," Stowy said, wiping the blade on a dirty towel and returning it to Zeke. "Literally! It fills every cell of my body with sustenance. I'll never tire of it."

"Beautiful. Just beautiful. You amaze me! But tell me, how did I do?" Zeke asked, as though looking for approval from the master. Another source of sustenance for the Snowman.

"Not bad," Stowy said as he inspected the work. "She's a perfect likeness to my sweet Maggie. Your selection is above and beyond, but you have to be more careful with the knife work. Be an artist, not a damned butcher, so that the fun can last longer. Unless you want them dead fast."

"I'm not nearly as patient as you are, but I'll learn." Zeke patted him on the back. "So, how's Mommy Dearest?"

"Wondering where you are. Fern thinks you abandoned her."

"I'll bet." Zeke laughed. "I'd love to be hitting that ass of hers, but I'm sticking with your plan, just like you want." He scratched his head. "I still don't get why you want her to think I abandoned her or that I tried to kill you. Makes no sense to me, but you're the boss." He shrugged. "By the way, did you ever figure out who sabotaged your plane?"

"Not yet. The guy covered his tracks, but I'll find him soon enough. In our circle, bragging is an affliction most of us never kick."

Zeke laughed. "We do love to talk about our accomplishments, don't we? Just so you know, I've been keeping my ear to the ground, too, and I haven't heard a word." He tossed the knife to a side table. "Any changes to the plan?"

"Nope, I'm dead and enjoying it, at least until Detective Quaid tracks my path. But for the time being, Mom waits on me hand and foot, and you invite me to the fun. So, I'll stay dead until I've no choice but to reincarnate myself." God, I'm a great liar. Idiot, him, and my mother both. Pull the wool over my eyes. I think not. Vengeance is mine, always will be mine!

"I read about that detective in the paper today. Are you worried?" Zeke asked.

"Not even a little bit." Stowy snorted and rubbed his nose. "Damn, how can you work in such a dump?"

"It's just for work. I don't live here."

Stowy laughed. "I've got to give you kudos for finding the perfect location, even if it does smell like ass," he said, offering his palm for a high five. "Come on, let's take Maggie May out to the tide flats. Then we'll wait around to see if Detective Quaid makes an appearance. If he does, we're going to this little diner I know, and I'll treat you to the best steak you ever tasted. If he doesn't, you're buying."

~~*~~

CHAPTER SIXTEEN

Deja Vu

September 2nd

Something about the day felt wrong. As Steven parked his truck in the lot of the Anchorage Police Department, an uneasy feeling of déjà vu swept over him, but he shrugged it off. After all, he'd worked here for the past ten years, so of course, he'd feel a certain sense of been there- done that when returning to work and parking in the same lot he'd parked in so many times before. No big deal.

Before he even made it into the building, he ran into Frank Stover and Captain Reed, who were on their way out. "Welcome back, Steve," the captain said, signaling that he should walk with them. "You're just in time. We got an anonymous call about a body on the tide flats."

Frank locked eyes with him and nodded grimly. "Same time and place as Jenkins' first kill."

They drove to the flats in silence, and when they arrived fifteen minutes later. Steven hopped out of the car and led the way. "This is where we found Margarette Caruthers' body ten years ago," he said, lifting the yellow crime scene tape and slipping under it to get a closer look.

The young blonde was posed exactly like the first woman they'd found here ten years earlier. Just like before, her bottom half was ensconced in a garbage bag, and a chewing gum wrapper lay beside her body. Everything about the scene was reminiscent of the first Snowman killing, which Steven had covered as a rookie. He stood and shook his head. "This might be another copycat murder. Then again, it might not. The way she's staged is the same but look at the cuts. Most are too deep, and there aren't enough of them. Jenkins made his victims bleed out slowly, but this girl died quickly." He continued to look at the body. So many similarities, now I get it…it's déjà vu all over again.

Frank knelt to examine the scene. "This one's different from the other copycat killings. They were sloppy butcher jobs, but there are some precise cuts here, too, more like Jenkins' work." He stood. "You think Jenkins is working with the copycat? He knows we're on his trail. He has no reason to hide now."

"That would explain it. Good observation," Steven said. "Maybe we'll have the answer after I visit Moose Pass." His phone pinged with a text from an unknown number with two cat emojis.

Hey, Detective. They call me the copycat, but I'm better than the Snowman ever was. I get off on the killing. There's no ART to it. It's just straight-up butchery. You'll see. I have many more tricks up my sleeve. Many more!

Steven looked around the gathering crowd. "The killer's watching us."

As Reed and Frank were reading the message, another appeared.

Get ready, Detective. This boogeyman is just getting started. Before I'm finished, Anchorage will be covered in blood.

CHAPTER SEVENTEEN

Tracking a Snowman

September 3rd

The team of trackers chosen to accompany Steven and his Uncle Sky to Moose Pass boarded the Chinook helicopter and took their seats. "So, is this a wild goose chase, or are we tracking the monster?" Helen asked her fiancé and partner, Brent Summers.

He shrugged.

"Are you all right?" she asked.

"I'm fine. Why?"

"Your attitude's a little off, for one. Is it because it's your first day back on the job?"

"Sorry. No, I was thinking about the files I read last night. This Jenkins guy is a real-life monster. You never had any dealings with him, did you?"

"Me? No, Jenkins was well before my time."

He blew out a sigh of relief and rubbed the back of his neck. "Good. That means he's not holding a grudge against you."

"It's sweet of you to worry about me," she said, squeezing his hand. "But I'm pretty sure he's already dead. I'm so sure I want to wager a steak dinner on it. My take is that we're on a wild goose chase. What's your bet?"

"I hope you're right, but sorry, I'm with the boss man. I say Jenkins is alive. Cockroaches like him always find a way."

Helen laughed. "What a suck-up! You're just covering your ass." She smiled at him and shook her head. "After the man gets you shot in Hawaii, you're still following his lead."

"Okay, smart ass! I'll take your bet. I say we find Jenkins tangled in his chute and hanging from a tree, begging to be sent back to prison."

"What an imagination! Okay, you're on. The winner has to buy steak dinners for the whole team when we get back to Anchorage."

The pilot twisted in his seat to look at her. "Does that team include us?"

Helen nodded. "Of course, but what's your wager?"

"We," he said, gesturing to include the co-pilot, "say he's dead. The wilderness got him."

"Smart call," Helen said, nudging Brent playfully. She looked out over the airstrip. "About time! Here's the boss and my favorite man, Quinn."

Steven responded to her salute with a nod. "Our crew looks impatient," he said.

"It's a good crew," Quinn said. "How does it feel to be back at work?"

Steven's sheepish grin told all. "Since I'm headed to the wilderness, pretty darned good."

Quinn patted his nephew on the back. "Thought so."

They climbed into the helicopter, and as soon as they took their seats, the chopper lifted off and headed toward the site of the Medevac plane crash. An hour later, they landed at Moose Pass, unloaded their gear, and the chopper took off again, leaving the team behind to do its job.

The trackers stood side-by-side, checking out the site of the plane crash. Although the plane fragments and body parts were no longer there, the enormity of the charred crater in front of them bore silent testimony to the magnitude of the impact. Comparing what they saw now to the crime scene photos provided by the first responders, they got a better understanding of the crash.

Helen pulled out her notebook. "Here's what we know. Someone tampered with both engines. The first engine's explosion provided ample warning that the plane was in trouble. There were parachutes and winter gear on board, so an escape before the second engine exploded was possible. The remains of both pilots were positively identified from DNA. A dental piece and Jenkins' DNA, along with a set of handcuffs, the paramedic's watch, with DNA, and a lab coat covered in blood were also found. Nothing of the two guards, though." She looked up from her notes. "Which means we have two more missing people."

"Interesting," Quinn said, looking around the area. "So, what's our first move?"

"The families of those two guards deserve closure, and we're going to try to give it to them. I believe Jenkins pushed those men out without parachutes. Quinn and I drew a grid based on the plane's descent and the wind direction, and we've given that information to two search teams, who are now looking for the remains. Those teams are working in recovery mode, but our mission is different." Steven paused to look at each of the team members. "People, we're tracking a living breathing bastard. Knowing Jenkins, he not only made it out alive, but he also left a trail a five-year-old could follow."

"You think he survived and has stayed quiet all this time?" Helen asked.

Steven nodded. "For Jenkins, being quiet means, he's burying the bodies, but when he's ready for the attention, he'll make his presence known. I believe he's alive, but nothing would make me happier than finding the bastard's body. This is one time I hope I'm wrong."

The team separated and began their search, moving northwest from the plane's crash site, and staying connected via walkie-talkie. Even though the witness had been confident of the coordinates, after a day of hiking and searching, they still hadn't found the parachutes. As darkness began to descend, they set up camp, and after a quick supper of ready-made sandwiches and coffee, they slept the sleep of the exhausted.

The next morning, while Helen and Brent packed the equipment, the others fanned out to search the surrounding area.

Sky radioed, "I've found ground zero." He shot up a flare, and the others converged on his location.

"This is where they landed," Sky said. "Their chutes were hidden in the rocks, but for whatever reason, they didn't bother hiding the evidence of their stay here."

Helen collected samples from two piles of human waste. "If nothing else, this shit will prove once and for all that Jenkins is alive."

Brent laughed. He looked at the piles and said. "I'm hoping it's bear scat. The bear ate the bastard, then had tummy problems."

"If only," Steven said and chuckled, too.

Helen, sick to her stomach for the job she had to do, didn't find the conversation funny. She glared at her partners and called Reed to inform him of the find, and he promised a helicopter would be there to collect the samples in a few hours.

Following the trail left by the two men proved to be as simple as Steven had predicted. When they reached the hikers' camp, the stench of death was still strong, even though scavengers had consumed most of the remains. After calling Reed to request a CSI team, they found a second grisly scene.

A man's skull lay in the remnants of a campfire, alongside a four-wheeler with a siphoning tube hanging from its gas tank. Steven considered for a moment. "I'm guessing there was another vehicle here, and Jenkins wanted to make sure he had enough fuel to get out." He nodded toward the skull. "And I'd say that's what's left of his cohort. Jenkins didn't need him anymore."

Steven turned to his uncle. "You ready to finish this?"

Quinn nodded

"Good job, everyone. You can all head back to Anchorage, and we'll take it from here. Just do me one favor, Helen. Find out who those campers were."

"On it, boss," she assured him.

With gasoline brought in by the CSI team, they filled the tank of the four-wheeler, and Steven and Quinn continued the hunt.

~***~

A day later, Steven, Quinn, and an entire team of other officers, including a CSI team, knocked on Fern Jenkins's front door. "Good morning," Steven said, handing her a search warrant.

"What's this? What are you doing here?" She scowled at him while glancing at the paper.

"Search warrant, Mrs. Jenkins. We know Stowy survived the plane crash. We tracked him to Anchorage, then to this house. His DNA was found in a truck he stole from a man he killed in the mountains south of Moose Pass. Just one of the seven men he killed during his escape. If we find evidence that he's been here, you will be arrested. Speak up now, Mrs. Jenkins. Or go to jail."

Fern stepped back to let him enter, and then walked to the couch and sat down slowly. Twisting her hands in her lap, she looked down and spoke quietly. "He handcuffed me to my bed. He abused me. My son beat me. He threatened to kill me, and I can prove it. Follow me."

She led him to the bedroom and pointed to the handcuffs still attached to the bedposts. "See? And here's further proof." She opened a vanity drawer and removed the pictures Zeke took of her their first night together and handed them to Steven. "He said you'd come. He wanted you to see his handiwork."

Steven flinched at the graphic photographs. "Why didn't you call us?"

Quinn pointed to the date and time recorded on the photograph, a date well before Stowy's escape. "The beast you seek was born of this lying creature," Quinn said under his breath.

Steven, understanding his comment, nodded, but Fern, hearing only the word beast responded. "Yes, a beast. Prison did that to my sweet boy. I couldn't tell you. I couldn't tell anyone. He'd have killed me. He's changed. My baby boy has been hardened by prison, and I blame you for that." She walked away, swiping at her eyes with a tissue, but neither Steven nor Quinn saw any tears.

"He left this for you," she said, thrusting an envelope into his hands.

Steven motioned to another detective. "Take her downtown. Get a full statement." He looked directly at Fern. "I'll let the Captain determine your collusion." Steven turned his back to her and opened the envelope. Quinn read the note over his shoulder.

Hello, Detective,

Took you a while, but I knew they wouldn't find me without your expertise. Sorry to interrupt your honeymoon. No. I'm not. But honestly, I can't wait to meet the lovely Sarah Davis, and I will. Count on it!

Good hunting. This time my capture won't be so easy. But it will be a lot more fun.

The Snowman

Quinn put his hand on Steven's shoulder. "Be extra careful, my son. This one is out for revenge. I will see to the safety of the family; you concentrate on capturing the demon."

CHAPTER EIGHTEEN

Sacrifice

September 5th

There was a definite chill in the air. Now that winter had arrived in the mountains of the Brookes Range, Sarah knew it was time for her to go, but that didn't mean she had to like it. She hated having to abandon their beloved cave-like mountain retreat, but she was hopeful that she and Steven could return for a few days before the year's end. She closed and secured the door with a sigh.

John smiled at her. "You don't want to leave, do you?"

"Leaving is harder than I thought it would be. Being here was the best part of our honeymoon. Even after Steven left to go back to work, I enjoyed being here alone. It's an ideal place to paint." She frowned. "But they say all good things must come to an end, right? And we'll be back."

"Leeann is dying to spend time here, but thank goodness, she's willing to wait until the summer," John said.

"Good morning," Elliot said as he joined them. "You ready?"

"As ready as I'll ever be," she said, stealing one last look at the cabin. "Bear, Dancer. Heel." The dogs took their places on either side of her, and the group began their journey down the mountain.

The end of summer and beginning of fall left the tundra burnished in colors of red, orange, and gold, colors Sarah had hoped to capture on a canvas before snow dominated the landscape. As they hiked down the mountain, she settled for capturing the beauty with her camera. She could convert some of the pictures into paintings later.

Once they reached the foothills and entered the forest, Dancer and Bear abruptly stopped walking, bared their teeth, and growled a deep, ominous warning. John grabbed his 30.6. "Protect," he told the dogs, and they immediately went to Sarah's side. "Elliott, don't move until I give the all-clear. Stay with Sarah."

Elliott nodded, and John moved forward cautiously, searching the path ahead with binoculars. Then he froze in place. "Oh, dear God." Shaking, he reached for his gun and fired.

The grizzly, who'd been bellowing over Gabriella's body a moment ago, was now lying motionless, but so was Gabriella. John whistled the all clear and then ran to check on her.

She was on her stomach. John turned her over, and a glimmer of light flashed in her eyes when she saw him. "Thank God," she whispered.

"Let's get you to the house." He picked her up, and cradling her close to his body, hurried toward the cabin with Sarah and Elliott close behind him.

Once inside, he laid her on the kitchen table so Elliott could dress her wounds, but Gabriella grabbed Elliott's hand.

"Too late," she said weakly. "Please. I must speak to Sarah."

Sarah wrapped her fingers around her friend's cold hand. "I'm right here."

"My girls," Gabby said. "Watch over them. Be their mother, please."

"But, Gabby—"

"Please, promise me." The seriousness of the situation was confirmed by Elliott's shaking head as Sarah looked to him for help. "Please," Gabby begged.

"You know I'll love them as my own, but isn't their family in Texas?"

"They're hateful people," she whispered as blood poured from the corner of her mouth. With her last breath and remaining strength, she pleaded, "They don't care about my Inuit babies. Please, promise me—"

Sarah squeezed Gabby's hand. "I promise. You have my word. I'll fight for your daughters."

"Thank you." Gabby sighed deeply and closed her eyes. She was gone. Sarah fell to her knees, her hands still grasping Gabby's, her grief raw, exposed, and heart-wrenching. The two men stood behind her with bowed heads and wet eyes.

John lifted Sarah from the floor. "Come now. Pull yourself together."

"I'll take Miss Gabby to her room," Elliott said.

Sarah nodded and tried to push back her grief.

"What's this?" John asked as he picked up an envelope from the kitchen counter. "It's addressed to you," he said, handing it to Sarah.

She accepted the envelope with shaking hands and removed the documents from it. "It's her will and a letter," she said, tears once again flowing freely down her cheeks. "I can't," she sobbed, handing the papers to John. "You read it, John."

Elliott rejoined them just as John finished a quick, silent read. "Listen to this," John said.

The bear started harassing us last week. I shot to scare the poor creature away and mistakenly injured him. Now I am out of ammunition; he's injured and enraged. For a while, he left, I thought to die. I began to feel safe but not enough to let the girls out. I went for water, and he caught me. I got away from him, but my injuries are severe. I would have called for help, but the day he attacked, I lost the phone in the creek.

I'm dying. Blood loss is too extreme, and infection has set in. The monster keeps trying to tear down the cabin. Our door will not withstand another attack. The time has come for me to sacrifice myself. If I die here, inside with the girls, he will tear the place down around them. I will take my best hunting knife. I must end him, yet I know that it means my end, too. It is with love that I surrender myself and hope that you will arrive in time to save my girls, or we are all lost.

I have secreted them in the safe room behind the

fireplace and put a small amount of sedative in their juice so they will spend more time asleep and not worry about my absence. Leaving my sweet babies is most difficult, but I explained to them that I had injured a father bear, and because of my error, it was my duty to guide him to the spirit world. I explained that once there, I could not return. I told them I was joining their father and that we would forever watch over them. I know they barely understood my words, but I saw no other choice.

Please watch over them.

Please honor my wishes. Gabriella Sunne.

Please love my sweet girls!

~***~

Steven met Sarah's plane in Anchorage, and the girls buried their heads against his neck as he carried them to the car. Emma secured them in their car seats, while Sarah showed him the documents from Gabby.

He quickly looked them over. "Are we ready for this?"

"Yes," she said without hesitation. "We are."

He sighed deeply and held her close. "The world is turning so fast, I don't feel as though we ever get a chance to catch up, but if you're ready, then I'm right there with you."

She hugged him and whispered, "We can do this. I know we can."

He nodded. "Yes, we can do this."

CHAPTER NINETEEN

Predator

September 10th

Darkness had fallen, but in the glare of his headlights, the snow looked like glitter falling onto a glitzy dance floor. Winter was in the air, but fall hadn't even begun. It was Detective Dan Reinhardt's favorite time of the year, and he breathed deeply of the cold air when he got out of his car and walked to the door of his former partner's house. Good old Sergeant Corey Mullins. They hadn't seen each other in quite some time. Although he was curious about the sudden dinner invitation, he was looking forward to seeing his old pal again. Whatever was on the menu was bound to be a step up from the canned soup and stale baloney sandwiches he'd been eating by himself most nights since his divorce. Mullins had an impressive stock of exotic whiskeys, too, which he was always eager to share. It promised to be an enjoyable evening spent rehashing old times.

After stuffing himself with baked salmon, German potato salad, and fresh green beans, topped off with blueberry pie, Dan wiped his mouth and pushed himself away from the table. "Man, I had no idea you were such a good cook!"

"Thanks. I used to dabble, but since retirement, I've taken several cooking classes. Next week, I start a baking class." He grinned. "It's purely coincidental that the instructor happens to be one hot momma."

Dan laughed. "Sounds like you're enjoying retirement. Makes me look forward to the day I can join you."

Corey poured two glasses of whiskey and handed one to Dan. "On a more serious note, I've been thinking a lot about Jenkins' return, and about the threats he made when we arrested him."

"Thanks." Dan lifted the glass in a salute and then took a sip. He nodded appreciatively, set the glass down, and met his old partner's serious expression with one of his own. "He's been on my mind, too. Do you think we have anything to worry about?"

Corey retrieved a flyer from a desk drawer and handed it to Dan. "You tell me. I got this the other day."

Dan looked the flyer over and shrugged. "Is this supposed to mean something? I don't get it. It's just a poster for the movie Predator, isn't it? Is it a collectible?"

Corey drummed his fingers on the table. "Read the back."

Dan turned the paper over and saw the message: Skinned Alive. What a way to go. He swallowed hard. "Who sent it?"

"Can't say for sure. No prints."

Dan reread the message and frowned. "You don't think it was him, do you?"

Corey nodded. "My gut says it is."

"Did you call it in?"

"Not yet, but I will, if you agree, it's a threat."

"I do."

They downed their drinks, and Corey refilled their glasses. After gulping the second shots, Dan pulled out a couple of Cuban cigars, but before they could light them, they both suddenly slumped in their chairs, stiff and motionless.

Stowy Jenkins sauntered into the room from the kitchen, clapping his hands. "Well, gentlemen," he said. "What can I say? You are correct! That was a threat from me, and I'm very much looking forward to fulfilling it."

~***~

An unexpected cold front blew in from the Arctic and covered Anchorage in a thick blanket of white. Responding to a report of two dead bodies found at Kincaid Park, Steven warmed his hands in his pockets as he tromped through the snow to investigate. When he arrived at the scene, he stopped in his tracks, his mouth filling with bile-flavored saliva.

Not only was it one of the most horrific murder scenes he'd ever seen, but the victims were a couple of cops who'd been part of the Jenkins take-down years ago. And the only way he even knew it was Mullins and Reinhardt was by facial recognition, because that's the only part of their bodies that still had skin. Steven swallowed the foul taste in his mouth and signaled the coroner to cut them down.

Later that day, he met the coroner in the morgue. "Got anything?" he asked.

"I found this note in Mullins's throat." He handed Steven an unsealed evidence bag containing the note. "Looks like it's written in blood."

The note was a bloody scrawl, but Steven carefully unrolled the document. Detective, I've started at the bottom of the food chain, but as I promised, all those involved will pay for their crimes, including you. Signed, the Snowman.

"Shit! Unbelievable. We found evidence they were killed in Corey Mullins's house. And we found a poster that we're assuming was a warning."

"Did they report it?"

Steven shook his head. "No, but I've no idea when they received it." He nodded toward the corpse in front of him. "What else can you tell me?"

"Cause of death was a loss of blood, and I can tell you that being skinned alive is one of the most horrific forms of torture there is. I believe they were incapacitated by a paralyzing sedative but remained conscious and fully aware."

Steven grimaced. "Sounds about right. We found a doctored bottle of whiskey." His phone pinged, and he glanced at the screen. "I've got to go. Let me know if you find anything else."

He waited until he got to the parking lot before opening the text from Sarah. I hope your day is going well! The girls wanted to say hi to Daddy.

He gazed at the cheery image of the girls waving at him, so full of light and life, but the darkness and death he'd seen that day weighed heavily in his heart. How was it even possible for two such opposing worlds to co-exist in the same universe?

~~*~~

CHAPTER TWENTY

Family vs. Murder

September 15th

The newspaper reported on the Snowman's return and the two officers he killed. It also ran a series of archived stories detailing the Snowman's earlier exploits, along with theories about his current ones, so emotions were running high. With their fears stoked to a fever pitch by the non-stop media coverage, the public demanded action. As for Steven, he was in no mood to make nice to reporters, so he did his best to do his job while keeping the press at bay and left the press conferences to Captain Reed.

The conference room was uncharacteristically quiet as the officers waited for Steven to address them. He strode to the front of the room, faced them, and with all eyes focused on him, began speaking. "We assumed that because Jenkins's prior M.O. was to kill in the privacy of his killing shop that he'd continue to do the same this time," he said. "But we were wrong. He isn't. He's become more brazen. Now, he's stalking his victims. He's stalking us, and he may even communicate his intentions." He pointed to the movie flyer posted on the whiteboard. "That's what he did with Mullins and Reinhardt, so he may do the same with his other targets. We believe Jenkins plans to target anyone involved in his first arrest, and I think he'll take advantage of the opportunity to strike if he finds any one of us alone, so now, more than ever, we have to watch each other's back. We can't leave anyone, and I mean anyone, unprotected. Understood?"

He scanned the sea of nodding heads before continuing. "Jenkins is still meticulous, but he's working on the fly, which could work to our advantage, but don't underestimate him. He's a wily bastard with a new identity and an arsenal of disguises. The surveillance cameras that caught a glimpse of him show someone unafraid of being recognized. He's taunting us, daring us to catch him.

"Trust no one — not even a man in a uniform. Anyone you don't recognize, question. Anything that looks out of place probably is. Doctors, firefighters, police, he'll use whatever disguise he needs to get him what he needs. If he can get to his former deposit sites, I believe he'll use them, so I want them left open but covered with a hidden camera. And I do mean hidden.

"Remember, his goal is revenge, and he's going after the men and women who convicted him. That means some of your friends and co-workers are in danger, so we're going to need volunteers for bodyguard service. As of now, everyone has a partner, and no one goes anywhere alone. Is that clear?"

"Yes, sir," the group answered.

Steven nodded. "Good. Stay on your toes, people."

He took a seat, and Reed replaced him at the front of the room. "Threats to Fern Jenkins' life have made moving her to a more secure place a priority," he said. "I know it's a job that leaves a bad taste in everyone's mouth, but I expect nothing but professionalism on all levels, and I'll not settle for less.

"We're also establishing a task force to search old abandoned buildings, either by warrant or owner approval. No one is to enter any building without proper permission. A quick assessment hasn't turned anything up, so we need to take a more in-depth look.

"Remember, it's always the unexpected that solves the case, so keep your eyes open for exactly that. No clue is too small. We currently have hundreds of leads and sightings, and we'll be following up on all of them. Details, Officers! We need and rely on details. As Quaid said earlier, if something looks out of place, there's a reason for it. Follow up, but don't do it alone."

~***~

The next day, Jenkins thumbed his nose at Quinn and the entire police force by proving, despite what they'd been telling the public, there was more on his agenda than simple revenge. After removing his four former sex slaves from his freezer, he put them on display on the playground equipment in the most public park in downtown Anchorage, staging them on a swing, sliding board, monkey bars, and seesaw. The gruesome scene was discovered just minutes after he left the park, and the police quickly found the U-Haul truck he'd abandoned nearby. The vehicle, blanketed with his fingerprints, had been rented in his name with his mother's credit card, and next to the truck, he'd spray-painted a message: Suck that, Quaid. The Snowman is back.

The Snowman case kept Steven in town and away from his family for nights on end. He talked with Sarah by phone and texted every day and stole an hour or two away from the office whenever he could, but for now, putting Jenkins behind bars had to come first.

Blessed with a rare break in the middle of the day, he jumped at the opportunity to go home, and when he got there, he found Sarah in the nursery with the girls. She was rocking Moya and singing a lullaby, and Myra was already asleep in her bed. He stood in the doorway, staring at his family, and his heart swelled with pride. During Gabriella's memorial service, he hadn't shed a tear, but now, looking at his new family, he was overcome with emotions.

The threats Jenkins made during his arrest and conviction played on a constant loop in Steven's head, and lurid nightmares of Sarah and the girls covered in blood, hanging from trees, and left to the elements in one of the bastard's so-called art exhibits haunted his nights. The dark circles under his eyes bore witness to his sleepless nights, and even though he knew the respite was temporary, seeing his family like this filled him with joy.

Sarah smiled at him as she put Moya in the crib and covered her with a blanket. Then, after tucking Myra in, she took his hand, and they left the nursery together.

"I think it's time Mommy got a nap, too," he said. "Those two have been running you ragged," he said.

"Nonsense! They invigorate me."

"Then you're saying it's my fault that our love life has suffered?"

Sarah laughed. "I won't hold it against you, but how is the search for Jenkins going?"

"He's disappeared, leaving a mind-numbing confusion in his wake, as usual. Sorry. It's the nature of the beast."

"I'm sure, but in no time, you'll have your man, and we'll be a very cohesive family unit," Sarah said with confidence. "Emma's helping, and tomorrow we're interviewing nannies."

"I hope you're right. But I do miss my wife."

She squeezed his hand. "I miss my husband."

"Then let's take advantage of the quiet and nap, too."

Sarah laughed, resting her hand on his butt cheek. "I'd love a nap. And because we're parents now, we talk in code," she said with a wink.

A few hours later, she awoke to find him dressing. "Going back so soon?"

He sat beside her on the bed. "I have to find Jenkins."

"I know." Sarah kissed his hand. "I'm sorry."

"What for?"

"That I can't help, and you're being pulled in a million directions. That such people exist. I guess for many things. It wasn't that long ago that you were talking about moving north permanently. I feel guilty because I took part in the push for you to return, and now I wish we'd never left our sweet mountain home."

"No. Don't," Steven said and sat beside her on the bed. He lifted her chin. "Learning Jenkins is at it again, I could never walk away, no matter how much I wanted to. I do worry about you and the girls, though, which I'd do regardless. Isn't that what having a family is all about?"

Sarah nodded.

"I'm grateful for our family. If anything, it makes me even more determined." He kissed her softly. "And it doesn't matter what job a person has. People like Jenkins affect all of us. I witness that every day, in every phone call. People are frightened. They want…no they need, this man caught. He's giving everybody nightmares."

CHAPTER TWENTY-ONE

Bear Attack

September 22nd

Just enough snow was falling to make the roads wet and slippery, so retired District Attorney Jonathan Franks erred on the side of caution and was getting home from his new job as a legal consultant later than expected. He punched in his girlfriend's phone number as he walked to the door. "Listen, Tracy," he said to her voicemail. "Sorry I'm late, but I'll change and be at your place in twenty minutes. I promise."

He ended the call, went into the house, and raced to the shower, leaving a path of discarded clothing behind him. After being divorced for ten years, he thought his best years were behind him, but being with Tracy made him feel like a giddy teenager again. Whistling and dancing in place, Jonathan bent over to adjust the shower's water temperature.

A sharp sting suddenly burned his right buttock, and he fell helplessly to the floor. Hands gripped his ankles and dragged him from the bathroom, down the hallway past the strewn clothing, and into his bedroom, where he was dropped onto a bedspread like dead weight.

Sprawled on his back like a rag doll, he looked up at the face of his assailant, and fear surged through his paralyzed body. His heart pounded erratically, and a torrent of urine soaked the cover beneath him.

Stowy waved. "Hi, Frank. Remember me? I told you we'd meet again. Sorry, but I'm afraid you aren't going to make it to your engagement party. Wait, no, I'm not the one who's afraid. That would be you. You're the one who pissed all over yourself, you big baby." He kicked Jonathon in the side and chuckled. "But don't worry. I'll drop you off at Tracy's later. I was going to leave your body in a park, but she has such a lovely front yard, don't you think?" He kicked Jonathon's immobile body two more times. "What? Cat got your tongue. You know, it's rude not to answer me when I ask you a question." He laughed and sat on the edge of the bed.

"You know, I thought long and hard about how you should die, and if you recall, I was considerate enough to send you notice of my decision. That article about bear attacks?"

Jonathon's fear-crazed eyes opened even wider.

Stowy smiled. "Ah, I see you do remember. The way I see it, with you being a gruff, no-nonsense DA like you are, it only fits that you be attacked by an animal just as cantankerous. Remember, my Jessica? She was one of my most artistic displays. Simply stunning! I used something similar to these on her, and this set my pal Zeke got for me should work just as well on you." He dangled the razor-sharp bear claws where Jonathon could see them. "Impressive, aren't they? Those nails have got to be at least five inches long."

He tossed the claws on the bed and picked up the tuxedo that Jonathon had laid out to wear to the party. "Time to get you dressed so we can start having some fun. Let's make it look like you ran into a bear on the way to Tracy's house. Good idea, don't you agree? After all, we wouldn't want her to think you intentionally missed your engagement party." He laughed and shoved Jonathon's legs into his slacks. "What she sees in a fat old man like you is beyond me. Must be the money. She won't be getting her wedding, but I'll make sure she sees you in all your glory."

~***~

Just minutes after the last guest left, Tracy picked up a few cocktail glasses and carried them to the kitchen. She was disappointed Jonathon didn't make it, but emergencies couldn't be helped. At least he'd texted her to let her know and said he'd be there as soon as possible. She sighed. Hopefully, she'd hear from him soon.

As if she'd summoned him through magic, her phone pinged with a text: Meet me outside.

She smiled. Think of the devil. After putting on her coat and boots, she opened the front door, wondering what kind of surprise Jonathon had cooked up for her this time. Shivering, she walked out into the yard but saw nothing. Then she heard what sounded like a moan.

"Jon? Is that you? Are you out here?" She walked around the side of the house, searching for the source of the sound she'd heard.

She heard another groan, and it seemed to be coming from those trees. After switching on her phone's flashlight app, she walked toward them. "Jon, is that you? You're scaring me. Where are you?"

"Tracy, I'm here. To your left," Stowy stage-whispered. "Come on, sweetheart, just a little bit closer. I've got a surprise for you."

Tracy smiled, and her shoulders relaxed. "What am I going to do with you? You and your practical jokes!" Then she spotted his shadowy form on the ground, and the smile fell from her face. "Ohmigod!" She dropped to her knees beside him. "Ohmigod! Jon! What happened?"

She directed her flashlight to his face and fell backward, screaming. "NO! Ohmigod, no!" She dropped her phone and covered her eyes, not wanting to see the blood, the torn flesh, or that one unseeing eyeball dangling from its bloody socket. With a shudder, she pulled herself together. Help. He needed help. She groped on the ground for her phone.

A hand covered her mouth. "There's no need to scream," Stowy said, pushing her closer to the mutilated body. "He just wants to say goodbye."

Jonathan's remaining eye watched Tracy's tears fall into his open wounds, and he moaned, desperately wishing he still had a voice box so he could speak to her. Tell her how sorry he was. How very, very sorry.

Stowy slid his hand up Tracy's dress. "Oh my. Mr. District Attorney, you sure know how to pick a winner. Nice firm ass. What do you say to a ménage à trois? While I have some fun with that fine ass of hers, she can give you a farewell blowjob. If you can still get that sorry piece of meat up, that is." Stowy laughed. "Not often you get the chance to come and go at the same time." He chuckled as he put a vice-like grip on the back of Tracy's neck. "Won't you, sweetheart? After all, that's how you won his heart, isn't it? Blowjobs in exchange for all that lovely cash he's given you?" He tightened his grip, digging his nails into her flesh. "I want to know why a street-walker who accepts money for sex is a whore, while someone like you is considered a lady. You're just a different kind of hooker." He spat in her hair. "That's all any of you bitches are."

He shoved her face down and stuffed Jonathan's flaccid dick into her mouth and down her throat. She could barely breathe, but she didn't want to breathe at all. Her eyes watered, and the scent of blood and an unspeakable stench from his shredded intestines filled her nostrils. She tried to hold the vomit back but couldn't. Fueled by party food and champagne, it rose from her stomach but had nowhere to go. Stowy pushed her head down harder, and the cock in her throat grew. Her eyes rolled back, and she convulsed, while Stowy continued pounding her from behind.

Jonathan died moments after she did. Their horror was over, but Stowy wasn't finished with them yet.

~***~

Steven's phone pinged, and a text from an unknown number appeared beside a snowman emoji. District Attorney Jonathan Frank and his beautiful fiancée cordially invite you to the scene of their demise. Stowy conveniently listed Tracy's address.

He immediately called Reed and, after directing James in IT to trace the call, raced to the scene.

James called back moments later. "Steve, the phone that sent you the text belongs to Tracy Gold. Its location is the address Jenkins gave you.

"Understood," Steven said grimly. "The bastard's caught up with technology."

CHAPTER TWENTY-TWO

Gruesome Details

September 23rd

Details of the two gruesome murders spread globally, and now the Snowman was trending on Facebook, Twitter, and any other social network where people could voice an opinion, which everyone seemed to have. Some were even placing bets on who the next victim would be, and according to oddsmakers, Quaid was a long shot.

Steven stood at the front of the room, about to begin the morning briefing, his eyes telegraphing how little sleep he'd had since the Franks and Gold murders. His officers all knew and respected the former D.A. Many had considered him a friend. So Steven wasn't surprised by the dark cloud of grief and fear that was hanging so heavily in the air. "What happened to Jonathan Franks should never have happened," he said, a bitter edge of frustration in his voice. "He should have had protection, but he didn't believe he was in any danger, so he turned it down."

He paused to get his emotions under control as he looked out over the somber faces in front of him. "Too many of our friends have forgone protection or delayed it, and the cost has been too high," he said. "Despite our warnings and offers of security, Jenkins has been able to get to his targeted victims."

Steven held up the bear attack story in an evidence bag. "He's also telegraphing his intentions. The first time, it was a movie flyer, and this time, it was a newspaper article, and in both cases, he was giving a clue as to how he planned to kill his victims. Pay attention, ladies, and gentlemen, and don't dismiss anything, especially if you've had any interaction with Jenkins in the past. We have to stop this bastard!" To quell his returning anger, he ran a trembling hand through his hair and took a deep breath. "Any suggestions, people?" he asked more quietly. "Any new ideas about how to find his hiding place?"

No one spoke, but a single hand went up in the back of the room. Steven pointed, and James Lawrence, the department's computer expert, stood. "I've been going through real estate records, looking for any sales in locations Jenkins might find workable," he said. "Would it be too much to ask for a few officers to go out and personally lay eyes on these places? I tried calling the owners, but I haven't been able to reach all of them, and some don't bother calling back."

"Good thinking," Steven said, pointing to two other officers. "Johansson and Bender, I want you two to help Lawrence with those follow-ups. Jenkins is a master of disguise and fake ID's, so you're going to have to check each place thoroughly. I expect a written report on each location and what you find there. Document everything!"

"Yes, sir," the officers said. "Understood, sir."

Steven nodded. "That goes for the rest of you, too. Your assignment is to fan out and interview each person within a five-mile radius of his crime scenes. I expect each of you to submit a written report to Captain Reed and me. Be sure to include anything you find that's out of the ordinary. And I mean anything. Some little detail you may think is insignificant could be precisely what we need to blow this case wide open. Someone saw something. Find out what." He looked around the room at his officers…his friends. "Be careful out there, people. Dismissed."

~***~

While Steven worked hard to find a hate-filled monster, Sarah concentrated on making a love-filled home for the girls.

"Those two are so sweet. How are they adjusting?" Leeann asked.

"The first few weeks were rough, but they're…we're all moving forward. Moya looks to Myra for her cues. It's adorable. I've tried to distract them from their grief by shopping and allowing them to decorate their room, and for short increments, it works. Yesterday, I thought I'd taken them backward."

"How?"

"I presented them with a painting of the girls with their parents at the cabin."

"I'll bet that was emotional."

"Very. They spent every waking hour yesterday just sitting in front of it. It was heartbreaking to see Myra wiping away her tears so Moya wouldn't notice."

"She's so protective, they'll be close like that through life," Leeann said. "They seem much better today."

"They are. It's turned out to be a good thing. Myra told me she feels their protection. They say a prayer for them every night. It's the sweetest, most heartbreaking thing I've ever seen." Sarah wiped a tear from her cheek but smiled. "Thanks for the gifts. The girls were delighted. It was very thoughtful of you."

"Please," Leeann said with a dismissive wave of her hand. "It was just a few stuffed animals. No big deal."

Sarah smiled. "Yes, it is. Believe me." She sighed. "I can't believe how much I love my new role. At first, I wasn't sure I could do it, but then, you just do. Your whole world changes, and you make the adjustments. I've never been happier."

"I'm not surprised. A family is what you've always wanted. You're glowing with happiness, and those little ones are lucky to have you."

"No, I'm the lucky one. Steven, too. When he's here, he's a changed man. They call him Daddy Hawk. It's adorable."

"And they call you Mommy Sarah. That's just too cute. It's a shame this Snowman character is back in his life. I think that's why John wants me to go away. Now that I've gotten through the first trimester, he's shipping me home to my mother."

"I suggested it," Sarah confessed.

"Yeah, I know." Leeann stuck her tongue out at her friend. "John told me it was your idea, but to be honest, I don't want to be here, anyway. Not until that man is dead or back in prison. John assigned me security, but it's still frightening, and really, that's not how I want to live."

"Tell me about it," Sarah said, thrusting her thumb toward the security guard standing a few feet away on the outside deck.

"Sorry. I'm an idiot. Knowing Steven, your security's probably so tight, you can't even go pee in peace." She smiled. "Thanks for the use of the plane, but I have a favor to ask. Would you consider going with me?" When she saw the look on Sarah's face, she held up her hand. "Wait! Before you say no, I'm only asking for a few days, maybe a week. It'd be fun for you and a distraction for the girls. Please?"

Sarah considered a moment and then cocked her head and grinned. "Sure! Why not? Steven wanted to send the girls and me off to France yesterday, but I dug in my heels because I didn't want to go without him. Instead, we're going to spend Thanksgiving and Christmas with his family, and then we'll both take the girls to France after the new year, so I think it's safe to say he'd be thrilled if we go away with you for a few days. And you're right. It'd be a fun distraction."

"Sounds perfect, but that last idiot managed to find you in France. Are you sure it's a good idea for you to go there again? Although I don't see how this guy could get out of the state, let alone the country."

"That's why security has tripled. Steven's sending Elliott home to France for the holidays so he can spruce up the security on the farmhouse before we arrive."

"Smart man."

"What I've discovered is that if there's a will, the monsters will find a way," Sarah said sadly.

"Too true."

The mood had soured, but Sarah wouldn't let it stay that way. "I'm excited. When do we leave for Hawaii?"

CHAPTER TWENTY-THREE

Knock, Knock

September 25th

"New homes under construction. People moving in, and people moving out daily. Life marches on, but no one would believe that a monster lives next door, especially in the richest of neighborhoods," Bender said in a Rod Serling-like voice.

"Not funny, you idiot," Johansson said as they pulled into a newly built neighborhood

"How many of these damned places are there?" Bender grumbled as they approached yet another new chalet north of Anchorage. "In my opinion, it's a monumental waste of time checking them, anyway. We should be looking in some of the more affordable neighborhoods. There's no way the Snowman could afford one of these places, let alone walk into a mortgage office and purchase one."

"That's not what I heard," Johansson said. "I heard the bastard got rich off the proceeds from his kills."

Bender frowned. "That's bullshit! Where'd you hear that?"

Johansson laughed. "Yeah, I know. That's what I thought, too." He shrugged. "It's just one of the online rumors that have been going around. It claims there's a huge black market for the souvenirs from Jenkins' kills. Says he stashed them and got his mother to sell them online for big bucks. If what they're saying's true, the guy's got more than enough cash to buy one of these places."

"Man, that's sick!" Bender said, shaking his head. "What kind of souvenirs are you talking about?"

"Pictures of the girls he killed. You know, the before and after shots, or jewelry that belonged to the victims, and his blood paintings. I hear those bring the most money. Supposedly, his mother's negotiating a multi-million-dollar deal with some wacko who wants to turn the Jenkins' house into a museum in memory of his serial killer status."

"Memory? The guy isn't even dead."

"Just a matter of time. Although I'm hoping it'll be just a matter of days," Johansson said. "You ready?"

Bender nodded, and the two exited the patrol car, walked to the chalet's front door, and rang the doorbell.

Moments later, an effeminate-sounding voice said, "Hello. How can I help you, gentlemen?"

They looked around but saw no one. "Hello? Is someone there?" Johansson asked.

"Hello, officers," Stowy minced with a slight lisp. "I'm Gavin Raya, and you're at the front door of the home owned by my partner Brian and me. Look up and wave. How can we help you?"

Both officers' heads rose in unison, and they waved at the tiny camera hanging above the door. "Sir, we're here to do a security check," Bender said. "We're looking for Stowy Jenkins. You know…the Snowman? We're checking all recent house purchases in and around Anchorage, and we understand you bought this place last year."

"Oh, yes! How utterly delicious to have such strapping young officers looking out for us! We do love a man in uniform." Stowy put a hand over his mouth to keep from laughing.

"Can we come in, sir?"

"Oh, sorry! I'm not there. I mean here. I mean, wherever you are! Oh dear, you got me all flustered. Right now, my partner and I are on our honeymoon in Hawaii. But this wonderful new security system lets us monitor our house, inside and out, no matter where we are. Say hello to the handsome officers, Brian."

"Hey, guys, nice to see our tax dollars at work," Stowy said in a deeper voice. Then he went back to his effeminate voice. "Oh, but don't worry," he said. "We can still let you in, and just wait until you see it! We just finished redecorating, and it's to die for!"

"Thank you," Johansson said. "It won't take us long. We need to take a quick look around for any signs that Jenkins has been here. He's been known to take over unoccupied homes to do his killing."

"Oh dear, then I'm glad you're there," Stowy said in his effeminate voice. "We certainly wouldn't want to find any unpleasant surprises when we get home, now, would we? Can you imagine how devastating it would be to walk in our front door and right into that monster's arms? Oh! It makes me shudder to think of it! Thank goodness he's into girls!"

Stowy slapped his hand over his mouth, and his shoulders shook with contained laughter. Jerking those incompetent cops around from his basement right under their feet was the most fun he'd had all day. In a baritone voice, he said, "Yes, officers, please look around. I'll unlock the door now."

The door unlocked, and the officers wiped the mud from their boots, pushed the door open, and walked in.

The living room was immaculate and modern, with clean lines, large windows, and walls painted in various shades of gray. Vibrant red paintings were scattered throughout. Plush leather furniture and marble accents completed the decor. It was a far cry from the taxidermist's cabin they'd captured the Snowman in ten years earlier.

"Wow! Nice place," Bender said. "Not at all the kind of place I'd imagine a serial killer living. And these paintings, so unique, especially the colors." He reached out to touch one, and Johansson slapped his hand away."

"Don't touch that. The oil from your hand will cause damage."

"Yes, please don't touch, but thank you," Stowy gushed. "Your appreciation means a lot. I'll let the artist know. He's a good friend of mine."

The officers walked through each room, taking particular notice of the exits and checking for any possible hidden compartments. "I wonder why the basement door's locked," Bender said, jiggling the doorknob. "Wasn't the Snowman's favorite hangout in the basement?"

"Yeah, you're right. I'll ask the owners."

Johansson walked into the living room. "Can you guys still hear me?"

"Oh, yes, officer. Is something wrong?"

"Not really, except the door to the basement is locked."

"Oh, and you'd best thank your lucky stars it is, because there aren't any steps." Stowy lisped. "Our contractor suggested the keyed deadbolt to prevent any accidents. Oh my God, can you imagine the lawsuits?"

"Good thinking," Bender said as he joined his partner.

"Eventually, we'll get rid of the door and put a wall there, but until the construction's done downstairs, we can use a ladder to get to and from it in an emergency. Our electrical box is down there, along with the furnace. All that's to be moved. Until then, the snow can make a real mess if we need to get there from the outside."

As the officers listened to his rambling explanation, true to their orders, they scribbled notes to include in their reports later. Bender closed his pad and was about to shove it in his pocket when Stowy started speaking again.

"You see, we're building an apartment down there," he continued. "A nice one, too, so we can charge a healthy rent. We figure the rental income will keep us doing all the things we love, like traveling. Oh, and if you'd like, I can send you the key overnight."

"No need for that," Johansson said, returning his pen to his pocket. "I think we're done here. Thank you."

"You're quite welcome, officers. We appreciate your service!"

Stowy, sitting in his new basement bunker, listened to their footsteps above him, followed by the front door closing. Then he laughed until his stomach hurt. "What idiots!" Messing with them was so easy, it gave him a hard-on. "Get over here, slave!" he yelled." I want to celebrate!"

CHAPTER TWENTY-FOUR

Judgment Day

October 5th

A fresh layer of snow covered the lawn and bushes with a brilliant sparkle that made Norman Groove squint as he bent to pick up his morning paper. He felt a sting in his left buttock, and his legs immediately gave way.

"Well, what do we have here?" Stowy said as he caught him. "A little tipsy today, are we? Not a good look for a recovering alcoholic."

Stowy dragged the judge into the house and sat him on the sofa. "Relax. It won't be long," he said. "Remember that day you sentenced me to life in prison times ten?" He pulled the slumped man's head up by the hair and laughed at the horror-filled eyes staring back at him. "Oh yeah, you remember." He dropped the judge's head to the back of the sofa. "Well, I made a promise then, too. Do you remember what that was?"

He laughed again. "Oh, of course, you do! I know you do because nobody forgot the Snowman. Now the whole state is up in arms. Calling for the return of the death penalty, and it's all because of me. Me! Can you imagine? I'm honored, and because I care so much about what the people want, I'm here to see that they get their wish." His grin made him look more like a snarling beast than a man. "And I want you to know, I've saved my most brutal death for you."

He walked to the table beside the door and picked up the pile of mail that was sitting there. As he leafed through it, he said, "You should've paid attention to the religious tract I sent you." He held up a leaflet and let the rest of the mail fall to the floor. "And here it is! A special message from me to you." He held it in front of the judge's face.

"That's a nice-looking cross. Remember, sweet Holly? I crucified her. It took more than two hundred nails. The ones through her bones kept her on the cross. But all the ones that went through the flesh and muscle…well, let's say when I was done, there wasn't much left."

Stowy lifted the judge and threw him into a fireman's carry. "As much fun as this has been, we'd better get going. I understand your cleaning lady comes at eleven."

He dumped the judge onto the backseat floor of his truck and covered him with a dirty blanket. "Stay cool, Judge. We've got a bumpy ride ahead of us, but I'm sure you'll enjoy every single one of those potholes we'll be hitting."

Six hours later, the same religious tract, with the judge's name written on it in blood, was found taped to the courthouse door, and an anonymous phone call informed the police of the body's whereabouts.

They found the judge on a cross that had been propped against the front door of an old abandoned church on the south side of Anchorage. Blood, tissue, and bone chips were splattered everywhere. More than two hundred nails had been driven into the judge's body with a nail gun. His bones were splintered, his flesh torn, and his muscles shredded. Only the judge's face remained, but a crown of nails had been skewered into his skull. The coroner surmised that the judge had been alive during most of the torture.

Steven's phone pinged with a text from Jenkins. Judgment Day has arrived, Detective. Are you ready? Next to the message was the now-familiar snowman emoji.

CHAPTER TWENTY-FIVE

Don't Come Home

October 8th

The day of the judge's funeral was beautiful, calm, and warm, which meant most of Anchorage turned out in his honor. He'd dedicated decades to serving the town he loved. To express their appreciation, citizens lined both sides of the streets as the procession wended its way from the church to the cemetery. They stood quietly, respectfully, as the procession crept past, led by the entire police department, who wore somber expressions and black armbands over their crisply pressed dress uniforms. It was an honorable goodbye for an honorable man. Still, it was happening far too soon for the good people of Anchorage.

The headlines read ANCHORAGE: A CITY HOSTAGE TO A MADMAN. Reporters and citizens alike were merciless in their criticism of the police department, and they were all demanding answers. One article asked, how is it possible for one man to outsmart our entire police force and hold our city captive? Is he that smart, or are our police that stupid? Our incompetent officials are still clueless as to his location, and it's beyond ridiculous that this monster continues to walk freely among us.

Steven read the headlines while he waited for the captain. "Ready?" he asked as Reed stepped into his office.

"Almost," Reed said, rubbing his chin. "I don't understand this one. Why didn't the judge want security?"

"He did," Steven said. "Judge Groove was originally out of town visiting family, but he came home a day early and didn't inform anyone. He called me that morning, probably moments before Jenkins showed up, asking for someone to be assigned."

"Dammit! Just like the papers said, a day late and a dollar short. Jenkins is making fools out of all of us. Who's the bastard going after next?"

"Good question. Unfortunately, only Jenkins has the answer." Steven pulled out his phone. "Would you mind starting the meeting?

I'm going to call Sarah and try to convince her not to come home. She's supposed to fly back from Hawaii tomorrow."

"Good idea. I'll see you in the conference room."

Steven stared at the skyline and hit speed dial. Sarah answered with joy in her voice. "Hey, handsome, how are you?"

"Missing you, my sweet. What are the girls up to?"

"Running in the waves with Auntie Leeann and Nana Lori. I've taken so many pictures, it'll take you a week to get through them all."

"I can't wait. I love all the ones you've texted me. The guys at the office might be a little tired of them, though."

"Too bad," Sarah said with a laugh. "So, how is the case coming?"

"That's why I called. Would you consider staying there another week?"

"I had a feeling you were going to ask me that, but no, I wouldn't. We've already overstayed our welcome. It was originally only for a week, and we've already been here for two. The jet is scheduled, and the girl's clothes are almost all packed. We want to come home. The girls miss their daddy."

Steven sighed. "Okay, you win. Not fair to use my position against me."

Sarah laughed. "Ha, now you know how it feels. See you soon, Daddy!"

"I'll meet the plane. Love you. Kiss the girls for me." He hung up and found himself smiling, but only for a minute.

Officer Cotton knocked on the door. "Troops are waiting, sir."

With a nod, Steven followed him to the briefing room. "Officers, thank you for your dedicated response," he said. "I wish I had some good news for you. Hell, I wish I had any news, but all I can tell you is to dig deep. Jenkins is playing us. He's trying to make us all look like fools, and he's doing a damned good job of it. When you continue your search today, remember this man can be anyone. Use your intuition, and keep it professional, but let's find this bastard. Stay on your toes, people. Dismissed."

CHAPTER TWENTY-SIX

Trick or Treat

October 31st

There were no jack-o-lanterns, spiderwebs, or glow-in-the-dark skeletons decorating the so-called safe house, nor were there any bowls filled with chocolate bars and candy corn, but befitting the holiday, Fern Jenkins was suffocating in a horror movie-like atmosphere of stress and fear. She'd reluctantly agreed to let the police move her here after the death threats began, but that didn't mean she had to like it, any more than calling this dump a safe house meant she felt safe.

Her cell phone rang, and she answered with irritation. "Hello."

"What's wrong, lover?" Zeke asked with a smile in his voice.

"Zeke! Where in the world are you, and why haven't you called?"

"But I am calling, my love. Don't worry. It's all proceeding as planned, and Stowy doesn't have a clue. Soon the cops will have him, and we'll be free. I promise. Just stay cool. It'll all be over soon."

Before Fern could say another word, the line went dead. "Son of a bitch! It'd better be over soon. I haven't suffered all these months because I love you. The only reason you aren't already dead is because I need your contacts." She emptied her glass and laughed. "Believe me, killing you will be the highlight of my life."

She paced the floors, relishing the fantasy of finally seeing Zeke take his last breath. Then, resigned to her imprisonment, she poured herself some wine and switched on the television. The movie Halloween was playing, one of her longtime favorites. With an appreciative smile, she quickly guzzled several glasses of wine. As its relaxing warmth spread through her body, she settled back on the sofa to root for Michael Meyers and his epic quest for blood.

A floorboard behind her creaked, and with an annoyed frown, she muted the television. Still watching the now-silent movie, she snarled, "Who's there?"

The breathiness of his voice sounded slightly eerie in the quiet room. "You've been keeping secrets, dear mother."

She tossed the remote control to the sofa and jumped to her feet, a big grin on her face, and her arms opened wide. "There you are! I was wondering when you'd show up. What'd you do with the two guards?"

"Exactly what Michael would've done," Stowy said with a smile. "I cut their throats."

"That's my boy! They just changed shifts, so that means we've got all night."

"That was my plan," he said. "As always, there's a method to my madness." He moved into her embrace and gave her a bear hug. "I've missed you, Mother." Then he pulled back and raised his eyebrows. "Exactly what did you do to rate this kind of protection? I expected you to have moved south by now."

"That's what I planned to do, but they said I'm a material witness, and if I don't testify against you, they'll charge me with aiding and abetting."

He laughed. "Sucks to be you, doesn't it?"

She pinched his cheek and then patted it. "Don't get cute with me, young man! You said something about me keeping secrets. What was that all about?"

"Zeke's in town."

"Oh, he is, is he?" she said, returning to the sofa. "Well, that's news to me." She picked at some nonexistent lint on her slacks without looking at him. "Do you know if he purchased his dream home?"

He sat on the arm of the chair. "Dream home?"

"Didn't he tell you about it? I'm surprised because outside of you, that's about the only thing he ever blah-blah-blahed about. He said he was going to buy some land in New Freeport, Pennsylvania, wherever the hell that is. To listen to him talk, it's heaven on earth." She shrugged nonchalantly, but there was an eager intensity in her gaze.

"Odd," he said, watching her closely. "He never mentioned it, but I take it you're supposed to join him there. That'd make sense, seeing as how he told me you two are getting married."

She shook her head and made a quick dismissive motion with her hand. "Oh, Stowy, that was all talk! If I had to, I would've promised him the moon. He was torturing me, for goodness sake!"

"Is that so?" he said, still watching her. "That's not how Zeke tells it. Matter of fact, he used the word love more than once."

She grabbed her wine glass and drained it. "Yeah, some love!" she said. "He loved my blow jobs, and he loved my ass, but me? No, he never loved me. He just loved to use me."

A slow smile spread across Stowy's face. "Then why are you blushing? Come on, Mom, I think you're protesting too much. I saw the diamond he proposed with."

She pulled a chain from around her neck and held it up for him to see. "You mean this thing? It's cubic zirconia. The man has no money, no taste, and he doesn't know the first thing about love."

With a laugh, Stowy took the ring from her to look at it more closely. "Fine. Then I'll just put it down the garbage disposal," he said, moving toward the kitchen.

Fern jumped up. "No! Please don't." She grabbed the ring from his hand and put it back around her neck. "If I'm not wearing it when he shows up, he'll kill me."

"Are you trying to play both ends against the middle, Mother?"

"No, never. I'm…I'm terrified of the man. You have to know what he's capable of."

He nodded. "I'll make sure he pays, and I'll replace his fake diamond with a real one. I promise. But if he has no money, how could he buy a cabin in Pennsylvania?"

"Knowing him, he robbed a bank. He's one crafty cuss."

"Speaking of home, why haven't you sold the house and moved to the mansion you always wanted?"

She snorted. "Sell our house? As if that's ever going to happen. I talked to a realtor who said the place is worthless. According to him, it's worth zero, and I have zero chance of selling it. He said nobody wants to live in Stowy Jenkins' house, because it's cursed."

"Why not use the dark web…you know, the same way you and Zeke sold most of my keepsakes." He smiled coolly. "I'm sure one of my fans would love to live in the house that murder built."

Fern's hand flew to her chest like a fluttering bird. "You know about that?"

Stowy laughed. "Of course, I know. I know everything. And I believe Zeke will be very disappointed when he finds out you thought you had to lie to me."

"You've got it all wrong! I did what he asked, and said what he told me to say, and it was all to protect you. Otherwise, he would've killed you, and if he's back in town, my bet is he's here to do just that. I'm telling you, that man is crazy, and I'd bet anything he's the copycat killer they're looking for, too. I wouldn't put it past him. I think he's trying to re-live your glory. I know he's jealous of you, but for him to claim I've been plotting against you. That's preposterous!"

"Such big words, Mother. Do you really think he's jealous of me?"

"I'd bet my life on it!" She picked up her empty wine glass, frowned, and put it back on the table. "I'm sorry, son. I'm sorry we sold your treasures, but I honestly didn't know what else to do. Zeke insisted that we needed the money to get you out of prison. He took care of everything. He hired the plane and paid that paramedic, and he told me it was all at your direction."

"And all that's true." Stowy stood and paced the small room. "Zeke's been working for me this entire time. He likes to play the boss, but he's not been that since my first week in prison. Did he ever tell you how he ended up with dentures?"

"What are you talking about?"

"The first night in prison, I was initiated into the life that was ahead of me. Five men ganged up on me, and Zeke was their leader. The other four held me down while Zeke brutally took what he wanted. Do you understand, Mother, or do I have to draw a picture?"

"No. I understand. I do. Zeke told me he used you like that for months, but you were so accommodating, he grew to like you, and the two of you became friends. He said you became his second in command."

Stowy laughed, but it was a hollow sound. Then he grabbed Fern's arms and shook her. "Zeke only used me once, Mother! Got that? ONCE! Three days later, I knocked every single tooth out of his head and made him my number one bitch. He's not as good as you are, but thanks to me, that man learned to give a decent blowjob. The rest of the time we were in the joint, I only let him fuck the new prisoners after I had first go at them, and while he was getting sloppy seconds, I'd make them suck the shit off my dick. I was king in that prison! I made every man who held me down that first-night pay for it with their teeth. It was one of my favorite brands of punishment, and I was so good at it, I became known as the Dentist. All of them now bow, drop to their knees, and remove their dentures the moment I walk into a room. I conquered that prison, and every man there, including Zeke. They're all my slaves, even now, on the outside. Whatever I tell them to do, they do. Understand, Mother?"

"That lying bastard!" she roared. "All those lies he told me…" Her voice faded, and her shoulders slumped. "Yes, I understand. God, I wish I'd known." She sighed. "I'm glad. Really happy for you, son, but that's not how Zeke tells it." Fern dropped to her knees and looked up at Stowy with fear in her eyes. "How can I prove what I'm saying? He's the one who's plotted against you, son, not me. I swear!"

"Yes, he has." Stowy sat on a kitchen chair. "Zeke and I, we had a plan…at least, we did until the plane went down. He arranged that explosion. Did you know that, Mother, or do you want to lie to me about that, too?"

He watched her face for a reaction. She shrugged but did her best to look thoughtful. "I don't doubt it, son. I've told you how devious he's been. He took every dime I had. Why else would he disappear? He knows you'll kill him."

"Don't worry. When I'm finished using him, I'll take him out. And in any method, you desire."

"Oh, son, that'd be wonderful." She laid her head on his knees. "Thank you, but I'd rather take him out myself if you don't mind. Just let me know when you're done with him, and I'll cook him a bowl of soup to die for."

Stowy smiled and helped her up from the floor. "So, we're still partners?"

"Even better than that," she said. "We're blood, and nothing comes before that." She hugged him. "I don't know what I'd do without you."

"I know what you mean. I wouldn't be who I am without you, dear Mother. I just wouldn't. I'm your creation."

She held him close for several minutes, and then he pulled away from her embrace and went to the dining room table. "I have a surprise for you." When he returned, he handed her a box. "A Halloween memory. Look inside."

"I love surprises!" She quickly removed the ribbon and opened the box. "Oh, Stowy!" she gasped. "It's beautiful!"

Reverently, she ran her fingers over the slinky white flapper dress before lifting it from the box and holding it against her body. "I love the way that fringe shimmies…and look at those beads and rhinestones. Oh, Stowy, it's just perfect!"

"Does it remind you of anything?"

She beamed. "Halloween night, many, many years ago."

"The night you made me a man."

She smiled. "You remember."

"How could I forget? That night was the turning point for me. My awakening, you might say, and in honor of that momentous occasion, I believe a reenactment is in order."

"Oh, Stowy, that'd mean the world to me. Just give me a few minutes to change, and I'll be ready for you." Giggling like a schoolgirl, she grabbed the dress and hustled to her bedroom.

He put on his costume and met her there.

"Stowy, you look so dashing! A pirate costume suits you. It was always your favorite, too, even when you were a little boy." She smiled. "You were wearing one that night, weren't you?" When he nodded, she hugged him. "It means so much to me that you remember." She rested her head against his chest and caressed his back.

"I'll never forget, Mother." His jaw clenched, and his eyes narrowed. "Never."

"Give me one more minute to put on my lipstick and mask. Then we can open the champagne."

She hurried to her vanity, and without speaking, he followed and stood behind her. Their eyes met in the mirror, and her body stiffened.

He put his hands around her waist and pulled her close. "We don't need alcohol this time, do we? That night changed my life. This time I want it to be perfect." His hands moved upward and settled around her neck. "You know what I need, don't you?"

She nodded.

"Love is such a complicated thing, isn't it?" he said.

Again, she nodded.

Cackling a high-pitched staccato laugh, he picked her up and twirled her like a rag doll. "Do your thing, Mother. Make me a man. Show me how much you love me."

Taking him by the hand, she led him to the bed. Then she sat on its edge and pressed her head to his crotch. Caressing his buttocks, she pulled him closer. "My sweet, sweet boy. Mommy loves you more than anything in the world." She lowered his pants to his knees. While caressing his cock with one hand, she dropped the top of her dress with the other and placed his hands on her breasts. "Tonight, your life changes in so many beautiful ways," she whispered, removing her dentures and setting them aside. "This is the night you become a man."

Stowy moaned in pleasure as she brought him to hardness, and as she continued to suck and lick, her moans rose to mingle with his. Squeezing his ass and pulling him closer, she took his rock-hard member to the back of her throat and stroked it with her tongue.

"So good, my son. So very, very good. You know what Momma likes," she said as she looked up at him with love. "This time, it's perfection. Sheer perfection." She wrapped her mouth around him again, bringing him closer and closer to climax.

Stowy pinched her nipples before slowly moving his hands to her neck. Writhing in ecstasy, he closed his eyes and recalled that night so long ago when he first became his mother's sex toy…he remembered the horror of it…and he remembered the thrill of it. It was an impossible conundrum. He was just a stupid kid and too weak to fight her. He trusted her, a mistake he repeated time and time again over the years, but she was a she-devil. It was time to be free of her, but first, she owed him this…just one more time.

As his throbbing cock grew and his climax built, he gradually tightened his hold on her neck. Then his orgasm came, sending fireworks through his body as only she knew how. He lifted her from the bed by her neck.

"You met with the man who set those explosions. He told me you paid him with cash, then toasted my death with champagne."

Her eyes grew wide with recognition, but she didn't fight him. Fern's arms fell limply to her sides, and she stared at him through tear-filled eyes.

After giving her neck a sharp twist to snap it, he dropped her body to the bed with a satisfied grunt and spat on it. "That was a worthy farewell performance, Mother, but I'm afraid there won't be any encores."

He smiled. "Farewell, Mother, may the devil welcome you home with open arms."

CHAPTER TWENTY-SEVEN

Masked Ball

October 31st

Halloween night was clear and bright, creating the ideal backdrop for an evening of family fun at the Anchorage Boys & Girls Club. Steven and Sarah were always happy to support the club's fundraisers, and they admittedly were looking forward to showing off their dance moves at the masked ball. And Myra and Moya were positively bubbling over with excitement. Not only was this going to be their first Halloween party. But to make the event over-the-moon perfect for them, the Quaid family dressed as characters from Frozen, the girls' favorite movie. They said Daddy Hawk was a very handsome King Agnarr, and Sarah was the most beautiful Queen Iduna ever. Like the little princesses they were, they sashayed around the house in their sparkly Elsa and Anna costumes, heads held high, wishing out loud that they could wear the gowns forever.

The club was packed when they arrived, which was no surprise. Coupling a ball for adults with a supervised party for the kids was a hard-to-resist combination, especially now that the Snowman was back on the loose and safety was more of a concern.

The mayor greeted them as they entered. "Mr. and Mrs. Quaid, it's a pleasure to have you attend our little soirée. And who do we have here?" he asked, smiling at the girls.

"These are our daughters, Moya and Myra," Steven said. Holding a hand beside his mouth, he stage-whispered, "But tonight, they're Elsa and Anna."

"It's an honor to meet such beautiful princesses," the mayor said, dropping to one knee and planting a kiss on each of their hands. "I'm at your service, your highnesses."

The girls curtsied clumsily and giggled.

The mayor's wife smiled at Sarah. "You all look enchanting. Just like the movie."

Sarah was about to answer when they heard a woman's voice rise above the crowd. "…an unfortunate omen. I mean, King Agnarr and Queen Induna both die in that movie!"

Sarah froze.

Steven gave her hand a reassuring squeeze, and the mayor's wife touched her arm lightly. "Ignore her, dear," she said. "It's Halloween, a night for fun. Don't let a thoughtless remark like that spoil it for you." She smiled again. "Will you and Steven be dazzling us with your dancing tonight?"

Sarah, more rattled by the remark than she cared to admit, forced an unconvincing smile onto her face and nodded.

Steven squeezed her hand again. "Of course. We're looking forward to it," he said. "Excuse us, please. We want to get the princesses to their party." He herded Sarah and the girls a safe distance away from the crowd and kissed her on the forehead. "Are you okay?" he asked.

"I'll be fine. It's silly to let something like that bother me," Sarah said as she searched the crowd. "Oh, good! There's Charlotte."

Their new nanny, dressed as Mary Poppins, rushed to their side. "Sorry, I'm late. It took me a while to find parking. This must be the most popular place in town tonight." She looked around. "Oh, dear. Where are Myra and Moya? Did you leave them home?"

The girls giggled. "We're right here!" Myra said.

Charlotte did an exaggerated double-take. "Oh, my goodness! Just look at you two! I thought you were real princesses!"

"We are!" Myra said, hugging the nanny's legs. "We're Elsa and Anna."

The nanny grinned at Steven and Sarah. "You all look terrific! Are you ready for your dance? The Princesses and I are going to play some games. Right, girls?"

Steven handed her a roll of tickets. "Find us if it gets to be too much," Steven told her, while Sarah pointed the ring toss out to Myra. "Look, sweetie. You can win prizes, too."

"Can't we see you dance?" Myra asked, disappointment coating her voice.

"Of course, you can." Sarah knelt. "Do you remember the music we practiced too?"

Myra nodded.

"When you hear it start to play, that'll mean it's time for us to do our dance. Charlotte will bring you to the ballroom to watch." She glanced at the nanny.

Charlotte nodded, and Myra grinned. "Oh, I can't wait!" she said, bouncing in place. "You and Daddy Hawk are going to win, for sure."

Sarah laughed and hugged both girls. "It's not a contest, sweetie. But we hope it brings in lots of donations for the club, so they can help all the little boys and girls who need it. You'll be contributing by using those tickets and having the best time ever." She kissed each girl on the forehead. "Now be good for Charlotte, and we'll see you in a little while."

For the next hour, Sarah and Steven nibbled on some snacks while mingling with the other guests. Then their dance was announced. Holding hands, they walked to the dance floor and took their position while waiting for the music to begin. Charlotte rushed into the room with one girl under each arm. She set them down, and they all waved. Then the music started.

Steven twirled Sarah, then pulled her close. "Are you sure doing this will raise more money for the club?" They spun around the floor, their intricate steps in perfect unison, both precise and passionate, their two bodies moving as one.

"I told you," she said. "Since we started dancing at these functions, donations have doubled. What can it hurt whether I'm wrong or right? Isn't this fun?"

Steven laughed as he danced her around the room. "I think you're pulling my leg about the donations, but I'm game. Although I think it's because you want to show me off."

She smiled at him. "Do you blame me?"

He pulled her closer, dipped her backward for the end of the dance, and kissed her. "Never."

The audience applauded, but it was the girls' response that made them the proudest.

They dedicated the rest of the evening to the girls, with more games, contests, and dancing. While holding both girls in his arms, Steven danced them around the room, too. It was a perfect evening. Thanks in part to their special dance, the club raised three times more than the year before, and their first big family outing was a huge success. Shortly before ten, they gathered their two yawning princesses and headed for home, and the girls were nearly asleep before their heads hit the pillows.

Sarah and Steven shed their costumes and crawled into bed, about to enjoy a more intimate celebration of All Hallows' Eve.

Steven's phone rang. With a curse, he planted his feet on the floor and answered it. "Quaid," he growled. He spoke to the person on the other end for a few minutes. Then he hung up, crawled back into bed, and re-gathered his wife into his arms. "Where were we?"

Sarah smiled at him. "Wow! You're not going in?"

Steven shook his head. "Not this time. I've spent the last three months chasing down every clue and every sighting of the bastard. Out of ten reports, only three are real. Of those three, the bastard has shown himself on purpose. We have him on film. He'll look straight into the camera and give us the finger. In one instance, the idiot pulled down his trousers and mooned the camera. Or the asshole will shout out to the patrons of whatever establishment he's in, that the Snowman was here! Then he'll run off. He knows what he's doing. He's leading us on a wild goose chase, and I'll bet he knows many of us will get out of our warm beds to follow up on the sighting, in the hope that this time we'll catch him.

"But tonight, he's not going to get what he wants. I'm staying right here unless the guys call back and say they've got him cornered." He smiled. "I remember exactly where we were." He pulled her close, and together, they sank under the covers, lips locked, and bodies entwined.

CHAPTER TWENTY-EIGHT

Copycat Die

October 31st

Despite the late hour, clusters of trick-or-treaters still roamed the seedy neighborhood, so Stowy's pirate costume blended in nicely as he trudged toward Zeke's new place. He was curious to see what kind of killing ground Zeke had found since he'd abandoned the warehouse because of all the cops nosing around. But mostly, Stowy accepted Zeke's texted invitation because of the enticing pictures he'd included of a nymphet dressed as Cleopatra. Seeing her strapped naked to a table and waiting for him was enticing, but even more enticing was the vast selection of knives in the background. The combination gave him such a raging hard-on, he was out the door and on his way to Zeke's before his mother's body had a chance to get cold.

He nodded his approval as he approached what was clearly the worst-looking property on the block, possibly the whole neighborhood. What was left of the charred house after a fire claimed an entire family made it look like something from a kid's worst nightmare. Judging by the number of eggs smashed against its front and the amount of toilet paper hanging from the trees, Stowy guessed kids had targeted it to prove how brave they were. He smirked, imagining the little brats daring each other to ring the doorbell of the half-burned haunted house. He bet some of them were so scared, they peed their pants. He had to admit it. Zeke had chosen well.

Stowy cautiously made his way to the garage, which was severely damaged, but still standing, and quickly found the fake barricade, just as Zeke had described it. He pulled back the hinged façade of un-nailed boards and slipped into the house. Then he went straight to the basement door, where he found the camouflaged digital lock, punched in the entry code, and slowly made his way down the dark stairs.

"It's about time you got here," Zeke said. "I wanted to give you first whack at her, but believe me, she hasn't been easy to resist. Our Cleo's a real beauty. May even be a virgin."

"Where'd she come from?"

"I got lucky. Saw her walking down the street," Zeke said with a grin. "She said she was looking for a Halloween party, so I invited her to mine."

Stowy moved quickly through the killing room, and his smile grew when he saw the girl stretched out on the table. "My, my, my. She's even lovelier in person." He removed the gag from her mouth and smiled. "Hello, Cleo."

"Untie me!" she demanded, pulling fruitlessly at her restraints. "I'll do anything you ask. Just please let me go."

"Anything? Like what, dear? What do you think I want?" He ran his fingers through her long dark hair, caressed her face, and wiped away her tears. Which he suspected were more from anger than fear, a situation he was looking forward to rectifying. "You said you wanted to party. Why'd you change your mind?"

"That moron tied me up! What kind of party is that?" Her voice sounded calmer now. Stronger and more hopeful. A tentative smile flickered on her face. "Is there a party?"

"Depends. You said you'd do anything I asked. What did you have in mind?"

"A blow job. I'm really good at that. The best…at least that's what all the boys say."

"Do they? And what else? What else can you do for me?"

Her eyes grew wide. "I'm not sure. I'm a virgin, and I'd like to keep it that way until I get married. Blow jobs are okay, though, because they can't get me pregnant, and besides, my boyfriend says that's what he likes best. He's good at doing me too, but he's never come inside me, even though we want to sometimes. He has a huge dick, and when it gets hard, I get so wet."

"Really?" Stowy unzipped his fly and waved his penis at her. "Bigger than this?"

Her eyes grew even wider. "No! I don't think that'd even fit in my mouth!"

"I promise you it will. I'll show you, and you can show me what you can do." He straddled her chest, lifted her head, and forced his penis into her mouth. Once she got past the initial gag reflex, she started sucking like a pro. His moans gave her confidence, and she looked at him with hope-filled eyes and sucked harder.

The tension in his groin grew stronger and stronger as she sucked and teased him closer to the edge. He closed his eyes and smiled as he relived the heady feeling of his hands tightening around his mother's neck. His breathing came in gasps as he pictured Fern's spent body lying on the bed, and then with a full-body shudder, his explosive orgasm drenched young Cleo's throat.

After she sucked him dry, she licked the overflow from her lips. Then with a surprisingly innocent-looking smile, she said, "See? Just like I told you. I'm an expert."

"Yes, Cleopatra. That you are."

"Can I go home now? I was supposed to meet my friends."

He shook his head slowly. "Oh, but I thought you wanted to party."

"I...I want to go home. Please."

Stowy got off the table. "But I want more, sweetheart. Much, much more. You could say I'm a selfish lover, but I want all of it. I want all of you." His fingers caressed her naked body.

"Will you untie me?"

"My pleasure." He undid the ties.

Stowy lifted her into his arms. Cradling her, he headed toward the corner of the room. "You're shaking like a leaf. Don't be afraid, little Cleo. I'd never hurt you."

"Promise?" she whispered as tears rolled down her cheeks.

Zeke, watching from the shadows, continued stroking his dick. "Oh yeah, give it to her. Give all of it to her," he said huskily.

"I want you, Cleo. Something awful. Let me be your first. Will you do that? Then I'll let you go to whatever party you'd like to attend. If you'd like, I'll even take you there myself. Make all your friends jealous. What do you say?"

"You'd do that?" she asked, a tinge of hope returning to her voice.

"Anything for you. Let me take you to womanhood. You're the most beautiful thing I've ever seen, and I promise it'll be the best thing to ever happen to you. Once you're a woman, you can best judge who should be your man. I can be very gentle. Haven't I proven myself?"

She threw her arms around his neck, feeding his ego with her desperate capitulation. He kissed her deeply while gently laying her on the mattress in the corner of the room.

With tears of hope still staining her face, she whispered, "Okay." Not that he needed her permission. In one brutal thrust, he penetrated her vagina.

Her scream came slowly as the shock of his attack took her breath away. "NO! NO! Ohmigod, no!" she screamed while trying to crawl away from him. "Please stop!"

He laughed and held her firmly in place. "Oh, sorry. Does that hurt?" he asked between grunts of exertion. "Not what you had in mind, huh, sweetheart? I knew you'd have a tight little vagina. So good!" He continued pounding into her while she sobbed.

Still watching and stroking his dick, Zeke was breathing faster now. "Hurry up, man. I can't hold this load much longer," he gasped.

After Stowy howled in orgasmic pleasure, he stepped back, and Zeke moved forward for his turn. He flipped the girl over and forced her tight anus open with two thick fingers then quickly shoved his throbbing penis into her ass. Her high-pitched screams sounded other-worldly now, so Zeke stuffed part of the sheet down her throat to muffle them. When he finished, he tossed her aside, sank to the floor, and lit a cigarette.

The whimpering girl wrapped herself in the dirty sheet and watched them through tear-filled eyes.

Stowy laughed. "That's not the first time we double-dipped, but it's the first time we used a girl. I believe this was more to my liking. How about you?"

"I got no complaints. I got my treat, and you got yours, so I'd say it's a win-win. But what's going on? I thought I gave you a taste for ass. You going soft on me?" Zeke asked.

"Nah, but that was my third helping, and I couldn't resist the opportunity to ream her tight virgin cunt. Ass is still my topper."

Zeke motioned toward the girl. "Then go for it. She's not going anywhere."

Stowy walked to the sink and ran the water until steam was rising, and then he filled a pot with it. "Don't mind if I do, but she needs cleaning first. Damned if you didn't make her ass bleed more than her cooch did when I popped her cherry. Not that I mind the blood, but that shits got to go." He carried the pot to the bed, yanked the girl to her knees, and dumped the scalding water all over her bottom. Her screams died in her throat, and she collapsed to the bed, unconscious, and blissfully oblivious to the rest of Stowy's cruelty.

"Damn! What I wouldn't give for your youth," Zeke said after Stowy finished. "That was what…three times in less than an hour? Impressive." He went for the high five, but Stowy gave him a right hook, and Zeke went straight to the floor.

"Hey, what the hell!" Zeke said, rubbing his chin.

"It was four times in one hour. A record, even for me," Stowy said. "My mother was the first. A regular Halloween treat. But now she's dead, and it's all your fault!"

"What the hell are you talking about?" Zeke stopped rubbing his chin and pulled himself up from the floor, a look of concern on his face. "Fern? Your mother…dead. How? When?"

"Yes, my mother, you asshole." Stowy finished adjusting his clothes and zipped his pants. "Broken neck."

"Broken neck," Zeke said, shaking his head slowly. Then his eyes narrowed. "You killed her!"

Stowy shrugged. "She had it coming."

"I don't understand. Why would you do that?"

"She betrayed me. Financially, emotionally, and sexually, and nobody gets away with betraying the Snowman."

"Holy shit." Zeke lit another cigarette, shoved the girl's body out of the way, and dropped to the bed.

"She betrayed me. What do we do when one of our own betrays us?"

Zeke ran his forefinger across his neck.

"Exactly. So, I took out the trash. But you know what? I got the truth first."

Zeke's face paled, and his hand shook as he raised the cigarette to his mouth. "Really? What'd she say?"

"She didn't tell me shit. But Rowdy told me everything. I had to pay to get him to spill his guts, but then he couldn't rat you out fast enough. He said you gave him ten grand to disable the plane's engines. Then the snitch accidentally fell on his knife." He smirked. "You could say the dumb shit spilled his guts all over again."

Zeke wiped the beads of sweat from his upper lip and took another drag of his cigarette. "How'd you figure it out? How'd you know to talk to him?"

"It wasn't all that hard, Einstein. It's not like there were
hundreds of jet mechanics in the joint with us. He was the only one."

"Oh, yeah." Zeke looked down at his deflated cock. "At least I had one last party." He looked back up at Stowy. "I guess I'm dead meat, huh?"

"What would you do, my friend? How would you deal with betrayal?" Before Zeke could answer, Stowy swung a machete that had been hanging on a nearby hook, and Zeke's head landed beside the unconscious girl.

~***~

A phone call dragged Steven from a deep sleep at one AM, and he quickly threw on his clothes and rushed to the crime scene. An anonymous call had drawn firefighters to a derelict house already half-claimed by fire in the past. And at first, they thought it was either a Halloween prank or some well-meaning arsonist's attempt to rid the area of an eyesore. They'd quickly extinguished the smoldering fire, and then they found the bodies. Right after the chief heaved his dinner into the bushes, he'd called the police.

"Stanley, what do we have here?" Steven asked after arriving on the scene.

The coroner nodded in greeting. "Two headless bodies. The female was on her knees. The male was situated behind her with his penis glued to her ass. Judging by the Cleopatra costume, we found on the floor and her general description, we're pretty sure this is the sixteen-year-old girl who was grabbed earlier this evening. We found the heads over there on the other side of the room. The sadistic son of a bitch super-glued their lips together." He handed Steven an evidence bag. "And he left you a message."

After pulling the plastic bag taut, Steven read the words scrawled in Jenkins's familiar handwriting: Copycats lack artistry.

The coroner shook his head. "Is he escalating or deteriorating?"

"Hard to tell. Either way is bad news." Steven's phone pinged, and he frowned at the image of Jenkins' dead mother before reading his latest text: The Snowman doesn't tolerate betrayal.

CHAPTER TWENTY-NINE

Multiple Victims

November 3rd

The headline covered half of the Anchorage Times front page: Snowman Kills the Copycat, but who Killed the Snowman's Mother? It was a question that greased the rumor mills at every coffee shop, restaurant, and office in town, including the police department. However, all speculation immediately came to a halt in the station's conference room when Detective Quaid and Captain Reed strode into the room.

Steven stood in front of the whiteboard and waited for the officers to get settled before speaking. "Stowy Jenkins wants to be the center of attention, and because of these killings, he's gotten what he wanted. The question is: what are we going to do about it? So far, there's no discernible pattern to these murders. He's been striking when he wants and how he wants, but we need to get one step ahead of him.

"Although some of his murders may be a matter of convenience and therefore wholly random, like the unfortunate young lady he brutalized most recently, I believe the driving motivation for most of the killings since his escape is revenge. In simple terms, he's eliminating whomever he believes betrayed or wronged him in some way, and that includes three of the most recent killings.

"Victim one, Zeke Savon, Jenkins's former cellmate, was the person he hand-picked to act as his copycat killer. We found ample proof of that at Savon's location. We also have a witness who saw Jenkins and Savon together at the diner where the anonymous call was made alerting us to Martha Ashe's body on the mudflats. We know they were working together, but once we figured out that Jenkins was alive, he no longer needed Savon." He paused and slowly scanned the faces of his officers. "But that isn't why Jenkins killed him."

The officers leaned slightly forward in their chairs; their attention entirely focused on Steven.

"It, too, was revenge," he said. "Savon and victim number two, Fern Jenkins, were behind the crash of the medevac plane."

"Holy shit," someone from the back of the room said.

Steven nodded. "My sentiments exactly."

After a brief collective laugh, the officers shifted in their chairs, and he continued. "You're wondering how Jenkins knew and how we know? Well, that brings us to victim number three, one Rowdy Kenner, a former airline mechanic who also spent time at Seward. He died the same day as Savon and Jenkins' mother. Fern and Savon paid Kenner to sabotage the plane. Jenkins got the truth from Kenner and then scrambled the poor slob's guts as a bonus. We were able to get Kenner's statement at the hospital before he died. A very agonizing death. I think he held onto life so that he could spill the truth.

"Please understand, people. We're dealing with a man who has no fear, and the bastard enjoys what he does," Steven said. "His brutality is endless. While our number one assignment is to stop him, whatever you do, don't underestimate him. Proceed with caution, awareness, and always with a partner."

A phone call came moments after he left the meeting, and the message was one he was more than sick of hearing. "Steve, we've got another body."

~***~

After arriving at the scene, Steven listened to the responding officer's report.

"Our vic was found in the same gravel pit where Jenkins pulverized Jewel, that young Inuit girl. He was a mayoral candidate who got people riled up at his campaign rallies by railing against Jenkins and calling him a worthless coward. Jenkins took offense."

"Obviously," Steven said with disgust. "Thank you, Officer Clark. Stan, what can you tell me?"

The coroner took a deep breath and blew it out through his teeth. "The bastard dragged the man through the gravel pit so many times, all that's left of him is bone and tissue. Once again, Jenkins recreated one of his previous murders, but this time, with double the brutality. And he left something for you, too."

The coroner handed Steven a note: How many more before I get to you, Detective?

CHAPTER THIRTY

Devastation

November 5th

Saturday morning's skies were dark with the threat of snow, but the Quaid breakfast room was bright with light, laughter, and love. From his vantage point at the doorway, Steven smiled as he watched Sarah and the girls. With a squeal, Moya upended her bowl of cereal, and without missing a beat, Sarah jumped up to take care of the mess. In her haste, she knocked over a glass of milk and a glass of orange juice, which made Myra laugh so hard, she began to choke. Sarah stopped cleaning to pat her on the back, while Steven smiled at the beautiful chaos and felt blessed.

"Well, if it isn't a typical morning at the breakfast table," he said, entering the room. "Good morning, ladies."

Shouts of "Daddy" filled the air. Myra hugged his waist, and Moya reached for him from her highchair. He picked her up, kissed his frazzled wife's cheek, and sat down with Moya on his lap. Myra climbed up to sit on his other leg. "I bet you'd both prefer eggs and bacon instead of oatmeal. Right?"

The girls giggled but nodded in agreement. "Eggs!" they shouted.

Emma stood. "I'll have your eggs in a few shakes of a cat's tail."

"Nonsense. You finish your oatmeal. I've got this." Sarah poured Steven a cup of coffee and handed him a dry towel, then took the wet napkins and cereal bowls with her. "Be right back with those eggs." She winked at the girls.

Emma poured another glass of milk for Moya. "My favorite part of the day."

"Amen," Steven said.

That feeling of bliss lingered long after breakfast was over, then an unexpected knock at the door changed everything. When Steven opened the door and saw George Steiner, their Seattle-based attorney, his first impulse was to close and lock the door in his face.

Having the lawyer who was handling the adoption show up out of the blue couldn't be good. Especially when he was wearing such a grim expression.

Without preamble, Steven asked, "How bad is it?"

"Not good." He looked past Steven. "Where's Sarah?"

"She's tending to the girls. Come on in, and I'll go get her."

"No!" George said, grabbing Steven's arm. "Let's talk outside. Away from the family."

Steven got his jacket and followed the lawyer to his car, his heart already aching for the bad news he knew was coming. They got in the car, and he took a deep breath. "Okay, George, let me have it?"

"Remember how I said the adoption would be a breeze, considering the circumstances of Gabrielle's will and her specific intent?"

"Yes. You said just a few papers to sign and file, and we'd be the girl's parents, but it's not going to be that easy, is it? Are the grandparents going to fight us?"

"Not exactly. It's their father. He's alive, and he wants his children. I'm sorry, Steven, but there's not going to be an adoption."

Steven shook his head. "No…How's that even possible? They told Gabrielle he was dead! She even received an insurance payout."

"But it came from his parents. Their son Gregg was in bad shape, but the racist bastards brought him home and had their attorney tell Gabrielle he died. Then they gave her that so-called insurance settlement to be rid of her. Gregg finally came out of his coma a week ago, and as soon as he learned the truth, he contacted his attorney. He wants his girls with him in Texas. It's his right."

Steven could barely breathe. It felt like someone had punched him in the solar plexus. "Yes. Yes, it is," he murmured, shrinking in his seat, head in hands. "Sarah," he groaned. "How the hell do I tell her we're going to lose our babies?"

"I don't know. I'm sorry. I didn't want to be the one to tell her. She's so happy. So attached, and the girls already call her mommy. I can't, couldn't break her heart. Not that you aren't affected by this, but—"

"Shattered," Steven said softly. "But you're right. I'll take care of it. Is there any way to delay the transfer? Did you say Gregg Sunne just regained consciousness? Is he capable of taking the girls? I refuse to deliver them to his parents, the bastards. If we can deliver them into his hands directly, we will. No questions asked, I promise."

"I'll see what I can do. A delay of days, maybe weeks, but that's all. I'll get you as much time as possible, but I don't think it'll be easy, no matter when it happens."

"No, but we can prepare the girls. Get them excited about the changes and introduce them to their father via pictures so we can build their hopes for a new family. It'll make the transition easier. Not for Sarah, of course, but at least she'll have a little more time to prepare."

"I agree. I'll take care of it. I promise. You'll get that chance. Good luck, Steven."

Steven watched the lawyer's car until it was no longer in sight, but he couldn't bring himself to go back inside. Not yet. He couldn't face Sarah with such devastating news until he first came to terms with it himself. He hunched down in his jacket and began to walk. Maybe after a long walk, he'd feel strong enough to face her, strong enough to help her cope. He hadn't gone far when his cell phone rang.

"Steven?" Reed said. "There's been another murder. Jenkins' handiwork. Pick me up at Tok Junction."

"On my way." Steven rushed into the house for his gear and kissed his surprised wife. "Sorry, sweetie. Don't wait up." He rushed back outside to his truck, secretly relieved at the excuse to put off telling Sarah about Gregg Sunne. He'd have to turn her world upside down later.

When he got to Tok Junction, Reed climbed into the truck. Steven nodded at him. "Where we headed? What's the address?"

Reed slammed the door shut and reluctantly recited it.

Steven frowned. "Glacier Road? Isn't that where Denise's family cabin is?"

Reed touched Steven's arm lightly. "I'm sorry, Steven, but there's no good way to say this. She's our victim."

With his jaw set, Steven put the truck in gear and hit the gas, shooting an angry spray of gravel behind them. Reed fastened his seat belt.

CHAPTER THIRTY-ONE

Twenty-four Hours Earlier

November 4th

The cabin sat nestled among the birch trees and evergreens as a natural part of the landscape, built for comfort, but also ecologically sound. Denise smiled as she pulled into the drive, and happy memories assaulted her. Family getaways, fishing, hunting, skiing, and just quietly sitting and reflecting in front of the massive fireplace. She still enjoyed those things, but she missed her father and mother terribly. Her dad had died two years earlier from a sudden heart attack, and in a matter of weeks, pneumonia claimed her mother. Denise knew that her mother had just given up. Heartbroken after the loss of her husband, she just quit fighting. Now, Denise's heart was broken from the double loss.

Once inside, she secured the cabin, built a fire, set up the cameras and the audio, and waited for the man she was to interview. It wasn't long before Stowy Jenkins knocked on the door. Denise opened the door and said, "Come in. I've got everything set up in front of the fireplace. Make yourself comfortable."

Stowy looked around. "Where are you?"

From the attic, via a microphone, she answered. "I'm safe. I have electronic control of the cameras, lights, and sound. We can have our discussion as planned. I'll edit myself into the interview later. I agreed to a private meeting, but I wasn't about to risk being your next victim."

Stowy laughed. "Very clever, Denise. I love it. Not sure I'd want to be in the same room as myself, either, if I were you." He removed his jacket and hat. "Shall we begin?"

"First, you may want to peruse the publishing contract that's on the side table. Read it over and then sign on the last page if it meets your criteria, but I can assure you that it does. There's an extra copy for you."

Stowy picked up the document and read it quickly "I trust you, dear. I promise you can trust me, too."

Denise laughed. "I'm no fool, Stowy. I prefer working this way. I hope you don't mind."

"Not at all, my dear, not at all. I understand completely."

~~*~~

CHAPTER THIRTY-TWO

Loss

November 5th

At first glance, it looked like she'd been preparing for a routine photo shoot. Numerous cameras and lights were set up, and they were all aimed at Denise Cochran's body. Her throat had been brutally slashed, so the former Miss Alaska's neck and chest were awash in blood, as was the bright white gown she was wearing. Despite the photo shoot-like setting, the police could find no video equipment or tapes.

Steven fell to his knees, breathing shallowly to blunt the acrid scent of bleach that permeated the air, burning his nose and throat. He bowed his head to avoid looking at her. He didn't want to see those former brown and gold eyes, once bright with life, now turned a shallow gray by death. He just wanted to remember her as he knew her. Alive and filled with color, laughter, curiosity, and love.

Reed put his hand on Steven's shoulder, "You don't have to do this."

Steven shook his head. "Yes, I do. I owe it to her." He pushed his emotions aside and began his investigation.

He noted each detail in a notebook for later consumption, but he made sure he went through the entire place and that the CSI team didn't miss a speck of lint. Fingerprints were taken, fibers collected, papers were gone through. Her luggage was obtained, and pictures were taken from every angle. CSI left the place wrapped in yellow tape and moved the investigation to their offices in Anchorage.

The coroner loaded her body into his van and gave Steven his preliminary report. "She died about twenty-four hours ago. I see no evidence of torture, but she's been sodomized. Brutally raped. There's bruising, and her wrists and ankles show signs of restraints. The cut across the throat is what killed her, but it wasn't a fast death. She bled out slowly. He only nicked the carotid. She might've survived if pressure had been applied."

Steven went outside, then stood and stared at the cabin; his face scrunched up in thought. Something was off, but he couldn't quite put his finger on it. Reed, who'd been waiting for him in the truck while making a series of phone calls, continued to wait.

Steven finally climbed into the cab. "The coroner said he didn't torture her," he growled. "What the hell? Doesn't he think being raped and dying slowly like that was torture? Dammit, she didn't deserve to go out this way! Not Denise!" He hit the steering wheel with both fists.

"I'm sure he—" Reed started to say.

"Yeah, I know what he meant."

"Then let's use that anger to catch Jenkins."

Steven nodded.

"Did you call Sarah?" Reed asked.

"Not yet."

"I called Brent and told him to double security," Reed said.

Steven looked at him. "Thank you. It should've been my first move."

"You were on point. Now, let's get this bastard!"

CHAPTER THIRTY-THREE

Home & Hearth

November 10th

Fuming, Stowy paced the floor, the evening paper crumpled in his fist. "Why haven't you told them I didn't do this? I didn't kill Denise!" he yelled to the heavens. "Prove it, you illiterate half breed! You know my work. That travesty wasn't my work!" He kicked a kitchen chair against the far wall, breaking it.

"What's the matter, Stowy? Pissed because you didn't get the opportunity, or because you had the chance and didn't take it?" He laughed.

Dangerous discussion, my boy, very dangerous. If I didn't know better, I'd say you've lost all your marbles. Maybe you did kill her and don't remember.

Stowy laughed louder. "If I killed the pretty little bitch, it's not something I'd ever forget!"

Then it's time to get to work. Get the man on the job!

~***~

Sarah stared out at the snowfall and sipped a cup of tea. She sighed deeply. "I'm sorry, Leeann. I'm lousy company."

"Sorry for what? You have a right to be blue."

"You flew back to this hellhole just to cheer me up. I appreciate it, but you shouldn't have done that in your condition."

"Oh, yes, I should. After all, I was already in Seattle on a rendezvous with John. And the doc says I'm doing fine. Good to go." She smiled. "I'll be honest. I love this pregnancy thing. I feel wonderful."

"It shows. How are Eddie and Andrea making the transition to Seattle life?"

"Beautifully. Those two have a new luxurious home, and Andrea is enjoying her position with the college. They're trying for a baby, too. Can you believe it? Soon we'll all be parents. I can't wait to celebrate…." Leeann's hand flew to her mouth. "I'm sorry."

"No, don't apologize. It's all right. Maybe not in the immediate future for me, but soon, I hope. We're going to try in vitro."

"You should, and the sooner, the better."

"Steven's distracted with this case."

"Did you ever consider that Steven will always be distracted? There's always going to be a case somewhere."

"I know, but we'll figure it out. Eventually."

"I know you will."

Sarah gave her friend a hug.

"Can you believe this belly?" Leeann rubbed her stomach.

"You look beautiful. April will be here before you know it."

"It will, and I miss sharing this with you. That's why I hope you'll come to Hawaii. I mean, after the girls join their father."

"You're sweet. Maybe. I honestly don't know." Sarah stood. "Let me get through this, and then I'll reevaluate."

"I'll hold you to that. I wish I could say something that would make you feel better, but I can't think of a thing." She touched Sarah's hand.

Sarah squeezed her hand in return.

"When do the girls have to leave?"

Sarah shrugged. "I don't know for sure. Could be today, tomorrow, or a week from now. The attorney said he did as Steven asked and got Gregg Sunne to agree to let us keep the girls until he can personally take custody of them." She wiped a tear from her eye. "It's a good thing. Really." She looked at her friend but failed to form a smile. "With this Jenkins thing, it's all for the best." Her voice lost strength. She walked to the windows. "Steven won't have to worry as much if they're safe in Texas."

"How does Steven feel about all this?"

"I don't know. He got the news the same day Denise's body was found, and he hasn't been home since, so we haven't even discussed it. I only learned about it yesterday, when the attorney called. Poor George. He thought I already knew."

"Steven didn't tell you?"

Sarah shook her head. "I'm sure he couldn't find the words. For hours after I learned the truth, I could barely speak."

Leeann put her arm around Sarah's shoulders. "Oh, sweetheart, I am so sorry. Come to Hawaii. He'll worry less if you're not here to be a target, too."

"Thanks. I'll consider it, but leaving feels wrong."

"From what John told me, he's spending most of his time in town."

"He's working, but he's also mourning. Denise meant a lot to him, and I can't hold that against him. I married him for better or worse, and right now, things couldn't be much worse."

Several seconds of silence followed, but Sarah quickly brightened. "Maybe it's time to let Steven know I'll always be by his side, especially when things get tough."

~***~

Snowflakes filled the air. Lightly falling, gently swirling in a lazy wind, they tickled the skin, and their slight chill teased the senses. Sarah walked down the sidewalk, unaware of their beauty. Brent took stock of the neighborhood while she stopped to stare upward at the apartment building housing her husband's condo. She knew he was there. Captain Reed told her Steven had gone home for a few hours' sleep, and the windows were dark. She hated disturbing him, but he never ate well when working a case, and she was sure that at this moment in time, his self-care was nonexistent.

Brent unlocked the front door of the apartment building and held the door open for her. He walked in behind her, but someone grabbed the door. Brent held it tight. "Do you have a key?" he asked the man.

"My friend lives here."

"No key, no entry." Brent pulled the door closed. He watched the man reluctantly walk away. "Elliott," he said into a walkie-talkie, "keep an eye on the man in the gray parka."

"You want me to follow him?"

"No, I want you to stay with the car. Just watch his direction and make sure he leaves. There's something eerily familiar about that guy."

"I've got it," Elliott said.

Sarah held the elevator for Brent. He caught up to her, and they proceeded to Steven's apartment. Again, Brent unlocked the door, checked, and spotted Steven asleep on the couch, so he backed out to stand guard.

She tiptoed into the small galley kitchen and turned on the light farthest from the couch where Steven was sleeping, determined not to disturb him.

He sat up and rubbed his eyes. "Is something wrong?"

"Darn it! No. Sorry, I didn't mean to wake you." She moved toward him and placed a cup of coffee and a Dunkin Donuts breakfast sandwich on the coffee table.

"Are you alone?" He went to the window to check the street.

She sat on the arm of the chair. "You know I'm never alone. Brent is outside the door, and Elliott is waiting at the car. Are you ready to come home?"

He rubbed the stubble on his face, smoothed his hair back, and shrugged. "Not yet."

"We miss you. You know how the girls love their bedtime story with Daddy."

"I know, but it's been crazy since Denise—"

"I realize that, and I've tried to give you space. It's just that, well, we need you, too."

Steven nodded. "I understand. But..." He searched for the right words.

Sarah's eyes grew wide with understanding, then anger. "Oh, my God!" She jumped to her feet. "I should've known! You're not just mourning, or even working. You're alone because you want Jenkins to show himself! You're baiting him! You want a shootout with the boogieman!" Ignoring the tears that were threatening to fall, she buttoned her coat and put her gloves back on. "I'm sorry I disturbed you. I'll get out of the line of fire."

"Sarah, don't! Please understand."

"Don't what? Leave...stay...care? Understand? I understand? You have a death wish," she said, her voice a pitch higher, and her face flushed.

"It's not a death wish!" Steven moved closer. "Please understand. I just want this man off the streets."

Sarah stood straight, took a deep breath, and spoke more calmly. "You do what you have to, Steven. I can't dissuade you. I'm not even going to try." She moved toward the door. "I'm sorry for your loss. I know how much Denise meant to you." She opened the door. "I thought you should know that we're to have the girls in Texas before Christmas. It all depends on when Gregg gets out of the hospital. They say he's making a miraculous recovery."

Steven's jaw dropped, and he felt like his world had just shattered into a zillion pieces Dumbstruck, he watched Sarah leave and close the door behind her.

~***~

Stowy circled the block and hid in the shadows. He saw Sarah leave the building with her bodyguards. "That was a short visit. Marital discord, jealousy, or are you just so busy trying to find me that you no longer live at home?" Stowy smiled at the idea. "I like that, Detective. I like that a lot. Divide and conquer. It's always the best way to defeat the enemy."

Steven's phone pinged. He picked it up and a number he didn't recognize, showed on the screen, along with the snowman emoji. How do you rate such sweetness? That new babe of yours, Sarah, is just too much. Your absence from her life won't protect her from me. That is a promise, Detective. And I always keep my promises.

Now get off your ass and solve Denise's murder! Isn't that what a great detective does?

~***~

Steven found Sarah at Eagles Nest, staring out at the snowfall. Clouds obscured the view of the city as snow fell at a pace of a foot an hour, intent on obliterating the land and everything on it.

She looked up as he approached. He walked behind her and gathered her in his arms. "I'm sorry, Angel. I didn't know how to tell you about George's visit, and then Denise—"

She turned to face him. "I know," she put her fingers against his lips. "Sometimes, words are impossible, and sometimes they get away from us." He pulled her close and kissed her hungrily.

Sarah opened her parka then his. "I'm your haven. Here only for you, always for you."

"Ditto," Steven responded.

The magic between them ignited with deepening kisses, tangling tongues, urgent hands, fiery touches, and deep moans. Forgiveness and love came together under the trees in the falling snow.

Shared loss, shared grief, shared love.

CHAPTER THIRTY-FOUR

Innocent by Murder

November 13th

The Anchorage police department was bursting with activity. Volunteers from other departments poured in from the lower forty-eight to help find the Snowman. Going door to door, talking with every streetwalker, and interviewing possible witnesses took human resources, and the lower forty-eight had answered the call for help.

From Captain Reed's office, Steven watched his men and the recruits prepare for their jobs. "All good men putting their lives on the line to find one psychopath. Unbelievable." Rubbing his chin, he turned to Reed. "I can't believe Denise would agree to meet with a serial killer without protection, but her text messages show that's exactly what she did. Why? For ratings? For a promotion?"

"What does her husband say?" Reed asked as he perused the paperwork on his desk.

"He claims to have no clue. Denise told him she was coming to Alaska to take care of her father's estate. I don't like the guy."

Reed grinned. "No man likes his ex-wife's new husband."

"It isn't that. Seriously, Hemp's reaction to her death was, well, odd."

"You think he did this instead of Jenkins?" Reed gave Steven his full attention. "I thought he was in New York when you notified him."

"He was, but he could've hired someone."

"Were they estranged? Was there a life insurance policy?"

"No, I checked all that first, but there's something about that crime scene that's bugging me."

"Like what?"

"There was no sign that Jenkins played his usual games. No braggadocios message for me, either. Instead, there was the note he sent later saying he didn't kill her."

"What if he's pulling your leg? A murder he did but denies gets you running around in circles, takes your focus off him. My gut says the guy did it. He lured her here with the story of a lifetime. Denise is the reason Jenkins was arrested the last time. He wanted revenge, and he's gotten it with just enough changes to play you. Be careful, Steven. Don't let the monster in your head."

"Are you kidding? The monster already owns my ass."

~***~

Just days later, a call came in at midnight. The Snowman had struck again. Three bodies this time. Three naked Denise look-a-likes had been hung side by side in a local park. One girl had been skinned. Another had been burned by fire, and the third had her skin removed with acid. The coroner said the slow torture of the three must've taken hours. Steven stared at the scene, and his blood ran cold when the coroner gave him the message from Jenkins.

This is my version of 'hear no evil, see no evil, and speak no evil.' Okay, maybe that's a stretch. This is just the Snowman doing his artistic thing. See all evil, speak all evil, and do all evil. So how do you like my thing, Detective? Have you uncovered Denise's killer yet?

Reed read the message. "There's your answer to whether or not the Snowman killed Denise. I'd say this display shows the man's true colors."

Steven was contemplating his answer when his phone pinged with another text. Again, from the Snowman. Prove my innocence. I did not kill the beauty queen. Find the real killer or someone close to you is next. All I have to do is distract those two bodyguards. It almost worked the last time I ran into my favorite artist outside your apartment. Such a pretty little thing.

Steven showed the text to Reed. "You're right. The bastard's playing games!"

~~*~~

CHAPTER THIRTY-FIVE

Crushed Dreams

November 17th

With Steven and Sarah on either side of her holding one of her hands, Myra walked into her surprise birthday party at the Anchorage Children's Home. With Moya in his arms, Steven escorted the girls into the stunningly adorned hall, bright with pink decorations, balloons, and ribbons. The children, dressed in their finest, yelled, "Happy Birthday!" right on cue, and then they rushed forward to greet the guest of honor.

After a delicious kid-friendly meal, Santa Claus made an appearance. One by one, he held each child on his lap while listening to their universal Christmas wish for a new Mommy and Daddy. Then he gave each of them a gentle kiss on the cheek and a beautifully wrapped present topped with a big shiny bow.

Surrounded by girls her age, Myra radiated happiness until one of them asked, "Is it true your mother killed a bear to protect you?"

Myra's smile disappeared, and she hugged her new dolly close. "Momma had to guide him to the spirit world. But she couldn't come back," she whispered as the youngsters hung on every word.

"You're lucky. Hawk rescued you."

Myra smiled. "Yes. I was very lucky. I hope you get rescued soon, too."

The games, food, and excitement of the day exhausted both girls, sending them to bed early, and leaving the evening open for the adults.

In the afterglow of a night where romance ruled, Sarah hugged her husband close. "Thank you for today. It was perfect." She got up on one elbow and looked lovingly at her husband.

"And just now?" Steven said, wallowing in the compliment.

"Well, there's always room for improvement." She laughed when his smile turned to a frown.

"That's not fair," was all he could exclaim as his deflated ego wilted.

She giggled. "Just kidding! I've got to keep that ego of yours from getting overblown."

Steven straddled her and started tickling. "Take your punishment, you little minx."

Sarah shrieked and did her best to fight him off. After a few minutes of play wrestling, he captured her in his arms and kissed her soundly. "Tell me what you want. Your wish is my command," he said as he looked deeply into her eyes.

"One thing. All I want is one thing," she whispered.

He winked. "Well, it is close to that time of the year when all dreams are supposed to come true."

Pleased with his answer, Sarah explained, "I saw Dr. Jennings yesterday, and she thinks I'm as ready as I'll ever be for in vitro. What do you say? Let's make a baby!"

Steven was immediately out of their bed and pacing, his agitation growing with each step. "Really, Sarah? You want to bring a child into this devastation?"

"I want to bring our child into our family unit," she said softly.

"We don't have a family! We're surrounded by murder, loss, threats, and death daily." Steven pulled his jeans on. "I'm glad Gregg is alive and taking his daughters back. They have a chance for a long life with him." In a huff, he stuffed his arms through his shirt sleeves, tried but failed to get the buttons to cooperate, and cursed. "I'm going to the office," he said as he picked up his socks and boots. His phone rang, and he dropped it all to answer. "On my way." He looked at his wife and shook his head. "And right on cue, there's been another murder."

"Of course, there is," she mumbled. Sarah grabbed her robe to cover up her nakedness. Her perfect day was quickly coming apart at the seams, but she couldn't allow the argument to end this way. She stepped in front of the bedroom door. "Give me one more minute."

Steven stepped back, arms folded across his chest. He nodded but didn't speak.

She began to button his shirt. He relaxed his arms and allowed the intimacy. Concentrating on his buttons, she said, "I know losing the girls is a blow, but we still have a chance for our own." She met his gaze. "Remember? The family we've discussed for years. Your work isn't our world. Please, Steven. Reconsider. Give it time, but you have to understand…your work…it's…just not our world."

"I used to believe that too, but despite this afternoon, I think the idea of us having a family is an illusion. Not with the constant threats and murder all around us, and Denise's death proved that no one is immune. I told you I was glad the girls are leaving, and I meant it. I'm glad for the normalcy they'll find." Steven was about to take her in his arms, but his phone dinged with a text from Reed. "I've got to go."

Sarah stepped aside and let him pass. Steven walked through the door, but seconds later, he returned, took her into his arms, and held her close. "I love you. Just give me some time. We'll talk again later." He kissed her forehead.

On tiptoes, Sarah put her arms around his neck for a more intimate kiss, grateful that the argument had ended on a positive note. "I love you," she whispered and sent him on his way.

~***~

Sarah sat in front of her computer. Her mind was on the discussion she'd had with Steven that morning. The world was full of ugliness, but it also held beauty, and that's what she looked for. They couldn't allow evil to influence their choices. We can do this, my love, it's all we've ever wanted. I know we can.

A bird landed on a branch outside the window. Sarah admired its freedom and the ability to fly away from danger. Then the computer alerted her to a Skype call, destroying all forays into fantasy.

"Hello, Gregg," she said to the man on the screen.

"Mrs. Quaid. Hi." He was sitting in a hospital bed. She recognized the background: fluffed pillows, stark white paint, medical accouterments, and devices for keeping a patient tethered. And he looked very nervous.

She smiled. "Please, call me Sarah. You're looking well."

He smiled back at her. "I am. Thank you for this. The ability to talk via Skype is a great idea. Telephone calls aren't nearly as personal as face-to-face."

"That's why I suggested it. The girls are excited, too. Are you ready?"

"Definitely!"

Sarah smiled. "Then, without further ado…" The girls, who'd been standing out of the picture, ran to Sarah's lap.

"Hi, Daddy," Myra said with an adorable shyness. With one finger shoved in her mouth, Moya just smiled.

"Oh my gosh, you're so beautiful! And so big!" Gregg said. "Did you get my birthday present, Myra?"

Before she could answer, Sarah put a package on the table in front of her. "This came in the mail for you this morning, Myra. I thought you 'd want to open it while your daddy watched."

Myra smiled, "From you, daddy?"

He nodded. "A special gift for an extraordinary girl. I hope you know, Myra, how proud I am of you."

Myra tore open the package to find a lovely baby doll. It looked almost exactly like her. "Oh, Daddy, this is so beautiful," she said, hugging it close. "Thank you!"

"You're so welcome. I know you had a great party yesterday. I wish I could've been there, but I promise to be with you for the next one."

Sarah saw the tears in his eyes. He did an excellent job of pushing them back, though, as he touched the screen. The girls pressed their fingers to the screen, too.

"What happened to you?" Myra asked.

"I was injured. Remember, I went away to a place called Afghanistan? You were there, Myra, at the airport when I said goodbye."

"I remember," Myra said. Moya shook her head.

"I was sick for a very long time, but now I'm getting better. Can you see my room? He moved his computer to show them. I'm still in the hospital, but as soon as I can go home, you'll join me. Would you like that?"

"Will Mommy Sarah and Daddy Hawk come with us?"

"They'll bring you to me, and if I can convince them to stay, I will. But Steven and Sarah live in Anchorage, and I live in Texas. You do want to come to Texas, don't you?"

"I do," Myra said. She looked at Sarah.

Sarah nodded and smiled to assure her.

"Me too," Moya agreed.

"Good! I'm so happy. My baby girls are coming home!"

"Do you know more about when?" Sarah asked.

"I wish I did. I have one more surgery, but the doctor said I'll be home before Christmas. If it's possible, I'd love to have the girls before then."

"We'll be ready when you are. Have you thought about a nanny?"

"No, honestly, I haven't, but I should have." He rubbed his head. "I can get my mother to start interviews."

"Would you like to meet the current nanny?" She waved to Charlotte, who was waiting off-screen.

Charlotte walked to where Gregg could see her. "Hello, sir. I've loved taking care of your girls."

"We love Charlotte," Moya and Myra chorused.

"It's nice to meet you, Charlotte. I know it's asking a lot, but would you consider a move to Texas to continue as their nanny? Don't answer now. I may be expecting too much, but considering all they've been through, some consistency in their lives would be a beautiful thing."

"I was hoping you'd ask, but you should know I'm planning to attend college on a part-time basis. I want to get my degree in child psychology."

"I think that's wonderful. We have great schools here in Austin, and I'd make sure you had transportation and time for whatever classes you needed."

Charlotte smiled. "That sounds wonderful. Thank you."

"I'll send you information on all of the schools. I promise."

"Thank you, Mr. Sunne. I'll let you know for sure as soon as I talk it over with my grandmother."

A nurse walked into view. "I'm sorry, Gregg. The doctor's waiting."

Gregg rolled his eyes. "Be with you in a second," he told her. "Give it honest consideration, Charlotte, and I'll send all the information I promised."

"I will, Mr. Sunne. Thank you." She waved and stepped out of the picture.

"Sarah, thanks again for this," Gregg said.

"My pleasure. Girls say goodbye! Daddy has to go, but you can talk again tomorrow."

"Bye, Daddy," Moya and Myra both said, then blew him kisses.

"I love you, girls."

"We love you, Daddy," they chorused.

"This was such a wonderful idea. I can't wait to meet all of you in person."

"Before you leave, Gregg. If you're up to it, call at seven this evening. Then you can read the girls a bedtime story. I think it'd be a great way for you to stay in touch and be part of their lives now."

His eyes grew wide, and his smile wider. "Thank you. I'll see you at seven. Nothing will stop me. Not even a little surgery."

Sarah's heart warmed and then just as quickly chilled. She was so happy for them but deeply saddened for her loss.

Preparing for the girls' departure was heartbreaking work, but Sarah did everything possible to make it a smooth transition. She would've loved Steven's support, but she knew that until Jenkins was caught, his attention was elsewhere. She carried on with Emma's help, but Emma was hurting as much as she was. Emma loved the girls too.

~~*~~

CHAPTER THIRTY-SIX

Close Friends

November 19th

To make up for his long absences, Steven tried to make breakfast with his family a priority, no matter what time he got home the evening before. At 2 AM, he was looking forward to stripping and slipping into bed beside his warm wife. Instead, he walked into the house to find his wife sipping a cup of tea by the fireplace.

"What is it, angel?"

She melted against him but didn't speak.

"A nightmare?"

She nodded. "So much blood," she whispered. "A devil was killing an angel. He ripped her to shreds and laughed the entire time. Snow all around. Even the flakes were red."

"I'm so sorry," he said. "I was hoping nightmares were a thing of the past." Concern filled his voice and pain hit his heart. This was precisely why he hated bringing his job home.

"Me, too," she admitted, but she didn't dare share the fact that she was the angel in the dream, and the Snowman was the devil.

"How many nightmares since the case started?"

"A few," she admitted. "Please don't worry. I'll handle it."

He hugged her close. "You shouldn't have to."

~***~

Kevin Cooper threw his suitcase on the bed and rushed to answer his phone. "Yeah, babe, I'm back. The waves were spectacular, but my plane was late, and I'm working the night shift, so I've got to get to work. The captain will have my head if I'm late. Sorry, I don't have time to talk right now. I missed you, but we can catch up later. I'll call after work. Maybe we can have breakfast together."

He hung up and pulled on his uniform. He buttoned his shirt, stuffed it in his pants, fastened his belt, and grabbed his gun and jacket. When he opened his apartment door, he felt a sudden sting in his upper arm. He stumbled backward.

"Officer Cooper. So good to see you again. I'm the Snowman. You probably don't remember me, but you and Detective Dickweed, AKA Quaid, stopped me for running a red light. I know it was years ago, but I remember like it was yesterday. You and that cute new native rookie Quaid and his long black hair left quite an impression. I've often wondered if you two got it on. Thought about you two in fantasies for ten years. Did you? Get it on?"

Kevin stared at the stranger, his eyes wide with confusion.

Stowy continued his tirade. "I almost hate using you to make a point, especially since you had no role in my original arrest, but, honestly, you know Quaid. He's not on the ball, and I need him to focus. I'd go after his family, but that'd make him insane. He needs to understand that I didn't kill Denise. I want justice. I deserve justice. And as much as I hate to admit it, he's good at his job when he concentrates. It's something we have in common."

Stowy stabbed the paralyzed man repeatedly, and left him on his couch, bleeding out slowly. As his life drained, Stowy sent a text to the detective.

Quaid, what the hell are you waiting for? I'm coming for you, but first, the people you love will die alone in their living rooms. Guess which one I've taken from you this time? Okay, one hint. He likes to surf.

Before Steven had a chance to react, Stowy sent a graphic picture of Kevin's bloodied body. With a muttered curse, Steven raced to his friend's condo.

Kevin Cooper was Steven's partner when he was a beat cop. Steven had all the ambition, but Keven was perfectly happy being a patrol officer and didn't aspire to anything more. He was extremely athletic and more into his off-duty hobbies than he was in a career, but despite Steven's meteoric rise, they'd remained friends. Losing him was a significant blow that delivered just the kind of message the Snowman wanted.

You'd better take me seriously, Detective, because I'm not playing games. I'm coming for you, but first, I'm going to decimate your world.

~~*~~

CHAPTER THIRTY-SEVEN

Striptease

November 28th

On Thanksgiving Day, the snow came down like feathers dropped from thousands of pillows at once, creating a hard-to-resist winter wonderland. When the girls asked to build a snowman, Steven and Sarah didn't even try to resist, and it was hard to distinguish which generation was more excited about it. For several hours, the four of them felt like a real family, even though D-day, or devastation day, as Sarah called it, was growing closer and closer. They built a family of snowmen and raced sleds down the hills on a track created by the security forces that protected them from danger. At least for a few hours, the sheer joy of being together overshadowed any thoughts of threats. After a huge Thanksgiving Day meal, warm baths, and hot chocolate with marshmallows, both girls fell fast asleep.

The rest of the evening meant alone time for Mommy and Daddy. Steven cuddled up with the love of his life on the couch in the den. "Where do they get all that energy?" he asked. "You're right. Those girls are refreshing."

"Told you," Sarah said, her face still pink from the day's fun. "You were a different man today. I think it's the happiest I've ever seen you."

"My stress always disappears when I'm with you." He pulled her into his arms. "Know what? We're going to make the best parents ever. Today was the kind of day I've always dreamt of." He kissed his wife with passion, and soon, necking on the couch began to raise the room's temperature.

When they both came up for air, Sarah asked, "Does this mean you're ready to have a baby?"

Steven smiled. "I'm sure I can be persuaded, although to be honest, it might take some doing. Right now, I feel like a tired old man." He winked.

Sarah took on the challenge and kissed him again, her body making suggestions for what could come next and her hands teasing a promise of ecstasy. She left him breathless when she stood. "Hmmm, it's gotten awful warm in here..." Watching him watching her, she removed her sweater and slowly undid a few buttons on her blouse. Then she glanced toward the deck and said, "Maybe I'd better do this upstairs." She picked up her sweater and winked at him. "If you're up to it, old man, you can watch." With a husky laugh, she sashayed up the steps.

Steven raced after her. Halfway up the stairs, he swept her into his arms and carried her to their bedroom. He nudged the door shut behind them, stood her in the middle of the room, and then sat on the edge of the bed. "I'm watching, Gypsy Rose," he said with a smile.

Sarah turned the stereo on and began moving to the music. As she danced, her fingers delicately undid each button of her blouse. Taking her sweet time, she finally removed it, revealing the creamy skin underneath. Flirting shamelessly, she moved suggestively while removing her bra, then she flicked her nipples to hardness. Still swaying to the music, she unzipped her jeans, turned her back, and slowly lowered them.

Heart pounding, he watched, mesmerized, as her hands and fingers touched places on her body that he couldn't wait to taste. When she was down to her panties, he was desperate for her to take them off, but she moved even slower, teasing him mercilessly. When she finally threw her panties at him, he immediately tossed them aside and pulled her into his arms.

Kissing her hungrily, he pressed her against the wall and lifted her legs. She wrapped them around his torso and reached down to unzip his pants. Feverishly, his mouth and hands explored. Worshiped her body, and then, with their lips fused, he thrust into her, stealing her breath and satisfying her deepest hunger.

He made love to her with a deep-seated devotion and vigor. Their pace was frenetic, his appetite, insatiable, and their matched desire, an inferno. She kneaded his back with her fingers, and her nails etched deep grooves in his muscles. Their moans commingled, feeding the flames as he brought her closer and closer to climax. Then they erupted in a shared explosion of pleasure.

Breathless, Steven continued to hold her in place. Sarah rested against him, her legs still encircling his hips, as their breathing slowly returned to normal.

"Promise me you'll do that every night for the rest of our marriage. I've never witnessed anything so hot," he said.

She laughed. "Every night is fine with me. If that didn't create a baby, nothing we do will."

"You're wrong. Every time you do that striptease, we'll end up with a kid."

CHAPTER THIRTY-EIGHT

Hope

November 29th

At five in the morning, Sarah awoke within the haven of her husband's arms for the first time in a long time, and she relished the feeling. Not wanting to wake him, she lay very still and smiled as she thought about the evening before. She said a silent prayer for the baby she wanted to create with him. If they had more nights like the one before, they'd have a houseful of kids in no time.

"You're thinking about last night, aren't you?" Steven whispered in her ear. He hugged her close and kissed the back of her head.

She turned to face him. "How did you know?"

"Because I felt your smile." He kissed her nose. "Good morning, wife."

"Good morning, husband. Thank you."

"For what?"

"For being here this morning. For loving me so fully. For holding me while you sleep. Thank you for being you."

"Ditto, wife. Ditto." He kissed her forehead. "What do you say to a quickie in the shower?"

"I thought you'd never ask." But instead of moving to the bathroom, she nestled closer, and before long, they were sound asleep again. Shortly after daylight, two giggly girls joined them and started bouncing on the bed.

"Sorry," Charlotte said from the doorway. "They got away from me. Come on, girls. How about a nice cup of hot cocoa?"

Squealing, the girls hopped off the bed.

Sarah laughed. "We'll see you downstairs in a little bit. Daddy's going to make pancakes for all of us." She winked at him. As soon as the girls left, they rushed to the shower, their earlier discussion not forgotten.

Such a healthy love-filled start to the day left them both aching for more of the same, but at eight, Steven left for work, and Sarah got down to the business at hand – preparing the girls for their move to Texas. At ten, another Skype connection was made with Gregg Sunne.

"Daddy? I remember a song," Myra said when Gregg came on screen.

Gregg grinned and began singing You Are My Sunshine.

Myra giggled. "That's it! You remembered."

He laughed. "Of course, I remember, and I can't wait to hold you in my arms and sing it to you again."

"Dada, sing!" Moya said.

Charlotte gave Gregg a little wave. "My grandmother says I'd be a fool not to take you up on your offer," she said. "I'm coming to Texas, too!"

"That's perfect! And I've got some more good news. The doc says I'll be home on December eighth!"

"That's wonderful, Gregg," Sarah said, steeling herself for what was to come.

"Would you be able to bring the girls home soon after?" he asked.

She nodded, even managed a smile to mask her heartbreak, and said, "What do you say, girls? Are you ready to see Daddy in person? For Christmas, Texas-style?"

"Yeah!" they squealed.

"I'll reserve the flight right away. You're getting out on the eighth, so how about if I bring them on the tenth, so you have a couple of days to adjust? Will that work?"

Gregg beamed, while Sarah's heart shattered. "It's perfect, just perfect. Thank you!"

After Sarah signed off, she went to her room and cried herself to sleep. Steven found her wrapped up in a blanket, tears still staining her face. He curled up with her and held her close. "I'm sorry."

"It's not your fault. It just hurts so much."

"I know, angel. I love them, too." He sighed and twirled her hair around his finger. "Emma told me what you did. She said you should be canonized."

Sarah grinned. "I'm not even Catholic."

"Doesn't matter. Emma's right. She described every excruciating detail. I know that had to be rough."

"It's not that I want them to go. Just the opposite, but it's the right thing. The only thing. He loves them so much." A tear slid down her cheek.

He kissed it away, then captured her mouth. He whispered in her ear, "Santa said you wanted a baby for Christmas. What do you say we try the old-fashioned way, and if that doesn't work, we'll make plans for in vitro after the new year?"

She threw her arms around his neck and kissed him with such passion, such warmth, and such fierceness, he opened his eyes to make sure she wasn't glowing with divine light.

CHAPTER THIRTY-NINE

Encounters

December 9th

Snow covered the ground, and a new storm was due before the day's end. The day was gray, and Captain Reed had just left his home for the office. His security detail had already pulled out, but he'd lagged behind to make sure the garbage was ready for collection. Then he hopped in his truck to follow, but before he made it to the main road, he spotted his neighbor squatting next to his car's flat tire, so he pulled over.

"Hey, Tony," he said as he got out of his truck. "How can I help?" He walked over to his neighbor

"Oh, you just did!" Stowy said, jumping up and spinning around to face him with a hypodermic needle in his hand. "I knew I could count on you to be the neighborly type." Reed reached for his gun, but Stowy moved faster. So did the paralytic he injected. Before Reed's fingers even touched his gun, he'd lost all control of his body.

"Don't worry, Captain," Stowy said, catching him before he hit the ground. "I've got you. I won't let a nice neighborly fella like you fall in the mud. But I do believe we need to have a little discussion. Does going to your place work for you?" He grinned. 'Since you have no objections, we might as well take your vehicle." He tossed Reed into the back seat, did a U-ey, and drove back up the long driveway to Reed's house.

Then he carried the captain into the house and arranged him in an upright position on the couch. "You people aren't paying attention!" Stowy said, pacing in front of the sofa. "I've been patient, so very, very patient, but the good detective isn't working hard enough to prove my innocence. I did not kill Denise! We had an agreement, and here's a copy of the contract I signed with her. We even made a tape of our time together. When I left, the lady was very much alive.

"Don't get me wrong. Believe me, I wanted to do the bitch. I mean lady/ But not until she made me the most written about, talked about serial killer in history," Stowy said dreamily. Then with the anger back in his voice, he reiterated, "I can't make it any clearer. Denise did not die by my hand! But you will." He pulled out a knife. "This is one of my favorite knives. It's the same one that killed Coop. You don't mind, do you?"

He caressed the shiny blade and grinned. "Maybe now that asshole will get off his duff and prove I didn't kill her!'

A car door slammed, and Stowy rushed to the window. "Fuck! Speak of the devil."

He darted to the rear of the room, and as soon as Steven opened the front door, Stowy threw the knife and sliced a chunk from the side of Reed's neck. Then he took off running.

Every step he took, Stowy imagined that the detective was right behind him, which made him run even faster. He kept expecting to feel the half breed's paws on him at any second, but other than being out of breath, he made it to his truck with no problem. He laughed as he got into the truck. "I keep forgetting you're getting older, too, Quaid. Whew! That was a close one. But exciting." He peeled out and raced back to town.

~***~

Steven immediately pressed a towel to the captain's wound and called for an ambulance. Then he ran after Stowy, but it was no use. He got to the road just in time to see the bastard take off in a dark gray truck. Even though he couldn't make out the license tag, he called in a description of the truck as he hurried back to the captain.

After an excruciating wait at the hospital, Steven was finally ushered in to see Reed. "Glad to see you so alert."

"That drug's brutal, but at least the cut was superficial," Reed said.

"What happened?"

Reed quickly brought him up to speed before asking, "Did you find the contract? Is it real?"

"Good question. We've got some people looking into it. It's an interesting angle."

Reed nodded. "Even if it is real, that doesn't mean they didn't argue over some of the finer points. Jenkins was convinced that Denise would make him the most famous serial killer of all time, but knowing her, I find that hard to believe."

"I agree. It's not Denise's style, but I do believe that she wanted to get the scoop. I wish it hadn't cost her life."

Reed closed his eyes.

"Rest up boss, I'll check in with you later," Steven said as he headed to the door.

Reed stirred. "Damn drugs! Thank you, Steven. You saved my life. I won't forget it."

"No problem. I'm sure you'll do the same for me someday. But right now, I need to find a dark gray pickup."

CHAPTER FORTY

Freedom

December 10th

After Reed's close call, Steven worked non-stop, but even though he spent the night in town, he promised to meet Sarah at the airport the next morning for the flight to Texas. He was a mile from the airport when James Lawrence, the department's computer expert, called him.

"Sorry. I know you're on your way out of town, but I had to call."

"Okay, so tell me what you've got."

"I may have found Jenkins' hiding place. You're not going to believe it."

"Try me."

"You were right about tracing Jenkins' cohort's activity. Zeke Savon had several aliases, and he used them to purchase some big-ticket items, including a new house. You're not going to believe where it is."

Steven laughed. "James, I'm aging as you speak. No guessing games, please. Just spit it out."

"Sorry, boss. It's in that new high-dollar Wellington neighborhood."

"Let me guess. It's the place where Jason and Craig didn't check out the basement."

"How do you always know?"

Steven made a U-turn. "Because it's been bugging the hell out of me ever since I read their report. I want you to get a warrant based on what you've found and tell those two blockheads to meet me there. And James, better send the calvary. We may just get lucky."

"You got it, boss."

As Steven raced to the address, all thoughts about meeting Sarah and the girls were replaced with the heady possibility of nailing Jenkins.

He was the first to arrive at the house, but when he saw the modern A-frame with eight tiny reindeer pulling Santa's sleigh up its roof and all the cheery Christmas lights and decorations dotting the yard, he began to doubt that this was the right place. It sure as hell didn't look like a monster's lair.

No one answered when he rang the bell, and a peek through the windows revealed no activity, so he decided to examine the exterior of the house. At the same time, he waited for the search warrant. With any luck, maybe he could find an entrance to that basement.

He didn't have any luck finding a door, so he wiped the dirt from a small window and peered into what looked like a storeroom. As he squinted into the dim room, an eerie sense of déjà vu swept over him. The unnaturally orderly stacks of boxes and storage bins were much too familiar. They looked exactly like the ones in Jenkins' last basement. Memories of the horrors he found in that other basement and how close he came to dying there made his skin crawl.

He clenched his jaw and kept searching. Where was the damned door? It had to be hidden there somewhere. It had to be. He pounded on the cement blocks and checked the mortar seams for a concealed break but found nothing.

Then he smelled it. Smoke.

With heart-pounding, Steven called the fire department as he ran to the front of the house. When he looked in the window this time, he saw flames stretching from the kitchen to the living room, and every instinct he had told him the fire was no coincidence. Jenkins was in there.

And he couldn't let the bastard get away again.

No big rocks in the area, so he took a deep breath and tried pounding on the window with his bare hands, but it was a waste of time. The three-tier safety glass was as impenetrable to his efforts as the reinforced steel door was to his kicks. How the hell was he supposed to get into this place?

A wailing siren signaled the arrival of the firetruck, and right behind it was a multitude of police cars. Steven nodded at his officers as he ran to the firetruck. "Do you have anything that can get through that door or window? This place is a damned fortress."

Their high carbon steel pry-ax created an entry point, but the fire was raging, so out of control, Steven wasn't allowed to use it. He had to stand back helplessly while the firefighters did their job.

He smacked the side of his head. Son of a bitch! What was he thinking? If he couldn't get in this way, Stowy sure as hell couldn't get out, either. There had to be another escape route.

Steven sprinted to the back yard, and the first thing to catch his eye was the entire rear wall of the garage sliding closed. And sure enough, as the hidden opening was disappearing into a seamless-looking seal, Jenkins' gray truck was tearing through the yard, down the embankment, and onto the road below.

Cursing his bad timing, Steven issued an all-points bulletin while jogging to his vehicle, where Jason and Craig were waiting. He nodded at them and growled, "The bastard got away again. He's still in that dark gray truck, and last seen, was heading north on Arctic Drive. We're closing in on him, boys. It's only a matter of time."

But it wasn't going to be this time. Despite the roadblocks and all the multitude of police cars swarming all over the streets of Anchorage, Jenkins got away again.

Meanwhile, the firefighters found a young girl chained to a support pole in the basement. She'd swallowed a lot of smoke, and burns covered most of her body, but she was still breathing. Barely. But Ellen Tran, a runaway from Pittsburgh, wasn't talking. She was in a catatonic state, and doctors feared for her sanity.

~***~

Just moments before all the chaos, Stowy had been enjoying a late breakfast, prepared by his newest slave. "I've been considering letting you live. If I did, what would you do?"

"I'd go back home to Pittsburgh. Even though I ran away, I've really been missing my family lately. Maybe it's because of the holidays, but I'd like to find out if I'm still welcome there."

Stowy laughed. "By all means, if you enjoy being a slave, go back. I'm sure they'll make you feel right at home."

"What do you mean?" she'd asked, but then the doorbell rang.

"Quiet!" he ordered. "Not a sound." He checked his phone to see who was at the door and ran his fingers through his hair while scowling at Quaid's image. Then he grabbed the girl and threw her onto the bed in the corner.

"I've got to get out of here, but not until I destroy this place," Jenkins said, looking around sadly at his latest killing room. "Such a waste." After lifting a plastic container of gasoline from a closet, he splashed it all over everything, including the girl.

Then he raced up the steps, oblivious to the girl's agonized cries. After throwing a lit lighter down the steps, he paused at the top of the stairs to watch the flames spread and to revel in the girl's escalating screams. The sound filled him with renewed energy, but it was time to move.

Stowy crossed the kitchen to the garage, threw his already-packed emergency duffle bag into the truck, and pushed the button that would lift the rear wall of his garage. And just that easy, Stowy Jenkins drove away. He laughed as he headed to his other hideout, a nondescript rental he'd leased under an assumed name in another neighborhood. He heard sirens but didn't see a single police vehicle.

Once he was safely inside the garage of his new hideout, he sent Quaid a message: That's twice, Detective. Both close calls. But close only counts in horseshoes. Enjoy your day. I know I will.

CHAPTER FORTY-ONE

Heartbreak

December 10th

D-day, or Devastation Day, as Sarah called it, arrived with a blast of spring-like weather. The sun was bright, the breeze felt like a warm caress, and birds sang love melodies in the treetops, but in Sarah's heart, it still felt like the darkest day of winter. The girls were leaving today.

She didn't get much sleep the night before, because she spent most of it in their bedroom, watching them sleep. Steven still wasn't home, and she wondered if he realized that today was the day. She picked up her phone a dozen times to text him but couldn't follow through. The Snowman had already turned his life into a stress-filled nightmare. It wouldn't be fair to add to it.

When the girls awoke, she made their favorite pancakes for breakfast and then dressed them in warm play clothes, promising to change them into their new dresses before they met their dad. Despite her own sadness, Charlotte and the girls were so excited about taking Sarah's private plane to Texas, she couldn't help but get caught up in their joy.

Until they were all seated, and the plane started to taxi away from the hanger. Then her heart hurt so much, it showed on her face, and Brent jumped up to make her a cup of tea.

"Stay strong, kiddo. You can do this. We'll do it together." He handed her the cup and sat down across from her.

"Thanks," she said, taking a sip of the soothing brew. She looked over at the Christmas pictures the girls and Charlotte were coloring for Gregg, and then turned back to Brent and gave him a weak smile. "You're not a bad substitute, but Steven really should've been here."

"From what I know about this case, he wants you and the girls as far away from here as possible right now. I'm sure all he's thinking is that they're safe. They're finally safe."

"You're right. I know you're right." She sighed and took another sip of her tea. "Maybe this trip will ease his mind. I hope so."

~***~

Steven missed Jenkins, but he sure as hell wasn't going to miss that plane to Texas. This was one trip, one goodbye, one obligation he couldn't fail to accomplish. His family needed him. Sarah needed him. He wasn't about to let that bastard Jenkins keep him from Sarah's side. Not this time. Not today.

When he got to the airport, the plane was already taxiing for takeoff, so he made a call to the tower, parked, and waited for it to return. As soon as he stepped aboard, the girls ran to him. "Daddy Hawk! Daddy Hawk! You remembered!"

"Of course, I remembered! I can't let you go to Texas without me. I have to make sure it's the best place on earth for our princesses!" He hugged Sarah. "Sorry, I cut it so close."

She kissed him. "You always do," she said with a smile.

CHAPTER FORTY-TWO

Texas

December 10th

The temperatures were in the seventies, a virtual heatwave compared to the weather they left behind in Anchorage. When they got out of the plane, all dressed in their holiday finest, they piled into the waiting limo, and long before Sarah and Steven were ready, their driver was taking them down the impressive entrance to Gregg's parents' house. White wooden fences as far as the eye could see enclosed the meticulous grounds, which contained stands of massive trees, vast gardens, and open meadows, where a handful of thoroughbred horses ran and grazed.

The house was half a block long, three stories tall, and had a widow's walk, which Sarah was sure offered a spectacular view of the grounds. They all gawked at the plantation-like splendor, and except for Charlotte, were awed into silence. After saying, "Oh, my!" and "Wow!" countless times, she said, "This is beyond anything I could've imagined. The pictures Gregg sent don't even begin to do it justice."

Sarah shook her head. "No, they certainly don't."

After being assured that someone would take care of their luggage, a butler ushered them into the house, which was beautifully decked in eye-popping holiday decorations. With eyes shining, the girls immediately ran to the two-story-tall Christmas tree with a Moya-sized angel on top, which sat in the center of the hall and was framed majestically by a pair of highly polished curved wooden staircases.

"Welcome to Texas," a man in a wheelchair said as he rolled into the room. He grinned at the girls. "Myra! Moya! My beautiful, beautiful girls." He held out his arms, but the girls just stood and stared.

Charlotte picked up Moya and took Myra by the hand and walked them over to their father. Then she placed both on his lap.

They leaned in against him as he hugged them tightly. "Daddy," they whispered.

"My babies, my sweet, sweet girls." Tears rolled down his cheeks.

Sarah smiled at the sweet reunion. Her heart was breaking, but she smiled.

"Sarah. Steven. It's so good to meet you finally," Gregg said. "Thank you so very much."

"Let's move into the sitting room," a tall, stern-looking woman said.

"Sarah, Steven, this is my unforgiving mother. Father will be home in a few hours."

Sarah extended her hand, but the woman glared at Steven and said, "Please follow me," and turned on her heel. She led them to the sitting room, where a maid waited in the doorway.

"Bring the refreshments, Hilda," Mrs. Sunne said.

"Yes, ma'am."

Gregg Sunne laughed. "Ignore her. She doesn't come alive until the sun goes down," he said, giving Sarah a wink. "Come on. Let's get this party started. Charlotte, would you mind?" He motioned to the back of his chair. "My arms are full. What do you think, girls? How about a ride? Are you hungry? I asked the kitchen staff to make peanut butter finger sandwiches and banana ice cream just for you."

"Ooh," the girls said, giggling as Charlotte pushed the wheelchair into the sitting room, where a smaller Christmas tree, covered with antique ornaments and brightly colored twinkle lights, stood beside a beautifully decorated fireplace.

Sarah and Steven took a seat on the couch.

"I'm sorry. I wasn't introduced to your bodyguard," Mrs. Sunne said from her perch on a high-backed chair.

"No wonder, Mother. You barely said hello," Gregg said. "Sarah, would you do the honors?"

Steven stood. "I'm Steven Quaid, Mrs. Sunne. Sarah and I are pleased to meet you."

"You're married?"

Sarah nodded. "Yes. Why does that surprise you?"

Before Mrs. Sunne could respond, Myra said, "We built a snowman! Daddy Hawk helped us make it really tall. As tall as he is."

"Yes, we did," Sarah said. "And we sent pictures of it to your daddy. Remember?"

Gregg smiled at Myra. "And I loved those pictures, sweetheart. One day, I'll build a snowman with you, too. I promise."

Mrs. Sunne surreptitiously watched Sarah's every move. "Married to a woman of your caliber," she muttered, shaking her head in disapproval.

The maid came in, pushing a tray of goodies and tea. Charlotte served the girls, seating them at the coffee table and making sure they showed good manners.

Mrs. Sunne watched Charlotte with fascination. "You handle the girls very well," she said. "I'm glad you decided to continue as their nanny."

"Thank you. I've grown very, very fond of them."

"I'm glad, too. As a matter of fact, my heart is overflowing with gratitude. Thank you," Gregg said, touching Charlotte's hand lightly. When their eyes locked, Charlotte blushed.

Sarah smiled at their sweet connection until she noticed the blatant look of disdain Mrs. Sunne was directing at Charlotte. Gabrielle told her Gregg's mother hated Inuit's, but it was unsettling to see the woman's bigotry in action.

"You're a native Alaskan?" Mrs. Sunne asked, barely looking at Steven.

"Yes, we both are," Sarah said.

Mrs. Sunne did a double-take.

"We're both Alaskan-born, but Steven is Tlingit Indian. Is that what you mean by native?"

"I guess. I don't mean to be impertinent, but how did your parents react to the news?"

"Mother!" Gregg scolded, his face red with embarrassment. "I'm so sorry, Sarah."

"It's all right, Gregg. I don't mind." Sarah faced Mrs. Sunne. "My parents died when I was nineteen, but I know from the way they raised me that they understood that we are all from one race, different nationalities, different colors, and different voices, but of the human race and all the same."

"I see." Mrs. Sunne stood, nose in the air. "Please excuse me. I must see the cook about dinner." After she strutted from the room, it immediately felt warmer.

"Ignore her," Gregg said. "My mother acts as though she lives in the early 1900s, but once she gets to know the girls, I'm sure she'll come around. And I promise you, my father's going to be a terrific grandfather, so you don't have anything to worry about. Charlotte and the girls will be fine. I won't let Mother do anything to hurt them. Besides, we'll be moving out of this mausoleum and into a place of our own as soon as possible. I'm having a place built about a mile from here."

Sarah smiled. "Oh, I'm not worried. I know how good these two are at melting hearts. If anyone should be warned, it's your mother."

"That means the world." He squeezed her hand. "Would you like to see the girls' room? We borrowed a lot of ideas from the pictures you sent. They'll be together until Moya is ready for her own room. Your observations and insight into what they need have been a tremendous help. Thank you." He still held her hand. "I know this is hard for you, but I also know that someday, you'll have little ones to love. I hope you'll consider us an extension of your family, and regular visits will be possible."

"Of course. We wouldn't want it any other way. The girls and Charlotte are family, so when we walk out that door, we won't be walking out of their lives."

"Good. I'm holding you to that. And I promise you that the first place we visit once I'm out of this damned wheelchair is Alaska."

~***~

After viewing the girls' room and making sure they were settled in, Sarah and Steven said their goodbyes, but before leaving, they took a moment to walk through the gardens. "I've never, ever in my life wanted to hit a woman before, but Mrs. Sunne sure put my resolve to the test."

"I'm sorry, Steven. If I'd known it was going to be that bad, I would've left an hour earlier, and you'd still be in Anchorage."

"No, it's all right. Just please, please make sure Charlotte isn't abused in any way, because if she is, those girls will be, too. And if that happens, I'll move heaven and hell to get them away from her."

Mrs. Sunne cleared her throat as she came around a large rose bush and stood in front of them with a basket of flowers in her hand. "I'm afraid you caught me doing a bit of deadheading and gathering the flowers for the table tonight. I do love fresh flowers."

Steven and Sarah didn't say a word. They knew she'd heard their conversation, but they offered nothing but a stoic front.

"Please let me apologize to both of you, but that's the easy part. The hard part is apologizing to Gabriella." The woman seemed to shrink. "She's gone, and I'll never get that chance. I was wrong. I'm proud, no, what I am is a silly old woman with airs I don't really have a claim to, but because of the money my husband has made, I've claimed. I've wondered repeatedly, if I had welcomed Gabriella to our family, to our home, would she have been in Texas instead of Alaska? Would she still be alive today?" She looked at them with tears in her eyes.

"I'll never know that answer. But I can promise you that I love those two little ones already. And I'll do everything in my power to make sure no one makes them feel the way I made you feel just moments ago. Please forgive an old woman who doesn't deserve forgiveness but desires it nonetheless."

~~*~~

CHAPTER FORTY-THREE

Kidnapped

December 12th

Steven and Captain Reed strode into the department together. "Thanks, Steve. I appreciate the ride. I understand you just returned from Texas. I'm so sorry for your loss. Sarah must be devastated."

"She's hurting. We both are, but it was the only thing we could do. Their father's a good man. The girls will be happy. What about you? How are you doing?"

"Better, but I get flashbacks. That drug Jenkins used on me was fast. I felt like a limp doll. Aware, able to feel, but paralyzed and unable to fight back. It was a hell of a feeling; I can tell you that. I keep wondering how he planned to end me. Not a fun pastime, especially when I'm trying to get to sleep."

"Understandable. The only suggestion I have is to imagine an outcome where you kill the bastard," Steven said.

"Believe me, that's exactly what I do."

"I should've taken you home like the doctor said, but if I had, I know you would've just gotten in your truck and driven here yourself. So, work it is. One last favor. Don't dismiss the two men I've assigned to protect you. Leave when they leave, not ten minutes later."

"I won't. With only one good arm, I'm not taking any stupid chances. Several of my friends insisted on moving in with me, and believe me, after that close call, I welcome the backup. Carrie's staying in the lower forty-eight with our daughter. I told her I'd try to make it down there for Christmas. Just tell me we'll have this damned case under wraps by then."

"From your mouth to God's ears. I'll check in with you later," Steven said when they reached Reed's office. Then he patted his boss on the back before continuing down the hall, where he found a huge surprise sitting in the hallway just outside his office door.

He hadn't seen Winifred Carter, Jenkins' former girlfriend, for nearly ten years. Frankly, he never expected to see her again. Not here. Not now. Not in his office. She was in Australia taking care of family business when they caught Jenkins the first time, and up until this moment, that's where he thought she'd remained. "Miss Carter!" he said. "I barely recognized you. How are you? I'd heard you were still in Australia."

"I have been. I mean, I am, and it's Mrs. Bell now," she said, rising as he approached. "I've been married for seven years and have two beautiful girls."

"Congratulations. What brings you back to Anchorage?"

"An attorney, but to be honest, I'm frightened. Scared out of my mind is what I am, and now I'm questioning the journey. I don't know why I came, but I was compelled to, I guess. I thought I could help you."

"Help? How?" He motioned her into his office. "Please sit down. Would you like a cup of coffee?" He signaled one of the officers outside his office.

Officer Cotton answered Steven's summons.

"Thank you. Black, please. I could use the pick-me-up. My plane just landed, and I'm exhausted, but I thought I should come here first."

"Make that two cups, Cotton."

"Coming up. I just put a fresh pot on," Cotton said. David Cotton was new to the Anchorage police department, but a seasoned officer, having cut his teeth in the Air Force as a Security Forces Specialist. He'd served part of his term at Elmendorf Airforce Base, and fell in love with the state.

"Please, make yourself comfortable." Steven motioned toward a chair. "Why have you returned now? You mentioned an attorney."

"Yes, my mother's attorney contacted me. He claimed there's a dispute regarding some property she owned. That came as quite a shock because I thought all that was resolved ten years ago."

"And?"

"Well, it's true. There's some property in my mother's name, and the government wants to purchase it, so I'm here to sign the papers, collect a big check, and leave. I'm planning to leave for Australia first thing tomorrow morning…unless I can help you."

"Help me how?"

Cotton knocked and opened the door. "Coffee for the lady. And for you, boss."

"Thank you. It's appreciated."

Cotton nodded and started to leave, but Steven stopped him. "Please stay. This is Winifred Bell, Stowy Jenkins' former girlfriend."

With raised eyebrows, Cotton offered Winifred a friendly salute. "Nice to meet you, ma'am."

"How can you help me?" Steven asked her again.

Winifred took a sip of coffee. "Hot, but good. Thank you." She smiled at Cotton and then turned back to look at Steven. "I thought you might want to use me as bait."

Cotton almost choked on air. Steven shook his head. "No. No way."

"But he's killed so many people. It needs to stop. I know if he finds out I'm here, he'll most likely want to see me. He's been writing to me for years, but I 've never answered. I never even open his letters. I burn them, but no matter how many times I've moved, he always finds me again. He frightens me. Quite honestly, I don't know what I ever saw in him."

"I'm sure Jenkins would love to see you, Mrs. Bell, but I don't suggest it, and I can't condone using you to catch him. If something went wrong…no, I appreciate your offer, but I won't allow it." Steven stood. "You need to look after yourself. Get your business taken care of and get out of here."

"I wouldn't have come if I'd known he'd escaped. I read it in the paper on the plane here. But I felt I had to offer."

"It's commendable. Truly. What I will do is make sure you have an escort. An officer for security, Sergeant David Cotton."

"But…"

"It's decided." Steven put his coffee on the desk and took Winifred's hand. "It'll ease my mind and yours."

"Thank you. It will ease some of my anxiety," Winifred admitted.

"Good. I've already introduced you to your bodyguard. He's a former Airforce Security Officer and will serve you well."

"It'll be an honor to escort you, Mrs. Bell." Cotton said.

And with that, Steven left Winifred in the competent hands of one of his best men.

Steven left work early. He was too distracted by his personal life to make sense of any active case in the office. He and Sarah had left the girls in Texas, but their loss wasn't something that could be left behind. Like a dark cloud, it hung low, and the feelings of grief were overwhelming. He hurried home to check on his wife. He wanted to put her back on the road, distract her. When he arrived home, he found Sarah in the den.

He leaned down and kissed her. "How are you?"

She smiled. "Fine. You?" She patted the seat. Steven sat down.

"I'll probably be called back to work, but I don't like the idea of you being here alone without the girls. Funny, but I worry more now than I did then. Odd, isn't it?"

"Is Bill all right?"

"The captain's doing fine, but we were this close to nailing Jenkins."

"Must be frustrating, but please stop worrying about me. I'll be fine."

Steven shook his head. She might as well tell him to stop breathing. "Would you do me a favor?" he said.

"Name it."

"Leave Anchorage. Go to Hawaii. Visit Leeann. Or better yet, go to Paris with Elliott for the holidays. I'll concentrate on my job better if I know you're safe."

"Sorry, but I can't do that. My job, as your wife, is to be by your side. I'm not going anywhere. And that's final," she said. "Now, if you don't mind, I need a bubble bath. Would you like to join me?"

He shook his head, dumbfounded by her refusal to go somewhere safe.

She got up, but he pulled her back down onto his lap and held her tight. "I wish, just this once, that you'd listen to me. That you'd hear me and do this for me."

She hugged him close and ran her hands through his long black hair. "I'm not playing a game, dear love. I know the monster will find me, no matter where I hide, so instead of running, I'm making sure the odds are in my favor."

"How?"

Sarah reached down between couch cushions and pulled out a Colt .45. "Now that the girls are gone, I invested in an arsenal of my own."

Steven kissed his wife passionately. "I've changed my mind. Can I still join you in that bubble bath? I've got a whole lot of doubt that needs to be washed away."

~***~

When Cotton didn't show up for work the next day, Steven found him naked and unconscious, bound and gagged, but very much alive, in Winifred's hotel room closet. There was no sign of her or her luggage. Steven's hopes that she'd made her plane were dashed when Cotton regained consciousness and told him what happened.

"She was ready to go. I opened the closet to get her bags when someone, Jenkins most likely, hit me with a needle, and I was out like a light. Sorry, sir. I still don't understand why I'm alive."

"You're lucky. Few people survive an encounter. Jenkins knew that if he hurt you, Winifred wouldn't have left with him voluntarily. She saved your life. He was only interested in getting her out of here without any trouble. Your uniform let him do that."

"So, I get to live, and she'll die." Cotton swallowed hard.

"Don't blame yourself. This is my fault. I should've provided more security. Winifred was afraid Jenkins would come after her, but we both thought she could get away without any trouble. I wish I knew how he found out she was here. Did she make any phone calls?"

"Not to Jenkins or anyone else in Anchorage. No, wait. Correction…she did call her attorney. Then her family in Australia. I took her to the attorney's office. She signed the papers and picked up a check. Then we had lunch and went back to the room for her luggage, where Jenkins was

waiting for us."

~***~

At his office, Steven paced as he waited for a report on the search for Winifred. His phone rang, and he answered without hesitation.

"Quaid."

"Hey, Detective. Your favorite killing machine here. I just wanted you to know that Winifred is with me. She's safe. Completely unharmed."

Steven signaled Cotton to trace the call. "If she's with you, she's already come to harm."

"Now, Detective, is that fair? She and I are old friends. I don't hurt my friends. Ask her yourself if you don't believe me." He thrust the phone at her. "Tell him, sweetheart. You're here because you want to be here."

"Detective." Steven heard the fear in her voice.

"Winifred, are you all right?"

"Yes, Detective. I'm safe. We're just going to have dinner and visit for a while. I'll call you once our visit is over. I promise. Stowy has assured me that I can call you for a ride to the airport after our reunion. I've already rescheduled my flight. Please don't worry, Detective. I'm fine. I trust Stowy."

The line went dead, and Steven blew out his breath slowly. "Winifred's a dead woman."

~***~

Cotton knocked on Steven's door before entering. "Boss, we found out how Jenkins learned Mrs. Bell was here."

"How?"

"He arranged the whole thing. He, or one of his cronies, bought that land in Mrs. Carter's name a few years ago. It's a piece of land that the government has been eyeing for several years. They want to build a new office building. It was all planned. He wanted her here, and he tricked her into coming."

"Of course, he did. The man had ten years to perfect his plans. Shit. What other surprises does he have in store for us?"

~~*~~

CHAPTER FORTY-FOUR

Goodbye Winnie

December 15th

Torture comes in many forms. For Winifred, it was listening to and trying to reason with Stowy Jenkins.

"What's with all the blubbering?" Stowy sat down beside Winifred on the bed.

"Please let me go. I need to go home to my children, my husband. You promised I'd be home for Christmas."

"But I need you. I've always needed you. Don't you see that? Can't you understand?"

She cried harder. "I've tried. Really, I have, but it's too much. You're asking too much.

"I'm asking for your love and support. I'm asking you to be my wife."

She shook her head. "But I'm already married. I have two children. I have a life thousands of miles from here. I must go back. You can't ask me to give up my children and join you in this world of murder and torture."

Stowy threw the pillow he was holding onto the floor. "Too much. I'm asking too much," he muttered, shaking his head. "I love you, dammit! I'd stop killing for you. I promised to end my vendetta because you said you'd stay. What happened? Why'd you change your mind?"

"You expect me to give up everything to hide out with you…my life, my husband, my children. And for what? So, you can keep me, prisoner? Stowy, rape isn't love. You and your sexual appetites disgust me." She folded her arms over her chest. "What am I supposed to do? Celebrate? You said you were going to let me go, but you aren't, are you?"

"Disgust? You don't love me? I knew it! You lied to me! You and every woman I've ever known." He backhanded her, and she landed hard on the bed. "I made love to you. It's called love when a man holds you in his arms. When he makes sure that you're happy, and that you reach climax first. I even used lube, and I never use the stuff. I was gentle, showed you how to hold your body so it wouldn't hurt as much. How can you call our lovemaking rape?"

He removed his belt and folded it in half. "You're just as selfish as any bitch I've ever met. But I can rape you. Oh yeah, I can rape you real good. Just like I was raped my first day in prison." He turned her over and ripped off her nightgown and panties.

"NO! Please, don't!"

He beat her with his belt, then climbed behind her. "Pay attention, bitch. This is rape. Fucked up the ass, without warning and without lube…that's rape! That's brutality!"

Afterward, Winifred hugged herself, sobbing. "How could you possibly imagine that I could love you? That anyone could love you? You're not a man. You're a monster. A savage beast that knows nothing about love."

"I thought you got me. Loved me!"

"Maybe once, a long, long time ago. No. Not even then. I barely knew you." She wrapped the blanket around her bruised body. "But now you disgust me, and the only feeling I have for you is pity. I shouldn't have said otherwise, but I was trying to convince you to stop the killing and turn yourself in. I wasn't volunteering to be your prisoner."

Stowy eyes flashed with fury. With a howl, he beat her unmercifully with his belt and fist. "My attraction for the ass came from serving ten years in hell. It's all that was available there, and what can I say? You get a taste for it. Maybe after you've experienced it a few more times, you'll understand."

He tied her to the four bedposts and left her there, naked and alone. When she awoke, she screamed and yelled until her voice was hoarse, but he didn't reappear, and rescue didn't occur.

Two days later, Stowy returned. "I'm sorry, Winnie, I was cruel." He lifted her head to give her a drink of freshwater. She was too weak to speak, but she drank thirstily. She'd soiled herself, and he cleaned her up. Ran her a bubble bath and gingerly put her bruised body into the warm water. "How about some Epson salts for those wounds and that swelling? You relax. See, I even have a pillow for your head. I'll get you a hot cup of tea, but first those salts."

With a sneer, he carefully poured the contents of the container into the tub with her. As soon as the acid hit the water, it began to bubble and boil.

Winifred screamed as her skin fizzled and burned, and each feeble flail she made caused more flesh to fall away from her body. It was an excruciating death, but thankfully, she passed out long before her body stopped functioning.

Stowy snapped a picture and texted it to Steven with the message: Merry Christmas, Detective. Winifred's ready for her escort home.

Steven had the IT department trace the GPS of the photograph, and his team arrived on the scene soon after. The body hadn't been completely dissolved, but the top layer of skin was gone. Winfred's head remained untouched, except for the bruises from the beating she had suffered. The home where they found her had been closed for the winter, and Stowy was long gone, as was Winifred Carter Bell.

CHAPTER FORTY-FIVE

Secrets & Lies

December 20th

The St. Nicholas Ball, a fundraiser held every year to raise money for the local food banks, relied on the support of Anchorage's most prosperous and generous residents, and Steven and Sarah always attended. They were planning to go this year, too, and they hoped the ball would provide a respite from the deep sadness they were still feeling over losing the girls. In preparation, they rehearsed their dance multiple times, and each session gave them a break from the horrors of loss and murder.

The night of the ball, Sarah wore a stunning red gown and a tiara atop her French-braided hair, and Steven wore a perfectly fitted black tuxedo. For their special dance, they waltzed to Josh Groban's hit song, More of You, and in the process of dancing, they recaptured the enchantment that belonged only to them. But on this night, they managed to share it with all who watched them glide seamlessly around the floor.

As they danced, Sarah said, "You questioned the need for these dances during our last outing, but tonight, you were almost quivering with anticipation."

Steven pursed his lips. "I don't quiver, my lady," he said, then softened his tone. "But a chance to dance with you? How could I resist? Besides, after I read the financial reports, this is the least I could do to make sure the funds are raised," he said before her next spin.

"I knew there was a reason I married you," Sarah teased.

"Because I don't have two left feet?" Steven said.

"True. Smushed toes can kill a relationship," she said and winked.

As the music faded, he pulled her close and kissed her deeply. "Nothing can kill our bond. We are eternal."

Steven's smile grew into a grin as they bowed.

The audience applauded and swarmed them with congratulations.

~***~

Steven thought long and hard about what he wanted to give Sarah for Christmas, and what he decided on was a trip to Paris. To make up for not making it last spring and as a precursor to getting her out of town, out of the country, and away from Jenkins' clutches for good. With Elliott's help, he bought tickets to the New Year's Eve Grande Palace's Masked Ball, one of Paris' most famous balls. He chartered their flight, made the hotel reservations, and had their itinerary printed on a scroll to present to Sarah on Christmas day.

~***~

Sarah stared at the test stick in her hand, then realized she had to wait the full five minutes before the outcome was visible. The test came with a handy countdown clock, but she knew to stare at it would only delay the result. She was more than confident, but this test was meant to clear all doubts. She couldn't think of a better Christmas present. She sank to the floor of her dressing room and laid the stick on the footstool next to her. She prayed. She cried. She prayed. When she opened her eyes, the perfect Christmas gift came to fruition.

She quickly found a gift box and colorful paper to secure the perfect Christmas surprise. After wrapping the rest of Steven's gifts, she happily placed the packages under the tree.

CHAPTER FORTY-SIX

Stowy's Christmas

December 25th

Stowy loved Christmas. The lights, the food, the eggnog, but he especially enjoyed a good Christmas murder or two. As the clock struck midnight on Christmas Eve, Stowy was thoroughly enjoying his gift to himself.

"Come on, ladies, put some heart into it! You're killing my buzz." The two young women engaged in cunnilingus seemed to be enjoying themselves. But Stowy was getting bored, even though he'd already been the first recipient of their talents.

He stomped to the side of the bed. "On your knees!" he told the blonde. Then he pointed to the brunette. "And you! Get behind her." Both girls did as he said, and the brunette began licking the blonde. "That's it. Fuck her ass!" He grabbed his camera and started taking photographs. Then he handed the brunette a huge cock-shaped dildo. "Use that. I want to photograph you, giving her a good ass-fucking."

The girl shook her head. "Nuh-uh. Are you kidding? We aren't into that kinda stuff. Besides, this is way too big. No woman in her right mind would want that thing stuck up her ass."

"I paid you to be into it. You agreed."

"Not for the bills you gave us. Sorry, but we won't go there."

"Fine," Stowy said, but instead of walking away, he backhanded the girl, knocking her to the floor. The blonde went to her aid, but Stowy threw her onto the bed face down. He handcuffed her to the bed, then picked up the other girl and threw her on top of her friend. "We could've had fun, but no...you won't go there," he said in a mocking tone. "Well, we'll just see about that." He finished securing both girls. The one at the top of the bed was secured to the bedposts. And the other was secured to the bottom of the frame, but both were on their faces, their bottoms helplessly exposed.

"What are you going to do?" the brunette asked.

"What you wouldn't," Stowy said, yanking her up onto her knees. He impaled her ass, not with the dildo but with his cock, and her scream brought his enjoyment full tilt. "That's it. Give me your best voice." Her friend tried to get loose but failed and began crying. She couldn't see what was happening, but she could imagine it, and her friend's screams filled her with dread.

"Oh dear, we've forgotten Blondie. I'll have to remedy that." Stowy stopped his abuse and told the girl, "Straddle, your friend. That's it, expose that ass for me, and stay on your knees."

"Perfect," he said when he got the girls positioned the way he wanted them. Then he forced the dildo into the ass of the girl he'd just been doing. Her screams were muffled as her head was pushed deeper into the mattress. He knew the hard-plastic toy was tearing her up inside, but it didn't matter. She wouldn't be breathing much longer, anyway, and what was more critical, Stowy wasn't bored anymore. He was having fun.

"This one vibrates, too," he said, switching it on high. The woman's screams grew louder and louder before weakening to animalistic moans. "That's it, baby, give me all you have. Come for me and keep coming for me."

The second girl whimpered while she waited for his abuse. Her wait was short. Stowy lifted her hips and skewered her ass with his cock. "Oh my God, a double ass fuck," he exclaimed, as he pumped his cock in one girl and used the oversized dildo on the other. Their screams fed his tortuous appetites and spurred him to heights of intense fulfillment.

Although he was usually desperate to climax, Stowy decided to slow down this time, so he could get even more pleasure from the torture. He'd bring himself close to nirvana, then stop and take a drink of beer before continuing. He also switched asses several times, but after a while, he finally let loose and had one of his best climaxes on record.

The girls were now whimpering rag dolls. Irritated by their response, Stowy used a variety of knives and finished them off slowly. That is until he found his favorite knife. The razor-sharp blade sliced into their hearts like butter.

He super-glued red and green bows in all the right places on the girls' naked corpses, and then he transported them to downtown Anchorage, where he placed them under the city's Christmas tree.

Using red paint, he left his message in the snow: Merry Christmas, Anchorage.

CHAPTER FORTY-SEVEN

Christmas gifts

December 25th

On Christmas day, they snuggled close. Sarah rested her head on his chest after their early morning frolic, and Steven caressed her back. "If only all mornings were this blissful," he lamented.

"Once the case is solved, they will be," Sarah said. Even as she spoke the words, she realized there'd always be more cases. "We just have to appreciate them when they're here." She cuddled closer. "I especially love these cold mornings."

"Me, too. But what would you say to a different locale?" Steven presented her with his gift. "Merry Christmas, my love."

Sarah sat up. "I didn't know we were opening gifts so early."

"Surprises are always unexpected," Steven said as he watched her.

She undid the ribbon around the scroll, unrolled the official-looking document, and read their New Year's Eve itinerary. Sarah gave him a dazzling smile. "Wow, a Paris ball!"

Thrilled with her reaction, Steven grinned back at her. "So, what do you say we waltz our way to the new year in Paris? After all the practice we've put in this year, I can't imagine a better way to celebrate."

"Really? You'll come with me?" Sarah shook her head in disbelief.

"Of course. Who else?"

"But Captain Reed…the FBI…are they going to let you travel during this case?"

"I already got it cleared. Besides, they still owe me time from our honeymoon."

"How can I say no? Why would I?" She hugged him tightly. "YES! Of course. Paris, here we come, but if you have to turn around and come back, I will, too." She kissed him soundly. "It's the perfect gift! Thank you."

She reread their itinerary and wondered if the trip would even happen. She'd have to see Dr. James for the all-clear before she could board the plane, but dancing at a real masked ball in Paris would be a dream come true.

"We can start our family while we're there. Paris has always been lucky for us in that way," Steven added.

Sarah's eyes filled with tears, and despite her determination not to cry, they fell. Steven pulled her into his arms. "Tears? Now that I didn't expect."

"You do want a family," she whispered.

"Of course, I do. I know I've been all over the place lately, and I'm sorry, but a family is all I've ever wanted. Especially with you." He kissed her tears away. "Then it's settled. We'll dance in the new year in Paris?" He searched her eyes.

She nodded. "I have a special gift for you, too. If you give me a minute, I'll run downstairs and get it. It's under the tree."

He kissed her softly. "What do you say to a quick shower before breakfast, and then we open the rest of the presents?"

Although Sarah could hardly wait to see the expression on his face when he opened the box and found out she was pregnant, she agreed to his suggestion.

They showered together, but Steven didn't bother drying his hair, so he was the first to go downstairs. Not long afterward, Sarah raced downstairs, excited for the festivities to begin. She lit a fire in the den fireplace, turned on some Christmas carols, and then went to the kitchen to help Steven prepare breakfast. But the kitchen was empty.

She picked up the phone and dialed the security office. Brent answered. "Merry Christmas, Sarah. How can I be of service?"

"Merry Christmas, Brent. Is Steven with you?"

"No. Steven just left. Said Reed called."

"Thought so. Thanks." She hung up, made a cup of tea, and then carried it to the den, warming her hands on the mug. Absentmindedly, she rested one hand on her stomach. "Our son. We're having a son," she said to the puppies, as they found their place on her lap. Her cell phone pinged with a text message.

Jenkins is at it again. Sorry, angel. Love you, and Merry Christmas. I'm glad we had this morning. Think about

Paris. We'll be there soon. P.S. You have my permission to buy a whole new wardrobe.

She texted back with a smiley face emoji. *You'll love each article of clothing I buy, especially when it comes off. Good luck. Love you, too. Merry Christmas.*

Steven's haste to get back to work told her she had good reason to doubt that they'd ever make it to Paris. At least, not while he was still working this case.

Besides, the trip also depended on whether Dr. James gave her the go-ahead. If not, she'd be perfectly happy waiting until later in the pregnancy. After all, who doesn't love Paris in the springtime?

CHAPTER FORTY-EIGHT

Disappointment

December 27th

The Christmas Day murders kept Steven tied up for days, and all the packages intended for him were still under the tree. Sarah moved most of them to their room. Due to the murders, there would be no New Year's Eve party this year, so Emma wanted to take the tree down earlier than usual. While cleaning up, Emma saw Sarah drop one of the gaily wrapped presents into the wastebasket. "What was that? Food that's gone bad?" she asked.

Sarah turned. "What?"

"The gift you threw in the wastebasket."

"Oh, that," she said, picking the package back up and turning it over and over in her hands. "A joke gift that's no longer funny. Nothing expensive. Just a joke."

She recalled the day she wrapped the pregnancy test. The perfect Christmas present, she thought at the time. Now she knew it was too soon to make the announcement. Steven wasn't ready.

"It's a shame you two never really got to celebrate. But with Steven having to deal with that monster, it's hard for him to find the time to relax, let alone imagine anything funny these days."

"I know," Sarah said, dropping the package back into the trash can. She hugged Emma. "I'm sorry. I had every intention of helping you today, but I'm not feeling well. I'm going to make a cup of tea and lie down."

"Sweetheart, you go right upstairs. I'll take care of this. Go on. I'll bring a cup of tea up in a few moments. Milly is stopping by, and we'll have the place to rights in no time. Try to relax."

"Thanks, Em. I'll put the water on before I go upstairs."

Sarah left the brightness of the den, filled a kettle in the kitchen, and headed for her bedroom. Once there, she dimmed the lights and sank onto the chaise lounge. She was tired. No, she was beyond tired. She was exhausted, and the day had barely begun. All to be expected in the first trimester, according to the baby books she'd read, but her melancholy mood wasn't helping.

If Steven weren't so wrapped up with this case, she knew his happiness would be overflowing. Instead, he was frightened, fearful for her, and all those he loved. She wished she could take the stress from him, but since that was impossible, the least she could do was not add to it.

She closed her eyes and faded into a deep sleep.

Blood was everywhere. It was on her and flowing from her, but in her arms, she held her son. He was beautiful. Healthy and hungry. She put him on her breast. As he suckled, her energy waned, and she knew her body was dying. Her son nursed while death waited. Steven was suddenly in front of her, fighting the monster he'd been hunting. The beast was covered in blood, too, but it was too late for her. Steven would win this fight, but she wouldn't be part of the celebration.

She jolted awake.

"I'm sorry," Emma said as she put a tray on the side table. "I never imagined that you'd fall asleep so quickly. The tea got cold while I explained to Milly what I needed. So, I had to reheat it. Are you feeling any better?"

Sarah shook her head and tried to shake off the dream. Her heart raced. "I'm sure the tea will help. Thank you." She took a sip. "Do you think Steven's right?"

"About what?"

"Starting a family."

Emma stopped fussing and said thoughtfully, "Maybe. You're considering that in vitro thing, right?"

Sarah nodded.

"I'm sure for him it's just the timing. I'm sorry you have to go to such lengths to get pregnant, but I've no doubt it'll be successful. He's so tied up with this Snowman case. Horrific the way that man operates. Try to be patient. I'm sure it'll all work out."

Emma placed the back of her hand on Sarah's forehead. "You're a bit warm. You might be coming down with something." She took a throw from the bed and covered Sarah's lap and legs with it. "Rest. I'll check on you in a little while."

"Thanks, Em. I don't know what I'd do without you." As the cup of tea warmed her hands, images from the dream continued to chill her heart.

CHAPTER FORTY-NINE

More Heartache

December 29th

Sarah spent the morning chatting with Charlotte, Myra, and Moya about their Christmas, and it made her smile to hear the happiness in their voices. Then Gregg entered the conversation to give her some welcome news.

"It's a miracle, Sarah. You said my mother would change, and that the girls would melt her heart, and you were right! I didn't expect it to be so quick and so dramatic."

"How do you mean?"

"That first day. It was like day and night."

Sarah smiled and told him about their meeting in the garden. "So, what sparked all that? Do you know?"

Gregg smiled. "It was Moya. Mother was in their room looking at all the lovely pictures you painted of the girls, and Moya strolled in and called her Gaw'ma.

"Mother knelt to hear her better, and Moya threw her arms around her neck and said. 'I love you, Gaw'ma. I love you.' What can I say? It turned her cold dead heart to cotton candy. Now both girls call her Gaw'ma, and she loves it! Myra told me that Gabby used to point to Mother in the family photo and tell them they had to pray for grandma every night. Moya couldn't say grandma. Instead, it was Gaw'ma. Still, it was Gabby that told them how Mother needed their love and their prayers because she had grown up without love. My dear wife told them that it's why she never smiled. And you know what, Sarah? She smiles all the time now. It's truly a miracle."

After the phone call, Sarah enjoyed a walk around the grounds with two bodyguards. She smiled every time she pictured Moya with her little arms around Mrs. Sunne, declaring her love. Knowing that Moya had melted the devil's heart, lifted her spirits.

Sarah decided to give up running until she was in her second trimester, and in general, was going to play it safe until her January 2 appointment with Dr. James. However, even though she'd been taking it easy, she still hadn't been feeling very well. When she noticed blood in the snow and on her white mukluks beneath her skirt, she panicked. She began running toward the house and safety but collapsed in severe pain outside the door. Seeing the blood trail, the bodyguards thought she'd been shot and called for a medevac helicopter.

Steven was holding a staff meeting, discussing the latest cases, and handing out the assignments when a clerk ran into the room. She hurried to Steven's side and whispered into his ear.

"Gabble, take over," he said as he bolted for the door.

Reed ran down the hallway beside him. "I'll drive."

The staff exchanged looks and began murmuring about what might have happened. The clerk who'd interrupted the proceedings cleared her throat. "His wife was just rushed to the hospital," she said, and the room fell silent.

~***~

Steven ran into the emergency room, his heart pounding, and so breathless, he couldn't speak.

"Mrs. Quaid?" Captain Reed boomed, in his usual commanding voice.

The nurse flinched and picked up a clipboard. "This way," she said before leading them to a room in the obstetrics department.

Dr. Listten closed the door behind him and faced Steven. "Sarah's being prepared for surgery."

"What happened?"

"She collapsed."

"Why?"

The doctor took a deep breath. "Miscarriage."

Steven dropped to his knees. "No. God, no!"

The doctor knelt beside him. "Dr. James is with her now." Dr. Listten put his hand on Steven's arm. "The news isn't all bad. There were two babies. There's an ectopic pregnancy, as well as a normal one."

When he saw the blank look on Steven's face, the doctor continued. "Ectopic means the gestation took place outside the uterus. It's a pregnancy that couldn't survive, no matter what we did. But, Steven, the baby in her womb, is still viable. Dr. James is working to make sure it stays that way."

Steven's mind clouded, and his stomach roiled. "I don't understand. She lost a baby, but there's another?"

"Exactly."

"And you can save her...them?" Steven's voice quivered.

"We're going to try, but you need to pull yourself together for your wife's sake. There's a risk, a high risk, that she could lose this one, too. The ectopic pregnancy ruptured, and she's lost a lot of blood, but we're going to do everything we can to turn that around."

Steven stood. "Take me to her!"

~***~

Sarah kept fading in and out of consciousness.

"It's all right, Sarah. Your time hasn't arrived."

Sarah opened her eyes to see a beautiful angel in white. "Are you here for me?" she asked. As Sarah spoke, the vision began to fade, and with it, the words the angel said, but Sarah would've sworn she heard: "No, dear, you still have eight months and a son to deliver."

Sarah's world went black once more.

~***~

Dr. Listten hurried Steven down the hall and opened a door. Sarah lay against the pillows with wires and tubing going in all different directions. Blood pumped in almost as fast as it was escaping. Doctor James worked feverishly. Wiping the sweat from her brow, the doctor yelled, "Get her to surgery! Now!"

Sarah's pallor was so stark it terrified him. Her eyes blinked open, and when she saw Steven, a tear ran down the side of her cheek. "I'm so sorry," she whispered.

They wheeled Sarah past him on the way to surgery. "It's going to be all right. I'm right here." He touched her ice-cold hand.

"I love you," she whispered.

I love you too, he thought as they wheeled her through the door. An invisible vise gripped his throat. He tried to swallow but couldn't. Please, Great Spirit don't take my life, my soul, my everything.

In the waiting room, Steven sat alone on the edge of a chair, ready to sprint into action, and no one dared to approach him. His body stiff, with elbows on his knees and head in his hands, it was apparent he didn't want to hear any words of sympathy, concern, or prayers. His only thoughts were of Sarah and their child. Please, Great Spirit, let this baby survive. Give me back my angel. The waiting room began to fill with family and friends, but no one spoke, not even in whispers. When Emma sat beside him, he reached for her hand but said nothing.

An hour later, Dr. Listten returned to the room. "Sarah and the baby are fine for the time being, but the next twenty-four hours are critical."

Steven closed his eyes. Thank you, Great Spirit. "May I see her?"

"Certainly." He led Steven and Emma to the recovery room.

Sarah was still unconscious, her color closer to life than death, unlike the last time he'd seen her. Steven said another prayer of thanksgiving and gently touched her stomach, directing his healing prayer to her and their child. He sat beside the bed and pressed her ice-cold hand against his cheek, transferring his warmth to her.

Emma said a silent prayer, too, and touched her cheek. "Sleep well, precious girl. Sleep well."

A few hours later, Sarah was moved to a private room. Emma kissed her goodbye and returned home, but Steven stayed with her and positioned security outside her door. In a comfortable chair, he dozed off and on. When a dream caught her, she whimpered and moved restlessly, but didn't awaken. Steven curled his body around hers and held her close. She slept more soundly in his arms.

When Sarah awoke, so did Steven.

"Steven."

"Hey, beautiful. How do you feel?"

"Are we still…?" She couldn't even say the word. Tears filled her eyes.

"Yes, love." He kissed her forehead. "We're still pregnant. Everything is going to be all right. I promise."

She threw her arms around his neck and cried tears of relief. He pressed her trembling body close, whispering words of comfort while knowing his vow was a precarious one.

"Good morning, you two," Dr. James said when she walked into the room.

Steven moved from the bed and straightened his clothes. Sarah dried her tears and offered the doctor a weak smile.

"Your color certainly looks much better. How do you feel?" She checked Sarah's vitals.

"Scared," Sarah said. "Is everything all right?"

Steven squeezed her hand.

"The uterine pregnancy is viable. But, due to the ectopic rupture, you need to take it easy. I won't lie to you. There's still a chance of loss. You'll need to be on bed rest until your twentieth week, maybe longer. And I mean full bed rest. Can you do that? I know how active you are, so it's not going to be easy."

Sarah looked at Steven. Her eyes swam with tears. "You married an invalid," she whispered.

"I married my hero!" Steven said and kissed her hand. "We can do this."

Reed walked into the room. "Sarah, I'm glad to see you looking better."

"What's happened?" Steven asked, his voice tinged with irritation.

"A break in the case." Reed's gaze went to Sarah. "I'm sorry to intrude."

She grinned. "I understand." She kissed Steven on the cheek. "Go. I'm fine."

Steven glared at Reed before hugging his wife, settling her back on the bed, and kissing her goodbye. "I'll be back soon. Just do what the doctor says," he said as he followed Reed out the door.

Then he turned on Reed. "So, what is it? What's so damned important you had to burst in like that?"

"Sorry, Steve. It's Jenkins. We found his truck."

"Go on."

Reed continued, "A local garage owner called when Jenkins came by to pick it up. The man recognized the Snowman, but instead of calling us, he told his buddies."

"Please tell me they killed the bastard," Steven said.

"Unfortunately, no. After a tussle with a few torches and pitchforks, the monster got away, but at least we have the truck."

"Figures. Well, let's go see if it tells us anything about his location."

They hurried to the CSI garage. "Gordon, did you find anything?" Reed asked.

Gordon laughed. "You mean besides two dead bodies wrapped in plastic and locked in the toolbox in the bed of his truck? Other than that, no. Coroner took those away five minutes ago. All we have here are the fingerprints of the men who tried to stop Jenkins, Jenkins' fingerprints, and a completely detailed vehicle. It was clean. Well, other than the bodies, cleaner than a brand new one off the manufacturer's floor."

Disappointment cast a shadow over Steven's face. "Damn it! What's he up to now?"

"Only heaven knows," Reed said. "Only heaven and the devil himself."

~~*~~

CHAPTER FIFTY

Letter to the Editor

January 1st

To the good people of Anchorage:

I will stop my vendetta of revenge on one condition. Detective Quaid must concentrate on the death of Denise Cochran. Family distractions do not wipe out his obligations to the people of Alaska. Denise deserves justice. I know he's convinced you that I did it, and while a part of me did want to add her to my collection, I denied my deepest desires out of love for her. She was someone who always told the truth. I couldn't kill her. She was going to write my story.

We signed a contract. I even gave a copy of the agreement to Captain Reed, but I've heard no word. Nothing. Plus, Denise taped our last interview, and, yes, it was at the cabin where she was found, but I did not end that beautiful lady's life. Where's the tape of that interview? Why hasn't it been seen? She photographed our entire session. The proof that I'm innocent is on those recordings. I've not heard nor seen any mention of that evidence, either. Have you?

I swear, as God is my witness, I did not kill the Beauty Queen. People of Anchorage, I beg of you, please demand justice for Miss Denise Cochran. Tell Quaid to get off his ass and get to work!

This is my vow, my promise to you: If Detective Quaid concentrates all his efforts on solving Denise's murder, I will not kill again. I will keep my word. I always have. It's a matter of honor.

Sincerely, The Snowman.

CHAPTER FIFTY-ONE

A New Focus

January 2nd

Anchorage was experiencing an unusually warm winter, and spring fever was rampant, but according to the calendar, winter had just begun. The Snowman was still running free, and his letter to the editor had caused a stir among the population. Opinion was varied regarding the Snowman's words. Was he responsible for the beauty queen's death? Was Quaid on the ball, or was he too caught up in matters of the heart? The citizens of Anchorage thought they were owed an explanation.

"Sorry, Captain. I have to give his words the attention they demand," Steven said.

Reed paced the floor of the bullpen. "You don't really believe Jenkins will stop killing, do you?"

"No. But what will it hurt? The way we found Denise has never sat right with me. You know that, and now, I know why." Steven entered his office and sat down at his desk with the file outlining Denise's case. The captain followed and settled slowly into a chair.

"My gut was speaking then, but I ignored it because it was too close to a Jenkins killing, but what if it was staged?"

"Staged. Why? What evidence do you have?"

"Bleach," Steven said.

Reed looked confused. "I don't understand."

"The only cases we've had where bleach was used were the ones committed by the copycat. It was the only way to cover the identity of the real doer. Stowy doesn't use bleach anymore. He's proud of his conquests and wants credit for them."

After a brief consideration, the captain nodded his agreement. "By God, you're right! Do you think he had a copycat do it?"

"Not necessarily, but think about it, Captain. Jenkins has never denied a victim before, and if he did Denise, he'd be celebrating, but he isn't. He's calling for justice."

"We all want justice, but if not Jenkins or a copycat, then who? And please don't say the husband," Reed huffed.

"That's what I have to find out, and if working on Denise's case keeps him from killing anyone else right now, I'm all for it."

Reed shook his head. "I still think it's because he wants to look like he's pulling all the strings. Just another way to muddy the water."

"So, let him. We need a new angle, and who knows? Maybe he'll become more involved, and this could lead to his capture. I say we go public with the investigation and keep Jenkins quiet for a while. If it saves even one life, it's worth it."

"Fine. Go for it, but you know as well as I do, Jenkins' compulsion to kill is too strong. I tell you, he won't quit, because he can't. Sure, he'll stop making them so public, but the man also likes to bury his victims. He'll go underground."

"I know. I don't doubt that he'll keep killing, but if we can keep him talking…maybe, just maybe, the asshole will write himself into a corner," Steven said.

"Okay, I'll release a statement to the press, but I'll also let them know the publishing contract was bogus. The publishing company was something Denise thought up. I'm sure she planned to self-publish, but maybe he realized that, and it didn't sit right with him. It could be his motive for killing her. I don't trust the man to tell the truth here. Just remember while you're on your wild goose chase, Jenkins is getting away with twenty-some murders. Our focus has to remain on him."

"And it will, but we've got eyes everywhere, and we've not had any breaks. What if he leaves the state?" Steven said.

"There's no way. We're running facial recognition at the airport, the railroad station, and every port, and we've got cameras monitoring all exits out of Alaska. The bastard isn't going anywhere." Reed yawned. "Sorry. I'm not bored. I haven't been sleeping well."

"Understandable. To ease your mind, I've discussed my plan with Frank, and he's agreed to put some new men on the case, including a few FBI recruits. Fresh eyes can't hurt, and he agrees that a new search of abandoned buildings should be conducted.

Jenkins has lost several of his favorite killing grounds. He'll be looking for another one, and some of the places we ruled out earlier may be perfect for him now. Besides, if chasing after Denise's killer is a waste of my time, that'll become apparent quickly." Steven stood. "Go home, Captain. Get some rest. I'll call you if I find anything."

"You don't have to ask twice. I'm exhausted. I leave it in your hands." Reed stood, his shoulders hunched, and his face drawn. The stress of this case had aged him ten years in the past few months.

After he left, Steven went through the Jenkins file meticulously, reviewing all the interviews conducted and the evidence gathered. He made a few phone calls, one to the IT Director,

"Hey, James, do we still have copies of the airport footage around the time of Denise Cochran's death? Say the day before, then the day of, and the day after? Good. Do me a favor. See if Tyler Hemp shows up on any of them. Thanks."

Then he called the airport and made arrangements to fly to New York, but first, he wanted to return to the cabin where Denise died. He took Cotton with him.

"Spooky, isn't it?" Cotton said.

"Very," Stephen said as they pulled up to the cabin in the early evening. The dark forest looked eerie in the subdued light, and the cabin windows reflected the sunset, which made it look as though someone was moving around behind them, watching. Steven turned on his flashlight and trudged to the porch, where the wind-blown police tape curled against the railing. He unlocked the door and toggled the light switch on and off before remembering the electricity had been shut off. "Cotton, do me a favor and start the generator. It's in the outbuilding around back. We'll need proper lighting to do a decent search."

"Sure," Cotton agreed, jogging to the back yard.

Steven entered the room and stood for a few moments, remembering the scene as he initially found it. "You should never have come back, and for what?" he said, as though the spirit of Denise still lingered. "An interview with a fiend like Jenkins? What were you thinking? How could you not know it'd end in death?"

Cotton popped into the house and switched on the lights. "Nice generator. Easy start. So, where do we begin?"

"Follow the electrical lines from these cameras. Something Jenkins said has gotten under my skin. I'll search the bedroom."

Cotton talked aloud as he followed the cords. "Each one is plugged into a surge protector, and the surge protector is plugged into the wall socket, but this cable…not sure where it goes." He shrugged, then followed it into the kitchen. "It disappears into a hole in the wall. But I can't tell you where it goes from there unless I cut an opening."

"Then cut one, and find out," Steven ordered.

"Roger that," Cotton said, pulling out a pocketknife. He cut a small hole in the wallboard and then ripped off a chunk. "The cable goes up the wall. To the attic, I assume," he yelled. "I guess we're going to have to figure out how to get up there."

Steven opened a bedroom closet door and looked around. "Found it!" he yelled as he pulled down the ceiling door entry to the attic.

Cotton joined him, and they climbed the stairs. Steven switched on his flashlight again. "This is where she conducted the interview. Look at this equipment. I'll bet my bottom dollar it was all done electronically. She was safe up here while he was downstairs. Smart girl. Stowy couldn't have killed her, because he didn't know she was here."

"Are you sure he didn't figure it out?"

"Check the attic door. It has a lock."

Cotton nodded. "You're right. It was re-enforced, too, and nothing's broken."

"Exactly. Denise did her best to stay safe, and I don't think Jenkins had any idea she was up here."

"Then who killed her?"

"I'm betting on the husband. Just don't tell Reed until I have the proof." Steven switched on the lights, so he could get a better look at the tape recorder and microphone that were sitting on a corner desk. "Well, well, look at what we've got here," he said. "A tape."

He hit play.

"Holy shit, she recorded her own murder!" Cotton shouted.

"Yeah, but what happened to the tape of her conversation with Stowy?"

~~*~~

CHAPTER FIFTY-TWO

Warmth

January 2nd

The second day of the new year found the weather calm, temperatures in the forties, and Stowy Jenkins with a new identity, haircut, and wardrobe. Wearing his best camouflage, military-style haircut, and a scruffy three-day beard, he watched the Tok Junction Restaurant door. At the same time, he waited and gobbled a stack of pancakes dripping with melted butter and warm maple syrup.

Finally! He wiped his mouth, jumped to his feet, and smiled at the elderly couple hobbling toward him. The stupid naïve elderly couple. His smile stretched wider. Talk about easy marks. Thanks to the Internet, it was easier than ever to prey on stupid people.

"Mr. and Mrs. West, it's so nice to meet you. Please sit," he said, pulling out two chairs. "How are you feeling now, sir?"

"Thank you, young man. Much better. The hip has healed, but this leg is still a bit weak. That's why the cane. And why I won't be doing much driving for a while."

The waitress stopped by their table. "Can I get you, folks, some breakfast?" she asked, offering a couple of menus. "Mr. Appetite here," she said, topping off Stowy's coffee, "has already had two helpings of buckwheat cakes. All you can eat."

Mrs. West laughed. "Oh, dear! We may have to get a few more groceries before we leave town. Just kidding, Owen," she whispered, touching Stowy's arm. "We stocked up plenty." She looked at the waitress. 'Thanks, dear, but we don't need a menu. We've already eaten breakfast, but I think a piece of that great-smelling apple pie would hit the spot."

Stowy grinned. "Sounds good to me. A man has got to have dessert."

The waitress laughed and winked at Stowy. "Coming right up."

"It's such a blessing to be on our way home. Thank God you need a ride south, Owen. Has your sister had her baby yet?"

"Not yet. The doc says she's still got another week or two to go, but I think she's more than ready, Mr. West."

"Please call me George."

"I will. Thank you, George."

"And call me Irma," Mrs. West said, patting his hand.

Stowy gave her hand an affectionate squeeze. "Thank you, Irma. I'm so glad I checked that ride-sharing website. It was just by chance that a friend told me about it." He looked at Mr. West. "I forgot to ask. Does your RV have chains? I checked the weather report for our trip, and it's supposed to be clear, but once we hit those mountains, well, you never know what we might run into."

"Yes, indeedy. We're all ready. We've got chains, and plenty of cat litter, too. Plus, heat, shovels, and plenty of hot chocolate." He laughed. "And I've got the entire trip mapped out. I figure it'll take us a good week to get there."

"Owen, we were thrilled to find someone with your background to drive us out of here. I don't feel comfortable behind the wheel of that behemoth," Mrs. West said.

The waitress returned with three generous slices of pie, and they all dug in.

"Mmm, good pie," Stowy said, smacking his lips appreciatively. He set his fork down and wiped his mouth. "It's worked out for all of us. I love to drive and did so in my unit. Big rigs, tanks, jeeps, you name it, but I hate flying, and I want to get to my sister's place in time for the birth of my first nephew. So, thank you both. You two finish your pie, and I'll take care of the bill. I don't know about you, but I'm kind of anxious to get started."

"So are we." Mr. West enjoyed the last bite of his pie while Stowy paid the bill.

When he came back to the table, he said, "My room is just a few feet away. And I assume you're parked out front?"

"We are." They walked outside, and Mr. West pointed to a large black and white RV. "That's our chariot right over there," he said. "Do you need any help with your luggage?"

"No, all I've got is a duffle bag and a backpack, and my room is only a few feet from where you're parked. Give me a minute."

Stowy trotted toward his room with the West's trailing behind him. He stopped outside his door; his keycard still held in his hand.

"Something wrong, Owen?"

"I don't know. The doors not closed, but maybe the maid was in a hurry and forgot to lock up." He pushed the door open, stepped inside, and looked around. Then he went straight to the closet, opened it, and yelled, "NO! This can't be happening! It's gone! It's all gone!"

Mr. West came into the room. "What's gone?" he asked, frowning at what appeared to be a ransacked room. An empty duffle bag lay on the bed, its contents strewn on the floor.

"My gifts…my backpack with all my papers in it…my passport!" He hung his head. "I'm sorry, folks. You're going to have to go without me. I can't cross the border without my passport."

"No, that can't be! We have to get home. The weather and timing are perfect. Don't you think the Border Patrol would make an exception? After all, you are a vet," Mr. West said. "That should count for something."

"If I had my papers, they might cut me some slack, but all that stuff was in my backpack." Stowy dropped to the bed and put his head in his hands. "This is unbelievable, just unbelievable."

Mr. West sat beside him. "Listen, we can still do this. We have a compartment under our bed. You can hide there. We'll smuggle you across."

Mrs. West gasped. "But what if we get caught?"

"No. Thank you, Mr. West, but your wife is right. The last thing I want is to cause you folks, any trouble."

"Nonsense! We can do it! If security takes a look-see, we'll be ready. That compartment is plenty deep, and we'll pile all the Christmas packages on top of you. I'm sure they wouldn't want to disturb those. It'll work! I know it will. Come on, young man. Let's get out of here." He pushed the duffle bag toward Stowy and smiled. "At least they left your clothes. And on the way, we can pick up a few gifts to replace the ones that were stolen. Come on. Time's a-wasting!"

After Stowy gathered his clothes and stuffed them back in the duffle bag and zipped it up, Mr. West reached for it. "No, you don't," Stowy said. "I've got it. I appreciate what you're willing to do. It means the world to me."

"No, let me take your bag. You should go to the motel office and report the loss, so they can file a police report. The management needs to know someone jimmied that lock, and the police may even recover some of your paperwork."

"I'll go to the office, but this is coming with me." He lifted the bag. "You need to be taking care of you, not carrying something this heavy. I'll be right behind you." Stowy headed to the office and watched as they boarded the RV.

"Hey, handsome. Sorry to see you go. I hope you and your parents have a great trip," the waitress from the restaurant said.

"You done for the day?" Stowy asked.

"No, just taking a smoke break."

"I'll be coming back this way in the spring. Will you be around?"

"I live here, and I'm not planning to go anywhere." She flipped her cigarette butt to the ground and winked at him. "Look me up."

"Count on it. Excuse me, but I have to turn my key in. The folks are waiting."

"I'll do that for you. Go! Don't make those sweet people wait."

"Thanks!" Stowy gave her the key, waved goodbye, and hurried to the RV.

"Okay, folks, it's time to get this show on the road. Farewell to this frozen state." He honked the horn as they pulled out of the parking lot.

~***~

"Sorry, folks. I enjoyed the ride, but now I want to be alone," Stowy said, looking down at the two-unconscious people at his feet. George and Irma West had befriended a killer. While Irma reminded him of his dead mother, and George, the father he barely remembered, murder was Stowy's favorite way to say goodbye.

Hiding in the storage compartment under their bed worked like a charm. The border guards never even looked. Who could doubt these two, these typical-looking Grandma and Grandpa, especially with their homemade cookies to share? They were a kind couple, and they said he reminded them of their son Cooper, who'd died in Desert Storm. It probably didn't hurt that Stowy claimed to be a veteran from the same war. He loved the attention and care they'd shown him, but he was good at biding his time, and once they crossed the border into the United States, they were no longer useful.

Stowy killed them, and because they'd been so kind to him, it was a gentle murder. He drugged them, and as they slept, he put them in plastic bags and buried them side by side in the same grave. Buried alive, they eventually died by suffocation. According to Stowy, it was his most humane murder, and no one could say he broke his promise. Nobody in Alaska died.

Pleased with his escape from the frigid weather of the north, Stowy headed farther south to the hot desert of Arizona.

CHAPTER FIFTY-THREE

New York

January 5th

When he landed at LaGuardia, Steven was met by a New York detective. "Welcome to the big apple, Detective Quaid."

"Thanks, but please call me Steven, Detective Arnold. I appreciate all the work you've done since we talked."

"My pleasure, Steve. You can call me Harry. I'm curious. What made you zero in on the husband?"

"Even though it's usually the first place we go when a spouse dies mysteriously, it took me longer to get there this time because of the Snowman."

"Based on the evidence I saw, I would've come to the same initial conclusion. Once you caught Tyler Hemp on camera at the Anchorage Airport. We found him on camera leaving and returning here, it was easy to get a search warrant and an arrest warrant. We haven't interrogated him yet, though. I thought you might like to do the honors."

Quaid grinned. "Thanks. That's why I'm here."

Tyler Hemp paced from one side of the small room to the other. He finished his coffee and threw the empty Styrofoam cup at the garbage can, missed it by foot, cursed, and resumed pacing. He checked his watch, shook his head, then collapsed in a straight-backed wooden chair, his head in his hands.

Steven and Detective Arnold had been watching him for ten minutes.

"Ready?" Detective Arnold asked.

Steven nodded. "So is your guest," he said with a smile.

They opened the door to the interrogation room.

Hemp immediately stood. "Detective Quaid. What are you doing here?"

"Please sit, Tyler. I'm here to close your wife's case."

"Well, good, because no one here has told me a damned thing. Have you caught the Snowman?"

"No, but I am here because of Jenkins."

"What can I do?"

"For starters, you can tell me why you killed Denise."

The man's jaw dropped, and his face paled. "What? Are you nuts? I didn't kill anybody. I was right here in New York when she died. You can check with the nanny. She'll tell you."

"You mean the one you've been sleeping with?"

Beads of sweat appeared on Hemp's forehead and upper lip, and there was now a noticeable tremor in his hands. "You don't understand," he said. "After Denise died, I needed someone, and she was there. I'm not proud of it."

"Is that so? Cathy says your affair began six months before Denise died."

"She's lying! Hell, you're probably lying! Isn't that what you do? Try to scare the shit out of the innocent?" Looking pleased with himself, Hemp sat back, his arms folded across his chest.

"The security footage from the Anchorage airport doesn't lie. It shows us you landed at 3:20 PM on the same day as Denise and took a return flight home at 10:00 PM that evening. And you arrived home just an hour before you were notified of her death.

"We didn't find Denise until the next day after her father's attorney said she never returned the keys to the cabin. So, tell me, Tyler. Who's the liar in this scenario?"

"Cathy is! I swear I didn't touch that girl until after my wife died. She's looking to file a harassment lawsuit because she knows I have money. And as far as those supposed pictures, the ones from the airport? No matter what you say, that wasn't me!"

"Denise's divorce attorney says otherwise. She knew you were cheating on her, and she was ready to file for divorce. Did you know she had a meeting scheduled with her attorney the day after she was due to return home?"

"No!" Hemp pounded the table. "You're wrong!" He stood and began pacing again. "I couldn't kill Denise. I loved her. It was that monster, the Snowman. Look at what he did to her! He brutally raped her, posed her in that wedding dress, cleaned her with bleach, and then cut her neck. You know it was him! I could never have done that."

"How did you know about the bleach?"

"What do you mean, how did I know? I was told or read it in the coroner's report. It's true, isn't it?"

"We've never shared that detail with the public."

"Bullshit! I knew it. Hell, I think Denise knew it. She told me many of the things Jenkins did during his killing spree."

"Exactly! Denise told you all about Stowy Jenkins and how he worked, so you thought you knew just what to do to make it look like Jenkins killed her. But you know what, Mr. Hemp. Jenkins says he didn't do it, and here's another interesting little fact. He no longer uses bleach. Also, he wants...no, he craves...the accolades of his kills, but asshole claims he didn't kill Denise, and I believe him."

Red-faced, Hemp stood and shouted, "What? You believe a batshit crazy killer over me? An upstanding citizen of New York?"

Detective Arnold cleared his throat. "Sit your ass down, Tyler!" Then he hit play on the remote controller in his hand, and the video of Denise's final moments began playing. "If I'm not mistaken, that's you posing your wife. And looky there. That's also you cutting her neck and walking out with her briefcase."

Steven said, "We found this tape in a secret room in the attic of Denise's cabin."

"And that's not all," Detective Arnold said. "We also found Denise's computer, laptop, and a taped interview with Jenkins in a trunk at your house. Her tape shows Jenkins leaving." He folded his arms and smiled. "Your luck just ran out. We know what happened."

Hemp shook his head. "Bullshit! That's Jenkins in disguise! Does the tape show my face? No, it doesn't. I'm being

framed, dammit. I want an attorney. NOW!"

Despite all the evidence and his attorney's advice, Tyler Hemp refused to confess. He'd be going to court, and all of Anchorage was abuzz with the fact that, for once, the Snowman might be innocent.

~~*~~

CHAPTER FIFTY-FOUR

Meet the Sandman

January 15th

The sky above Phoenix, Arizona, was blue, and the desert sported various shades of brown, brown, and browner. There were also muted splashes of red, orange, and yellow, plus a dash of green, courtesy of some tired-looking cacti, but all Stowy saw was an uninspired landscape of brown bordered by some so-so mountains. He failed to see the beauty in any of it, but the warm weather more than made up for it. That and the fact that he could wear cowboy hats and boots and could drive with a shotgun slung openly across his pickup's rear window.

Today was going to be a good day. Quinn finally did his job and caught Denise's real killer. About damned time, too. Stowy would be sure to congratulate the detective later. But now, it was time for him to enjoy his own private celebration. In his own unique way. With a killing.

Every city, no matter how glitzy or glamorous, has a seedy side, and Phoenix is no different. Flashing neon lights, attached to tacky strip clubs and classless bars, provide the sole illumination on Tanner Street. Numerous derelict buildings and empty lots covered in garbage round out the scenery, but despite the lack of amenities, there was never a lack of customers. Nor was there a lack of miniskirted hookers.

Stowy felt right at home.

It didn't take him long to spot what he was looking for. He wanted someone new to the game, someone who wouldn't be all used up and soured by the life she'd chosen. This gal was standing in the most brightly lit part of the street, and she was smiling. It looked like she was on the prowl, just like him, and he was drawn to her positive attitude.

"Hey, pretty lady! Want to party?"

"If you got the music, I've got the dance." With a cheeky grin, she hopped into the cab of his truck. "Wow, your ride is so new, it even smells new. I love it." She ran her fingers along the dash. "Real leather?"

"Of course! I only go first class, little lady. How about you?"

"Every chance I get, cowboy." She settled into her seat and fastened her seat belt. "You mentioned a party?"

"I did. I most certainly did," Stowy said, handing her a joint. "Here you go. If you'd like to mellow out a little, help yourself."

"Cool! Don't mind if I do. Thanks!"

She toked while he drove, and then, as though suddenly remembering her manners, she offered the joint to him, but he pushed her hand away. "Not while I'm driving, babe. I'm not losing my truck over a bad decision. I'll partake once we stop for the night."

"So, it's going to be an all-nighter, huh? You sure you got enough cash for that?" She grinned at him through a haze of smoke.

Stowy laughed. "Does this ease your mind?" He pulled several hundred-dollar bills from his shirt pocket and tossed them at her. "And there's plenty more where that came from, if you get my drift."

She smiled. "Oh, yeah! I get it, all right, and I totally want it!"

Stowy pulled up beside the travel trailer. It was lit up, inside and out. The strings of brightly colored twinkle lights helped create a cheerful-looking party atmosphere.

"Where is everyone?" she asked.

"Don't worry. They're on the way, but it'll be nice to have a few moments alone with you before they get here. You know, to get into the party mood." He stepped out of the cab.

She hopped out, too. "Then let's get this party started!"

~***~

Stowy sighed deeply as he lay back in the king-sized bed. It was the same one that once belonged to Irma and George, but silk sheets and a plush red velvet coverlet had converted the room into the perfect bachelor pad. "You were right, little lady. You know exactly what to do with that tongue of yours."

She smiled as she licked the dribbles from her lips. "I started giving blow jobs when I was eleven. I'm eighteen now, and truly the best there is. It's how I make the most money. But it's my turn now.

Can I?" she asked as she straddled his cock, her hands expertly bringing it back to life.

"Mmm, hmm. Oh yeah! You know what I want." Stowy jumped up, leaving her on her knees, waiting.

"Go for it, big boy," she said as he positioned himself behind her.

But it wasn't her vagina that he wanted; it was her ass. He poured a drizzle of beer down her crack. "Can't invade without a little lubricant, so say all the ladies." He set his cock at the ready.

"No, wait! I'll need more than that." But it was too late. Stowy had already thrust forward. Holding her hips with a vise-like grip, he took what he wanted.

"After ten years in prison, you only crave the tightness of the ass."

Sandra screamed, but did her best to relax and take his abuse without causing more damage. When he finally came, he held her in place until his dick softened, and then he pulled out. "Yep, your ass was much, much better than your mouth."

"That's not fair! Did you have to be so brutal?" she said as she crawled away from him. "That kind of sex is always negotiated beforehand. I have lubricant. I have condoms. You took advantage. How do I know you don't have AIDS?"

Stowy laughed. "I might. I very well might. I was in prison for ten years, and it was the ass-fucking capital of the world."

He laughed at her shocked expression. "But now, I'm bored." He smashed her in the face with a beer bottle, breaking her jaw and knocking her unconscious.

"I'm going to take a long, well-deserved nap, and then early in the morning, we'll visit my favorite garden. You, my pretty, will be the third flower planted there." Stowy shoved her off the bed and pulled the covers over his naked body.

~***~

The sun was almost entirely above the horizon when Stowy finished digging the hole. "Five feet exactly," he said as he took the final measurement. "Perfect." He jumped out and went to the bed of his truck, where Sandra was lying beneath a tarp, her wrists, and ankles tied securely. "Come, my pretty. Time to get you planted."

The semi-conscious girl blinked at him as though trying to focus. Unshed tears clung to her lashes.

He dragged her to the pit he'd just dug, pushed her in, and positioned her on a mound of dirt so her head would remain above ground after he refilled the hole. Then, he made a series of precise cuts on her legs, feet, torso, and arms. If things went as planned, it would take a few hours for her to bleed out.

Before slipping into unconsciousness again, she whispered, "Please...don't..."

Stowy doused her with ammonia before filling in the pit. Then he combed her long black hair and checked his watch, wondering how long it'd take her to die. While he waited, he decided to dig a few more graves. The Boy Scouts had nothing on him. Stowy Jenkins was all about being prepared.

He stood back to admire his work, a beautiful garden of corpses, and then snapped a few pictures and smiled. His fans would pay big bucks for these shots. And well they should. He'd put a lot of careful planning into this project.

It would be a garden like no other. The sizable circular plot was outlined with similarly-sized rocks, which he'd painted black. While that simple border gave his garden a professional look, the crowning beauty would come from its unique flowers...from the different colors of long-flowing hair blowing in the desert wind.

He stopped digging from time to time to check on Sandra's progress and guzzle another beer. When her end was finally imminent, he was covered in sweat and had nearly a case of beer in his belly. To amuse himself, he stood in front of her, masturbated, and shot a wad right onto her sunburned face. And he recorded the entire thing. Including her death.

"Deeper cuts the next time. That took longer than expected. But truly, what a wonderful addition to my garden of lovelies."

~~*~~

CHAPTER FIFTY-FIVE

Valentine's Day

February 14th

Stowy Jenkins had kept his word and gone silent, and while Steven was sleeping better, he wasn't a fool. He'd done what the job asked of him and arrested the man responsible for Denise's murder, but no matter what he or the department did, they couldn't locate Jenkins. Captain Reed, Frank Stover, and Steven decided to meet at the Saloon.

"Well, what's the bastard up to?" Reed asked as they took their seats.

"He's left town. At least that's what my gut says. I've been monitoring other cities for an uptick in the murder or disappearances of young women," Steven said. He smiled as the waitress approached.

"Gentlemen, what will it be today?"

"Drafts all around," Frank said.

"You got it. Need menus?"

"None for me," Steven said. "The house special's fine."

"I agree," Reed said, and Frank nodded.

"Wonderful. I'll be right back with your drinks."

"How could he leave?" Reed asked. "We've been monitoring every exit."

Frank laughed. "Someone smuggled him over the border. Simple as that."

"Then, good riddance. At least Jenkins isn't killing any more of our citizens," Reed said.

"True, but he'll be back. He has unfinished business here," Steven said.

The waitress delivered their drinks and smiled. "Your meals will be up shortly."

"Thank you," Frank said, tipping her with a ten. After she walked away, he looked at Steven. "You mean he has unfinished business with you."

"Yes. With me." Steven stared into his drink before taking a long swig. "I think he's waiting for the birth of my son. The bastard haunts my nightmares."

They fell silent as each of them digested Steven's words. Pretending preoccupation with their drinks, their glasses were emptied in no time. Frank motioned to the waitress for another round before breaking the silence. "So, what's your plan?"

"I've reached out to several large cities, mostly western and southern states, because I doubt Jenkins would go to another cold location," Steven said. "My plan is to catch him in another state and keep him from coming back here."

"That's a good plan, but he is known as the Snowman.

That makes me think he might choose another cold locale," Reed said.

"Anything's possible, but I'm trying to cover all the bases as well as we can. Our officers have been reaching out to police departments all over the country, and most of them seem to be appreciative of the information and willing to cooperate. At least, that's what they say. They may start laughing in their coffee as soon as we hang up the phone." Steven chuckled. "Not that I blame them. A serial killer called the Snowman sounds more comical than dangerous."

"I wouldn't worry about it. If Jenkins shows up in any of their cities, they'll gladly cooperate. No one will be laughing then," Frank said.

Steven nodded. "True." He smiled at the waitress. "This one is on me." He handed her a fifty. "Keep the change. A toast, gentlemen." He held his glass high. "To warmer weather and early melting of all the snow."

Frank laughed. "Hear, hear!"

It didn't take long before Steven's outreach produced a response. Detective Archer from the Phoenix Police Department called with a favor.

"Detective Archer," Steven said as he answered the phone. "How can I help you?"

"Detective Quaid, I hate to admit this, but we have several missing women. All from the red-light district. They're in their early to late twenties and new to the streets. We have six women that we know of so far, but we haven't found any bodies. If this is Jenkins' handiwork, he's keeping them for himself. Any ideas?"

"Sounds like he's repeating former habits. After we realized what Jenkins was up to, he began burying them."

"I was afraid you'd say that. You do know, Detective, we have hundreds of acres of sand out here. Where do we even begin to look?"

"I wish I could tell you. Other than it being a remote location, I can't even guess."

"I didn't think so. Would you do me a favor, though? Send me everything you've got on this Jenkin character so I can issue a heads-up bulletin to my men. Anything about his habits, MO, strengths, possible weaknesses, and whatever else you think might help. On second thought, do you think there's any chance you could deliver it in person? I'd be much obliged if you'd come down here and help us get our new task force off the ground. We'd like to get ahead of this if we can."

"You've got it, Detective Archer. I'll text you my arrival time. See you soon."

Now all he had to do was tell Sarah he was leaving, and he had the perfect solution. He double-timed it up the steps to their room. "Hey, beautiful! How'd you like to visit your most favorite place on earth?"

"Don't tease! You know I'm stuck in this bed." She closed her book and set it aside.

Steven sat beside her. "I know it's been tough, but I know just the thing to cheer you. Dr. James just told me I could take you outside to Eagles Nest, as long as your feet don't touch the ground. She says you and the baby are both healthy, and while she wants you to wait until you're halfway to delivery before you get out of bed regularly, you can enjoy a trip in my arms right now. What do you say?"

"No joke? For real?"

He scooped her up. "For real, my love. Emma's getting your coat and boots ready as we speak."

Sarah threw her arms around his neck and kissed his cheek. "This is just what I need."

Once she was bundled up to Emma's satisfaction, Steven carried her to their favorite bench at Eagles Nest. For a long time, they sat there in silence under her favorite tree, just breathing in the fresh air and enjoying the panoramic view.

Then she sighed and turned to him. "Okay, so tell me about the case."

"You know me too well." He squeezed her mittened hand. "I don't want to feed your nightmares."

"Not knowing only makes them worse, because then my imagination takes over. Just tell me."

"Jenkins has gone quiet, and I'm betting he left Alaska."

"And you think you know where he is, don't you?"

Steven nodded. "Definitely a warmer climate, because we know he hates our winters. To get a bead on him, we've been monitoring the murders in other cities for look-a-like crimes, unusual disappearances, call girl murders, anything that looks like Jenkins' MO."

"And you found something?"

"Yep. I just got a call from a detective in Arizona, and from what he tells me, I'm pretty sure that's where Jenkins is."

"Good job."

"Thanks. That's not what I wanted to discuss, though. No matter where Jenkins is now, we know he's planning to come back, and I don't want you to be here when he does."

"Fine. Then let's move north. The Tlingit Nation came out in force to protect the family in the south. If a stranger shows up, they'll give warning."

Steven hugged her tightly. "You can read my mind."

"I try." She giggled. "But truthfully, I heard you talking to Emma about the possibility. Just because I'm an invalid doesn't mean I don't have good hearing."

"Then it's decided. I'll have the cabin prepared for our return, and as soon as the weather permits, we'll move north."

Sarah looked so serene, he hated to burst her bubble, but he had no choice. "There's one other little item that we need to discuss."

"You mean the one where you tell me you're going back to work, and this time it'll take you out of town?" Sarah said matter-of-factly.

"You love spoiling my surprises, don't you?" he teased.

"You're too easy to read," she said with a smile. "I could tell the minute you entered our bedroom. The way you held yourself, your confidence, and that look of freedom on your face, like, 'I've escaped. I've finally escaped,'" she said with a chuckle.

"Now, I feel guilty. You're the one on bedrest, and I have free will to do as I please, but I've got to get Jenkins. I can't rest until he's back in prison."

"I know, and I've appreciated you spending more time with me, but I'm the one on bedrest, not you, so go! Get your man."

"If I could take you with me, I would."

"Don't worry about me. One more month and I'll be so pregnant, I'll be waddling like a duck and wishing for time off my feet. Our son will be happy and healthy, and I'll get fatter and fatter."

"Never. You're my beautiful little doll," Steven said.

She smiled. "Be careful. Pregnancy weight is catchy. We could both turn into couch potatoes."

"Impossible." He chuckled.

"So where are you off to?"

"Phoenix. I think Jenkins is vacationing there, and he's found it hard to break old habits."

Sarah kissed his cheek. "Then go catch him in the act. Does Arizona have the death penalty?"

Steven laughed heartily. "They do! Bet the idiot didn't even think about that!"

~~*~~

CHAPTER FIFTY-SIX

Crossing Borders

February 15th

When Steven landed in Phoenix, Detective Archer, another Phoenix PD detective, and an FBI agent were all waiting to greet him.

"Thanks for meeting the plane," Steven said. "I wasn't expecting such a large welcoming committee."

"It's our pleasure," Archer said. "We appreciate the hell out of you coming. This here's my right-hand man, Detective Chadwick, and this is our FBI liaison, Agent Dean Haskins. After we get you checked into your hotel, we're looking forward to picking your brain over some good steaks."

After handshakes all around, the foursome made a trip to the hotel and then to the restaurant, where they enjoyed dinner and a lively discussion of the Jenkins case, followed by an exchange of files.

They lingered over their post-meal coffee while perusing the files. "That is one meticulous character," Detective Archer said.

"That he is," Steven agreed. "That's what makes him so hard to find. He always manages to stay one step ahead of us. Despite an increase in security measures, he still got to his targets. He's a fearless master of disguise who loves taunting us, and as much as I hate to say it, we deserve it. We failed to capture him by a matter of inches."

"He had ten years to plan, didn't he?" Haskins said. "By the way, I've worked with Frank Stover, and he speaks highly of you and your skills."

Steven nodded. "Thank you. Frank's an old friend, and the feeling is mutual. And yes, Jenkins had ten years to plan his revenge, and to make things more difficult, he's got plenty of friends willing to give him a helping hand."

"Does he know anyone from Phoenix?"

"He knew one that we know of, but that man died in prison three years ago, and to the best of our knowledge, he no longer had family or friends here. Doesn't mean Stowy didn't learn all about Arizona from this man before he died, though."

"But you're convinced he intends to return to Alaska?"

"I am. Jenkins has unfinished business there."

"Unless we can put him out of business right here?" Agent Haskins suggested.

Steven laughed. "That would be ideal. My wife reminded me that Arizona has the death penalty. A win-win situation."

~***~

Stowy sat in his wading pool under the rollout canopy of the RV, downing beer after beer. Between the psychedelic paint job, colorful lighting, and hip furniture, the RV barely resembled the Wests' frumpy grandma/grandpa cottage anymore. Now, it looked more like an in-your-face 70's disco palace. Parked on this secluded piece of property, he didn't even have to worry about drawing attention to himself, because there was no one around to notice. It was mighty nice of his mother to buy this sweet little piece of land. It was supposed to be for her retirement, but he was putting it to much better use, and even though she bought it in her maiden name, just to be safe, he made sure all evidence of the purchase was expunged from her paperwork before he left Anchorage. Otherwise, those nosy detectives would've been all over it like flies in a dumpster, and Steven would've visited him by now.

He picked up the newspaper and frowned at the headline. Alaskan Detective Offers His Expertise. He shook his head. No! It couldn't be!

According to the newspaper, it could: The man who caught the Snowman in Alaska ten years ago has come to Phoenix to help solve the disappearances of half a dozen young women. Has Stowy Jenkins, the Snowman, decided to exchange the cold North for the soothing warmth of Arizona? Is Phoenix in for a bloody visit by one of the most brutal killers of our century? Citizens of Phoenix hope not, but several signs point to that being the case...

Stowy read the entire article. As he did, the cold water became hotter and hotter, until he was sure someone had filled his wading pool with a scalding liquid. He got out and threw the paper down.

"Asshole! How dare he come to Phoenix?"

If the half-breed was here to play, it was time to change the rules of the game. Just because it was too risky to prowl Tanner Street right now didn't mean there weren't other options. He went straight to his computer and set up multiple profiles on a dating site.

Stowy was stunned by the number of responses he got. The only downside was these bitches would expect something in return for sex, like dinner, a movie, or both. Not that they'd get it.

His first date was with a successful young woman who owned her own graphic design company. Stowy couldn't resist. After all, computers were his first love. Chantal Parker agreed to meet with his alter ego, attorney John Lincoln, at Starbucks. Stowy walked in carrying a bouquet of yellow roses and a note.

"Hello? Chantal?" he said as he handed her the flowers. "I'm sorry, but John was called away on a family emergency. He was going to text you, but he thought that'd be too impersonal, so he asked me to offer his apology in person."

"Oh," Chantal said, as she accepted the flowers.

Stowy smiled. "He also sent you this gift certificate to your favorite restaurant, so you and your friends can have dinner on him. Of course, he's hoping that you'll agree to another coffee date next week, if not sooner."

"Wow," Chantal said. "I'm impressed. Thank you so much. I'm sorry, but I didn't get your name."

"Stone. My friends call me Stone. It's my pleasure." He touched his fingers to his head in an airy salute. "But if you'll excuse me, my date is waiting. John said to tell you he'll know he's done right by you when he receives your text." He smiled again. "I'll be sure to tell him he missed meeting a very charming young lady." With that, he turned and walked away.

Chantal got up from the table and quickly caught up with him. "I'd love another opportunity to meet with John. Would it be all right if I walk with you? Are you parked in the garage, too?"

"Yes, I am, and it'd be my pleasure." Stowy made small talk as he escorted her straight to her car. There was no need to ask for directions because he already knew where she was parked. His truck was right next to it.

"Thanks again. You're a good friend."

"John makes it easy. As you can see, he's very generous. It's a character flaw," Stowy said.

When she reached for her car door, he quickly plunged a needle into her arm. He caught her as she fell, and after a quick scan of the vacant parking area, threw her limp body onto the floor of his truck. It was simple, fast, and because he'd disabled the camera earlier, unrecorded. He'd thought of everything.

~***~

Several hours later, Chantal woke to a manic kaleidoscope of glittery lights all around her and the sound of Donna Summer singing Lady of the Night. When her eyes focused, they flitted frantically from the mirrored disco ball spinning above her to the shelves filled with languid lava lamps. She had absolutely no idea where she was.

All she knew for sure was she was lying on a hard-cold surface, and her arms and legs were tied securely. She could barely move.

"Well, little lady, it's about time. I was beginning to get worried. Did you sleep well?"

"Where am I?"

"You're in the Sandman's lair on a little journey back in time. How do you like the disco ball and my favorite singer?"

"What? I don't understand. Is John here, too?"

Stowy laughed. "Leave it to a stupid woman to think her date was still going to happen. John doesn't exist," he said as he moved closer to her. "It's just me. I'm the date you showed up for."

"Oh," was all she could say. Then she began crying.

"Oh, come on! You can do better than that. Beg for your life, scream, fuss and cuss…anything but cry! God, I hate tears!"

She cried harder.

"Fine. Wallow in your self-pity all you want. I'm going to go eat."

After abandoning her in his storage shed turned torture room, he prepared and ate dinner. He hated killing on an empty stomach, but after stuffing himself with a thick T-bone steak, baked potato, corn on the cob, and strawberry shortcake, he was more than ready for some after-dinner fun and games.

When he returned to the shed, she turned her face away from him. He forced a ballcock in her mouth and fastened it. "You don't want to communicate with me? That's fine. I'm going to have fun regardless."

He showed her the knife. "I'm going to use this on you. Are you ready?"

She shook her head. Her eyes, wide with terror, filled with tears, and he imagined her begging for her life.

Stowy shrugged. "I'm not ready, either." He set the blade down and turned off the lights and music. "I need a nap first. I overate."

Lying alone and naked in the dark, Chantal listened to the night sounds of the desert. The wind whistled across the sands, a coyote howled in the distance, and from somewhere nearby came some skittering sounds. Lizards, maybe? Or mice? Scorpions? Her heart thumped against her ribcage, and she tried to will whatever creepy-crawly it might be to stay away from her.

The next morning, Stowy returned to the shed, a bounce in his step and a smile on his face. "Good morning! There's nothing like a good night's sleep, is there? I slept like a baby, and now I'm like a tiger raring to go." He laughed as he removed the ballcock. "How about you, sweetheart? You ready for some fun?"

"Please, please, let me go," she begged.

"Don't be silly. We haven't had any fun yet. My usual girls are always willing to play my games, but something tells me you may have a different outlook. Maybe if I'm gentle...?" He caressed her breasts and smiled when her nipples hardened. He touched her skin softly, gently, arousing himself and watching closely as he also excited her, despite her reluctance.

She rolled her head from side to side, an expression of horror on her flushed face. "Please stop. I can't."

"I can see that you're torn. You want to enjoy sex, but something tells you it's wrong. Honest, it's not. It's truly not!"

He blindfolded her. "You don't need to see. Don't think. Just feel. Imagine John is here, and he's everything you've ever desired," Stowy said softly, as he slowly caressed her body and pinched her nipples. His fingers moved lower, circling her belly button, and skimming between her thighs. "Let me show you how good it is when you let those inhibitions go."

He continued to assault her with gentle feather-soft caresses, playful bites, and expert fingering. A soft moan escaped her, and her juices flowed.

"That's it, sweetheart. That's right. Just allow yourself to feel. Celebrate the pleasure," Stowy whispered.

He teased her clit. Used one finger and then another to explore her vagina. Soon she was panting and pushing her hips forward toward his touch. "That's it, sweetheart. That's it. Come for me. Show me how much you want to be fucked." Faster and faster, deeper and deeper, he pushed until she exploded in orgasm.

Stowy ripped her blindfold off and laughed. "Such a whore. I love it. But I'm not here to please you. You're here for me!"

He freed her legs and one hand. Then he pulled her to the side of the table and rolled her onto her stomach. With her legs dangling off the end of the table, he grabbed her ass. "This is what I want, my dear. I want to fuck your ass until you scream my name."

While holding the back of her neck so she couldn't move, Stowy thrust hard, then harder and harder into her virgin ass. Chantal screamed.

"That's it, bitch. Scream! Let me know how much you love this."

The more she screamed, the more his orgasm built. He roared as it exploded through him, and then he stepped back and zipped up his pants. "Finally, a little satisfaction. Time for breakfast."

After he left, Chantal pulled herself up and climbed back onto the table. Curled into the fetal position, she was too broken to care what happened next and barely responded when he returned late that afternoon.

"How's my little novice?" he asked. "Ready for your next lesson?"

She stared at him with empty eyes.

"Oh, come on! You had to have learned something. Would you like to go home?"

Her nod was barely perceptible.

"Then, let's act alive!" He unfastened her tied hand. "You have to please me, just once, and then I'll drive you home. No questions asked. We'll call it a bad hook-up and leave it at that. What do you say?"

A faint light filled her eyes, and her nod was a little more vigorous this time. "I can please you. I know I can."

"Excellent! Use the sink over there to clean yourself up, and we'll try that again."

On shaky legs, Chantal made her way to the sink in the corner, which was nothing more than a metal tub and a hose. She quenched her thirst and cleaned herself as best as she could with the towels provided, and when she turned back around, Stowy pointed at a mattress in the corner of the room.

"Shall we start with you on your knees?"

Stowy unzipped his pants and lovingly caressed his growing cock as she took her place opposite him. "Well, what are you waiting for?"

She leaned down, opened her mouth, and he inserted his cock. Despite the roiling in her stomach, Chantal sucked, licked, and prayed he was a quick blow, but she had no heart for what she was doing, and Stowy knew it.

He laughed and grabbed her by the shoulders. "Good try, sweetheart, but not nearly good enough to save your life." He laid her back and spread her legs. "I can be gentle, and I can be rough, but women like you, like my sweet Freddy, want it both ways. Slow and gentle in the beginning, but a little rough at the end. Am I right?"

"Yes," she whispered.

"Then show me. Wrap those legs around me. Pull me in deep and show me how much you want to be fucked."

Chantal chewed on her lip, closed her eyes, and hooked her ankles behind his back. He slapped her hard enough to leave a fiery handprint on her cheek. "Eyes open!" he barked. "So, I can watch you come. I want to see your pleasure."

Stowy lifted her hips and took her by the ass again, relishing the look of hatred on her face. He even enjoyed her tears, and the snot trickling into her open mouth. All of it turned him on. When he came, he grabbed her breasts and squeezed, and her screams brought him full throttle.

As he filled her with a hot load, he simultaneously plunged a butcher knife into her heart.

Stowy had achieved his goal. He saw death take his victim just as he reached nirvana. He collapsed on top of Chantal and held her close until his blood and hers began to cool.

"The best sex ever! My God, how am I ever going to top that? Shit, that was good. So good."

Stowy hosed the blood from their bodies before abandoning her again. Then he went to bed and slept the sleep of the righteous.

The next morning, he wrapped Chantal in a blanket, loaded her into his truck, and set out for his desert garden. He wasn't burying this one alive like the others, but that was okay by him because that little lady gave him the time of his life.

Thanks to her, he'd discovered a new and exciting kind of victim. Someone not experienced in the sex trade, someone ashamed and embarrassed by how the body reacted to an intimate touch. He liked it. Hell, he loved it, and he couldn't wait to do it again.

As soon as he got back to the RV, he went online to find the next flower for his sand garden. His garden needed some more color, so this one had to be a redhead.

It didn't take him long to find her.

Paula Douglas was lovely. Her red hair didn't look natural, but he didn't care. It would flow beautifully beside his other flowers. He made a date with her, but he wasn't going to apologize or show up with gifts this time.

Paula only waited for him in the coffee shop for fifteen minutes before she got up and left. When she drove off, he followed her, and when they reached a lonely stretch of road, he pulled up close behind her and flashed his blue emergency lights. She stopped, and Stowy, wearing his freshly pressed blue uniform and dark sunglasses, walked up to her window.

He asked her to step out of the vehicle, and when she did, his syringe was ready.

Stowy's killing techniques were improving all the time. By promising to release them, he got his victims to cooperate, which added to his fantasy and satisfaction. His favorite coup de grace was the stab to the heart, which he'd also perfected.

And each success only made him hungry for more.

CHAPTER FIFTY-SEVEN

Jack the Ripper

February 25th

The day was bright, the sun was hot, and Stowy was whistling while he worked. He'd just planted another flower, and after a quick shower, he began frying bacon to go with his eggs when the news came across the radio: Detective Steven Quaid, the famous sleuth from Anchorage, Alaska, is still in our fair city, doing his best to help the police solve some unusual disappearances. If these disappearances genuinely are the work of the serial killer known as The Snowman, he's obviously changed his tactics. He is now targeting victims outside of the red district.

Stowy threw the spatula at the radio. It fell off the counter and broke. "Goddammit! I don't want you here, Quaid! Shit, Sherlock never left London. Go back to your igloo, you fucking Eskimo. The Sandman wants to be left alone."

He raced to his truck and drove to the nearest service station to buy a paper. After he read the full story on Quaid's visit, he finished making his breakfast, then started kicking ideas around. All he had to do was come up with something that'd punch so many holes in Quaid's theory, the local cops would tar and feather his ass and run him out of town. Time to do a little research.

Stowy turned on his computer, opened his browser, and typed infamous serial killers. After reading about good ol' Jack the Ripper for more than an hour, he knew exactly what he was going to do to muddy Quaid's investigation.

The original Jack took out hookers, but Stowy would troll for any girl alone on the streets, especially in the parks around Phoenix. Anywhere that gave him a way to disappear as soon as the job was complete. He'd harvest souvenir body parts like Jack, too. His favorite Ripper killing was the one where he practically severed the head from the body and took the heart. He liked the idea of ripping out hearts. He could do that.

With a wistful smile on his face, Stowy contemplated the future. He'd preserve each heart in formaldehyde. Then when he was ready to let the world know the killings were his, his keepsakes would bring in more money than ever. Once the world found out the Sandman and the Snowmen were one and the same, he'd make millions. His underground fans would expect no less.

Stowy waited for midnight to begin trolling, and he decided to make the Margaret T. Hance Park his starting point. After leaving his truck near an isolated apartment complex, he walked to the park at a jaunty pace, swinging his arms and whistling quietly. He was wearing black slacks and a reversible hoodie, which was now showing its white side. A detail people would likely remember if they should happen to see him.

He walked deep into a dimly lit wooded area and switched his hoodie to the black side. Then he hid in the shadows behind a bench to wait and watch for the perfect target. After a while, he shifted positions. What he wanted to see was a lone woman, but so far, nothing but couples. He rolled his neck and stretched his stiffening back, but he wasn't ready to give up the hunt yet. Not if it meant screwing Quaid.

A young woman ran past, and then she doubled back and flopped onto the bench in front of him, breathless. Stowy could hear a male voice counting slowly from somewhere nearby, and he smiled. A couple playing hide and seek, and she chose this bench…his bench…as her hiding place? How lucky could he get? When her boyfriend reached fifty, she jumped up and ducked behind the bench.

Stowy grinned at her from his hiding place in the shadows.

Her giggle died in her throat as she stared at him, immobile and wide-eyed, and before she could recover, he pounced. When her boyfriend yelled, "Ready or not, here I come!" Stowy was stuffing her heart and uterus into a plastic baggy.

With his trophies secured inside his hoodie, he sprinted across the park to his truck, and he was on his way home before the police arrived on the scene.

~***~

Steven had been invited to address the Phoenix Police Department detectives, as well as a group of local FBI agents. He did so with the aid of a whiteboard showing the recent disappearances. As he talked, he made his case by pointing out the similarities to Jenkins' habits. As far as he was concerned, there was no doubt that these killings were more of the Snowman's handiwork.

After what turned out to be a long meeting, some of the men gathered in a local sports bar to unwind. While they were there, Detective Archer got a call. He stood, shaking his head. "We've got another body," he said. "And you're not going to believe this, gentlemen, but Jack the Ripper's in town."

The men pushed away from the table and followed him out the door. "Micky says it's a sight she never thought she'd live to see in this century," Archer said. "I sure hope she's exaggerating."

They soon found that she wasn't. If anything, it was worse than she'd described on the phone. When they arrived on the scene, Officer Micky Reynolds, the first to respond to the call, brought them up to speed. "The boyfriend says they were playing hide and seek, and this is what he found when he finished counting. He said this is how he found her, except for the puke. That's his. He's with the paramedics now. Needed to be sedated."

Archer turned to Steven with a grim expression on his face. "Well, Quaid, what do you think now? Jenkins's work, or are we watching a city come unglued?"

Steven rubbed his chin. "I don't believe in coincidences. I'm sorry, Detective Archer, but I believe my coming to Phoenix was a big mistake. Jenkins is playing games for my benefit, and your cities caught in the middle."

"You think this is a message for you?" Archer didn't sound convinced. "You're taking things a bit personally, aren't you?"

"Anything is possible, especially where Jenkins is concerned. Anything."

~***~

Steven realized his visit was coming to an end when a missing persons update said two of the women who'd been reported missing had shown up in California. Then one of the officers floated the theory that the other missing girls weren't actually missing, either. They'd just been passing through Arizona on their way to California, Vegas, or Seattle. Then a graphic designer disappeared, further sinking the plausibility of Steven's theories.

"You said he preferred hookers because they went willingly," Archer said over breakfast. "That graphic designer sure wasn't a hooker. As a matter of fact, this case doesn't fit any of your parameters. Not a single one. And our copycat Ripper case doesn't include any of the sexual sadism Jenkins is famous for, either."

"In other words, I've overstayed my welcome," Steven said, setting his fork down and wiping his mouth.

"Well, the city is picking up the tab."

Steven nodded. "Understood. I'll be on the next flight out of here. My apologies if you think I've wasted your time."

"Not at all. I don't think knowledge is ever a waste of anybody's time. But we've got a few new crimes to figure out that obviously have nothing to do with Jenkins. I may have overreacted to your suggestions, but I appreciate the way you dropped everything to fly down here to help us out. Especially with a pregnant wife at home."

"It was my pleasure. Always glad to lend a hand, especially when Jenkins is involved, and mark my word, he is. He's the fiend you're looking for, Detective. I guarantee it."

Detective Archer pursed his lips, stood, and shook Steven's hand. "Good hunting, Detective Quaid."

They left it at that. Steven flew back to Anchorage, but he'd continue to monitor the Phoenix newspapers.

Meanwhile, Stowy was planning his next kill.

This time, the victim would die in Anchorage, Alaska.

~~*~~

CHAPTER FIFTY-EIGHT

Two for One

March 10th

The task force that was created when Steven came to town was now tasked with investigating the Ripper murders. The missing persons division was still working on the other cases, but bodies, the kind Jenkins was famous for, never appeared, so the task force moved on.

Steven's visit quickly forgotten, Stowy continued killing, using the same timeline as the Ripper. But to make things interesting, he decided to stage a Snowman killing in Anchorage to coincide with one of his murders in Phoenix. It'd be one last nail in Quaid's ego and would put an end to his theories about the Snowman vacationing in Phoenix. At least, until Stowy was ready to tell the world. In his own time and on his own terms.

He made a phone call to Anchorage. "Earl, did you get the supplies?"

"Got 'em. I've gone through your instructions, and I understand perfectly. Thanks for the cash."

"No worries, my friend. Ten thousand more where that came from if you do this right."

Earl laughed. "How could I not? Your directions are so detailed, an idiot could follow them. I can't miss."

"Just remember. Clean up using bleach. Leave no hair, no fluids, nothing. Got it?"

"Understood. Don't worry. I've trolled the avenue a few times, and I've already found the perfect girl. You'll approve. I guarantee."

"Send me her picture."

"Will do," Earl assured him.

"Remember, it has to happen on March 15, the Ides of March. No later, no earlier. Got that?"

"Don't worry, friend. I won't let you down. Have I yet?" Earl asked.

"No, you haven't. That's why I called on you this time. You always come through for me."

"And I will this time, too. Guaranteed."

Satisfied that his plan would succeed, Stowy hung up and thought about today's entertainment. The police wouldn't expect him to go hunting in the same park, so that's what he'd do. It wasn't enough just to stay in practice. He had to keep 'em guessing, too.

This time, he had no trouble finding his victim, and even less nailing her. She thought her running speed would ensure her safety, but several strategically placed stones tripped her up, just as he planned. As soon as she hit the ground, he swooped in for the kill.

After an immediate cut to the throat, Stowy slit her entire body open and removed his favorite organs. He dropped her heart and uterus into a plastic to-go bag and displayed the rest in a tidy row beside her on the grass.

This time, there was no one to interrupt him, so he could enjoy his play at a more leisurely pace. In fact, he enjoyed it so much, he decided to pick out another girl on his way home. Killing would do as a nice preliminary round, but now he was ready for some sexual action. Time to pay a visit to Tanner Street.

Once in his truck, he removed his dark blood-covered clothes and put on a pair of jeans and a t-shirt. As usual, Tanner Street was crawling with willing victims, and he quickly chose his mark. Carol was a bit older than his usual twenty-something, but she was in a good mood and ready to party when she jumped into his truck.

He drove her to a secluded spot just outside the park, and while she sucked him off, he watched the swarm of flashing police lights surrounding his dead runner. Imagining their horror at his handiwork, he came hard, and as soon as Carol raised her head, he hit her with a syringe. "Time to go home and finish the job," he said, pushing her inert body to the floor. He pulled back into traffic and drove home carefully, obeying every traffic signal and driving law, and he still arrived in record time.

He ripped off the hooker's clothes and tied her naked body to the table in his storage shed. Then when he was sure she was securely in place, he drove to a nearby diner for a steak dinner cooked by someone other than himself.

His waitress was a young pregnant woman, who looked even more tired than Stowy felt when he was digging those graves in the hot desert. He had fun flirting with her and making her laugh, and he slipped her a generous tip, hinting that she should buy something extra special for her baby. To thank him, she gave him an extra big piece of apple pie to take home with him. "You can top off your dinner with this later," she said with a smile.

He accepted her gift and returned her smile. He'd certainly enjoy that pie later, but right now, he was hungry for something else.

Carol was awake and waiting for him. "I don't understand. I thought we had fun."

"Maybe you did. I felt cheated. It didn't feel like you were really into it. I was a little disappointed with my purchase."

"I can do better! Let me show you."

"Is that so? Tell me, how would you do things differently?"

She closed her eyes. "First, I would undress you. Kissing and sucking, and even playfully biting you, if you like, while I removed all your clothes."

"Sounds like a good start. Then what?" Stowy asked as he turned on the music and lights.

"Well, I'd caress your balls and cock with my hands, while I lick and fuck your ass with my tongue. Then when you're good and hot, I'd suck every drop of cum out of your dick. And after you've had a chance to catch your breath, I'd offer my ass for your pleasure."

"Now, that's what I call a plan! Care to show me?"

"Undo these bindings, let me use the john, and then I'd love to rock your world."

He untied her, and she sat up. "Can I have a drink? Water is fine if you don't have anything else."

"I have a full bar. What's your pleasure?"

"A cold beer would hit the spot."

Stowy smiled. "A girl after my own heart. The john is in the corner." He pointed to the bucket and hose. "There's a lovely white rug over there for your comfort, too. Why don't you spread it out while I get those drinks?"

She peed in the bucket and cleaned up with the hose. Then she laid the rug down as Stowy had instructed.

He joined her with the drinks. "A toast. To better sex!" Stowy took a big swig of his drink, but his guest had something else in mind.

Escape.

Carol tried to smash Stowy's skull in with the beer bottle, but she failed. Stowy didn't.

He laughed at her unconscious body bleeding on the white rug. "Seems to me you promised me some ass," he said, lifting her hips. After his cock was satisfied, he pushed an empty beer bottle so far up her ass, it disappeared entirely. Then he tried to shove another bottle down her throat, but it broke. Carol died from blood loss and suffocation.

Stowy added her to his flower garden and stood back to admire his work. "Now that's what I call a great way to recycle."

~~*~~

CHAPTER FIFTY-NINE

Broken Promises

March 15th

Earl received a burner phone from Stowy, along with detailed how-to instructions for the killing he'd agreed to commit, which he studied until he knew them by heart. He'd kept his nose clean since he got out of the joint, and the last thing this three-time loser wanted was to go back to prison, but the amount of dough Stowy was offering was too tempting to pass up.

And today was the big day.

He'd been trolling the red-light district for a while, so he knew precisely which nubile young lady he wanted, and it didn't take him long to spot her. He beckoned her over to his truck and gave her his sincerest smile. "I'd love someone to keep me warm tonight. What do you say, little lady?"

Then he flashed the cash at her. Seven hundred dollars. Stowy told him to use the full thousand, but why waste money? Not that it mattered, because once he killed her, he'd be getting it all back, anyway.

She smiled at the wad of money and immediately hopped into his pickup. Then, following Stowy's orders, he headed for the secluded cabin where Denise Cochran was murdered. Not that he liked the idea of going there. He didn't believe in ghosts, but he sure had his doubts about that cabin. He'd already gone there once to check things out and stock it with the supplies he needed for the job, and the place undoubtedly gave him the creeps, but no way was he going to buck Stowy. Obeying him was paramount for success, money, and a long life. When the Snowman called on you to do a favor, you damned straight did all you could to fulfill his wishes. He was the undisputed master criminal, and when his desires weren't fulfilled, his vengeance was extreme.

Earl learned that valuable lesson his first day in prison, when Stowy wanted a box of cookies, one of the other prisoners got in a gift package from home. The prisoner refused to give them up, so

Stowy broke the man's jaw. The guy had to eat through a straw for two months, but Stowy enjoyed the cookies.

"The drive to the cabin is going to take a while," he said. "What do you say we get to know one another?"

"What would you like to know?" the cute blonde asked.

"Well, for starters, your name. Mine's Earl."

She laughed. "Jenny. I'm from South Carolina. I came up here for the summer because I was told you could earn a good living quick here."

"And have you?"

She shook her head. "Not so much. I've earned a living, but it barely covers my bills. Anchorage sure is an expensive place to live, even when you share rent with several people. And the cost of food…oh, my God, it's crazy!"

"Tell me about it. But there's no place like the North."

"It is beautiful, but I'm not really into the outdoorsy stuff."

"Oh dear, and here I am taking you to my cabin in the woods. Should I turn around?"

"No, not at all. I'm thrilled for the opportunity. By the way, you are talking about a place with four walls and a warm fire, right?"

"Better than that, it has electricity, and all the accoutrements of luxury, and by that, I mean a real working bathroom."

Jenny laughed. "Now you're making fun of me."

Earl chuckled. "Not me."

Jenny scooted closer to him. "I like you, Earl. You're funny."

As they drove up the long winding mountain road, she nuzzled his neck and teased his cock through his pants. He was so distracted, he could barely keep the truck on the road, but he wasn't about to complain, especially when she unzipped his pants and slipped her fingers inside.

"Sorry, I just couldn't wait to feel that love machine you're hiding in those tight jeans," she said, blowing her sweet breath into his ear.

He laughed. "You're going to get us both killed if you don't stop these shenanigans."

"What a word. Shenanigans," she said slowly. "I love it. I do hope you show me some shenanigans real soon."

"Missy, I'm going to do more than show you. Just you wait and see."

Her fingers undid one of his shirt buttons, and she rubbed his hairy chest, tweaking his nipples unmercifully. "I'm sorry. I can't help myself. I feel like I'm on a real adventure with a true mountain man," she gushed.

"Well, missy, what do you think?" he asked as he pulled up outside the cabin.

"It's lovely, just lovely. But it looks abandoned."

"I'm sorry. I told the caretaker to have a fire going by the time I arrived, but he's a slacker. His next check will account for this breach of etiquette."

She laughed. "How you talk. Are you trying to impress me?"

"Of course! I want you to have the experience of a lifetime," he said.

"Can I do you now?" she asked.

"Before we get inside?"

"Of course. I just want to show you how much I appreciate your kindness. I've never been treated so sweetly.

Everyone's always in a hurry. I like people, but most of the time, the man just wants what he wants. You took the time to ask about me and get to know me. You made it feel like a real date, and I just wanted to say thank you."

Earl lifted the steering wheel out of their way and turned toward Jenny. Then he unbuttoned his pants. "I'd love to feel that gratitude. Show me."

Jenny got on her knees. She grabbed his scruffy face between her hands and kissed him. When her tongue explored his mouth, his tongue came alive and ventured forth. It was a kiss that outdid all other kisses.

She broke the kiss, and with her hands around his cock, took him into the back of her throat. Her warmth and skill brought him to climax in a matter of minutes, and his throaty groan was barely expressed before Jenny was kissing him again. "That was so good. Thank you, Earl."

"I should be thanking you, Jenny. That was the quickest I've ever come. Amazing. And because of those skillful hands, I'm ready again. But what do you say we take this one inside?"

"I can't wait. I want to ride that beast until the cows come home."

Earl smiled broadly as he fastened his jeans, and then he and Jenny walked into the cabin. Damn, I like this girl. But I've gotta do what Stowy says. Or else.

Once inside, he lit the kindling in the fireplace and spread a fluffy white rug in front of it. Then he set out a tray of iced champagne and chocolate-dipped strawberries. Hidden beneath it were his tools, but he was in no hurry to use them.

Jenny slowly undressed for him before joining him on the blanket. He hand-fed her several strawberries and poured her several flutes of champagne. At the same time, he took his time enjoying her large breasts and other attributes. Finally, he let her undress him and ride his cock to her first explosive orgasm.

Earl held her in his arms and wished he'd met her on any night other than this. How could he kill someone he liked so much? Yet how could he not? He kissed the top of her head. "Jenny, do you think we'd be friends if not for the cash changing hands?"

"I'd like to think so. Why?"

"I was just wondering. I mean, I'm not an ugly man, but I still have problems meeting women, forming lasting relationships. What do you think my problem is?"

"I don't know, Earl. You have kind eyes. I saw that immediately. And you smell good. I like that in a man. Maybe you're trying too hard?"

"Yeah, maybe you're right."

"Come on, cuddle me," she said. "It's starting to get cold again."

"First, I'd better stoke the fire. Then I'll make you my famous hot toddy, and after that, I'll be ready to go again. How about you?"

"Sounds good. And this time, I'm gonna blow your mind with my tricks!"

Earl smiled, kissed her, and tended to the fire before going to the kitchen to make their drinks. He returned with two more flutes of champagne. "I changed my mind. How about if we save those toddies until after our next go-around?"

"Perfect," she cooed. "Tell me, lover. What do you want? Tell me about your fantasy."

"You'll probably laugh."

"Never. Tell me."

"I want that ass of yours. More than anything else, I want to fuck that beautiful ass."

"Okay," she said.

Earl nearly choked on his champagne. "Really? It wouldn't bother you?"

"Not at all. As long as it's done right, it can be a lot of fun. How about if we do it in the shower? But first, I have another gift for you."

Earl never felt so free. Damn, he wanted this girl. No, he needed this girl. All he had to do was find another hooker to kill. Then he could keep this one for himself.

Jenny got on her knees and began sucking him off while he played with her long brown hair. "It's okay," she said, winking at him. "You can play with my ass."

He didn't need a second invitation. After changing positions, he was able to pump her ass and pussy with his fingers while she performed fellatio. She soon milked him dry, and he had her panting and ready to climax.

"Whoa, Earl, you're one talented man! Let's finish that champagne and strawberries, and then you can do me in the shower."

Basking in the afterglow, Earl gladly filled her glass and alternated feeding her strawberries with giving her deep heartfelt kisses. After she emptied her glass, they walked to the bathroom, hand-in-hand.

She washed his hair and bathed him slowly, spending most of her time lathering and stroking his dick while he lathered and squeezed her ass, anticipating the fun to come. Jenny hugged him tightly, and her kisses told him how much she could love him. If only he'd let her.

He turned her around. She immediately bent over, and with her hands resting on the shower bench, spread her legs wide and handed him a jar of lubricant. "Use it generously," she directed.

"First, I want a taste," he said, lowering his face to her bottom. He circled her anus with his tongue before shoving it inside to tease her inner walls. As the water rained down on them, he continued flicking his tongue while stroking her clit with one hand and finger-fucking her with the other.

"That's so good, Earl. So good," she moaned. "I'm ready for you. Give me some loving."

He could hardly wait to put his dick into her sweet little ass, but he stayed where he was. "Not yet. Come for me first, Jenny. Come for me."

"Oh, God, Earl. I'm coming!" Her body shook, and her juices covered his hands and arms. Wearing a self-satisfied smile and quivering with anticipation, he coated his cock with the lubricant.

"Fuck my ass, Earl. Give it to me as hard as you want. I am so ready for you."

"You got that, baby." He pushed his cock in deep, and it slid in like a well-oiled pole.

She threw her head back, moaning with pleasure. 'That's it! Harder, baby! Deeper!"

Even though she was begging him, he hesitated to step up the pace. "Are you sure?"

"Yes! Oh, Earl, give it to me. Give it all to me!"

So, he did. Thanking his lucky stars that Jenny liked him so much, he went for it. He dropped all reluctance, and it was the best fuck he'd ever experienced. In prison, Earl was always the recipient, never the fucker, but he'd dreamed of taking someone that way ever since. She'd made his dream come true, and now, he had to make Jenny his girl. Had to. With that thought in his mind, he came and came hard. She followed suit, and as the water washed them clean, she kissed him as only a lover would.

"Did you like that, honey?" she asked as she toweled him dry.

"Are you kidding? It was the best I've ever had," he said.

Jenny smiled. "That's what my boyfriend always says, too. Whenever I want to rock his world with something special, that's the trick I use. But you're special, too."

"I am?"

"I've never done that trick with any of my johns before. I like you, Earl. I think my boyfriend would, too. Well, maybe not if he knew what we just did, but only because he's the jealous type."

The word boyfriend taunted him, echoing in his head like a nasty schoolyard jeer and filling his rejected heart with rage. He was a fucking idiot. What made him think anyone like her would ever want to be his girl? He was just another john to her. Oh well. Her loss. Looked like Stowy was going to get the kill he wanted, after all.

He made her that special hot toddy he'd promised, and before she finished it, the sedative kicked in, and she keeled over.

Earl carried her limp body back to the shower and scrubbed all traces of his DNA from her body with bleach, just as Stowy had instructed. Her mouth, her vagina, her ass… nothing was spared. Then he gave the shower a good cleaning. Just like Stowy told him to do.

Still following orders, he stuffed the white rug and all of her belongings into a plastic bag. After dutifully placing them in the back of his truck. He dressed Jenny in the clothes Stowy had sent him. A white pageant dress and a Miss Alaska satin sash. Before arranging her in her final position, he shoved a dildo way up her ass and turned it on high. Not part of Stowy's plan, but he figured she deserved something more personal for leading him on like that.

After placing her on a new white rug, he arranged her body like the way Denise had been staged. Then, using a straight razor, he carved deep cuts from her shoulders down her arms to each of her fingers. Down her legs, from her hips to each of her toes. Deep wounds that bled bright red. He then carved a pentagram into her chest. And finally, he slit her throat from ear to ear.

Jenny would never give her gifts to anyone else. And, in an odd way, knowing that, filled Earl with satisfaction.

He texted Stowy and sent him a picture of the finished product.

Stowy responded immediately. Told him to make sure everything was clean, to stoke the fire and to send a picture to Quaid, along with this message:

I couldn't resist. Hemp told me what he did to Denise. I just had to relive that experience for myself. Did I get it right, Detective? I tried so hard not to overdo.

He also told him not to forget the snowman emoji.

Earl did as he was told. He sent word to Quaid, cleaned the burner phone of fingerprints, and left it on the rug. Then he hightailed it out of the cabin and drove to Valdosta. Stowy had warned him that they'd trace the text via the pictures and to make sure he was as far away as possible.

Meanwhile, Stowy, after getting the news from Earl, proceeded into the park. He'd already spotted his victim.

~***~

Steven got a text while watching an old black-and-white Sherlock Holmes movie with Sarah, and for a few minutes, he was beyond confused. Had Jenkins come back to Anchorage? He immediately called Reed, Frank, and then Detective Archer.

"I'm sorry, Detective Quaid. I don't have time to talk right now. We've got another Ripper murder. I'm on my way there now."

News of the Anchorage murder and the Ripper murder made the headlines in both Anchorage and Phoenix. But no matter the games Jenkins played, Steven knew in his heart what the residents of Anchorage and Phoenix did not. Jenkins was behind both murders, and someday he'd prove it.

~~*~~

CHAPTER SIXTY

The Snowman Returns

April 15th

April, the month of breakup, gave the residents of Anchorage another snowstorm instead of the spring flowers they were hoping for. Whether it was an omen or just the last winter storm of the season, hope was still in the air, despite the killing of another young girl.

To get back to Anchorage, Stowy pulled the same sort of con game, but on a younger couple, he'd met in a bar near the Canadian border.

Sitting at the bar, he overheard them talking about their plans for their trip. "You're on your way to Alaska?" he asked as he settled onto a barstool beside them.

"Yes, our honeymoon. We just got married. I'm Joe, and this is my wife, Karen."

"Nice to meet you, Joe, Karen. I'm Owen. I know you'll have an exciting time. I was going to ask for a ride, but not if you're on your honeymoon. I won't bother you. Have a wonderful trip. You'll love Alaska. It's unlike any other state in the union."

Karen nudged her husband. He shook his head, but she pleaded with her eyes. He finally said, "Wait, maybe we can help each other."

Stowy settled back down. "I hope so. I have to get to Anchorage before it's too late."

"Too late?"

"Never mind. On your honeymoon, the last thing you need is a third party with a sob story."

The couple exchanged a look. "No big deal," Joe said. "We've been living together for two years. If we can help, we'd be glad to."

"After my sister moved to Anchorage last year, she found out she has cancer. Now, my brother-in-law says she's dying, and it's only a matter of time. And here I am without a passport or the time to wait around for one to be issued."

"Why don't you fly?"

"Besides the fact that I'm deathly afraid of flying, I'm pretty sure I'm on the no-fly list," Stowy said, looking around the room. "I was in the army during Desert Storm, and our plane crashed behind enemy lines. Now, if I get on a plane, flashbacks haunt me. I can't do it without alcohol, but the last time I tried, I got so drunk, they kicked me off the flight. I figured I was on the no-fly list, so I haven't tried again."

"That's understandable. We don't like flying, either. We can try to get you there. All we ask is that you pay for half the gas because we're running low on funds. You can hide in the camper when we get to the border. We won't open our mouths if you don't," Joe said. "Sometimes they look, sometimes they don't."

"If we get there right before shift change, I'll bet they won't," Karen said.

"Thanks. You're very generous. If it doesn't happen, at least I can say I tried."

~***~

At the border crossing, Stowy hid under the bed again. Border patrol never looked. Although they did board the RV and they did check the closets, they never looked in the storage compartment under the bed.

Once across the border and in Alaska, Stowy didn't waste time. He had someplace to be, and he needed their RV to get there.

Stowy wasn't particularly kind or gentle when he killed the young couple. He tied them up and made Karen watch while he raped Joe. Then he made Joe watch while he raped Karen. They died staring at one another while hanging upside down from a tree branch. He slaughtered them, gutted them, then left them in a desolate area, half a mile from the road. He knew they'd be found but hoped it wouldn't be too soon. He wanted the police and the people of Alaska to think he was keeping his promises, but when you're a serial killer, that's what you do. You kill!

CHAPTER SIXTY-ONE

Taunts

April 30th

Break-up was finally over, and the spring flowers were now in bloom. While Sarah painted, Emma and Sky were setting out planters of wildflowers around the cabin, and Steven was working at his computer. No other Alaska killings had been attributed to Jenkins since the girl in the cabin. But the disappearances and Ripper murders in Arizona had continued until the middle of April. Then, they suddenly stopped, an omen Steven didn't take lightly. In fact, it was the reason he was working from home. He was about to join Sarah for lunch when his phone pinged with a text.

Hey, Detective, what's up? Did you miss me? Stowy signed off with a smiley face and his usual snowman emoji.

Stowy texted again and included a picture of his gruesome garden of corpses. I'm ready to go public. Beautiful, aren't they? Too bad I couldn't include the girls from the park, but their hearts will always be mine.

Steven put on his coat and boots, kissed Sarah goodbye and told Elliott, "Get the chopper out of mothballs. I need to get to the airport."

Quinn was immediately at his side. Steven nodded at him, grimly. "Triple the protection, Uncle. The bastard's back in town."

Steven called Reed to fill him in, then forwarded the picture. "Please tell me IT can trace the GPS on this photograph."

Reed stared at the photo, which showed more than a dozen heads in various stages of decomposition, surrounded by sand. They were contained within a circle of black stones and spelled out in the sand with white rocks were the words The Sandman.

"Unbelievable," Reed said. "Can you trace it?" he asked James in IT.

"I'll get right on it," James said.

"You were right, Steven. Jenkins has been in Phoenix this whole time. He must've used a surrogate to kill Jenny Dutton. You were right about the bleach, too. Damn, now who has egg on their faces? But he's back in Anchorage, isn't he?" Reed said to Steven over the speakerphone.

"I'd bet my life on it," Steven answered.

Reed sighed. "Shit. It's going to start again, dammit!"

"I'm sure it already has," Steven said. "James, do you have it?"

"Yep, this photograph was taken in the desert just north of Phoenix, Arizona," the IT director informed them. "I even have the coordinates."

"Send everything to Detective Archer and tell him I'm on my way. They'll want answers, despite the egg." Steven was already boarding a plane for Arizona.

CHAPTER SIXTY-TWO

Bail

May 1st

The snow was gone, the days were growing longer, and after making it through another long dark winter, Anchorage was reveling in an annual rebirth of hope and expectation. Shortly after Stowy returned to town, he found out Tyler Hemp was out on bail. Sure, it cost him a cool million dollars and an ankle bracelet, but the privileged bastard was sitting pretty in an apartment in Anchorage while awaiting his trial.

That didn't sit well with Stowy. Not well at all.

Expecting his attorney, Hemp immediately answered the door. "I thought you'd never get here…sorry, but I didn't call a cleaning service." His voice faded as he slowly recognized Stowy Jenkins. "Nice disguise. What are you doing here?"

"You know me? Does that mean you watched the interview?" Stowy strolled into the apartment.

"Who doesn't know you? Papers all over the world are talking about the Snowman. What are you doing here?"

"A very cool response. A famous killer shows up at the door, and you have the balls to invite him in. Interesting."

"I'm not afraid of you. Besides, the cops are all over the place. Idiots are afraid I'll skip. So, why are you here?" Hemp demanded as he poured himself a glass of whiskey.

"Good to know. So, tell me. Was Denise your first kill, or have there been others?"

"Why?"

"You're part of a fraternity…well, you will be if there's more than one killing. But the real reason I'm here is to rescue you. You don't want to go to prison. I'm here to make sure you don't ever see the inside of the penitentiary."

"Fat chance. My lawyer assures me I have a winning case."

"What does your lawyer know? He's in it for the cash. If the cops have that tape, they'll see that I didn't kill Denise." Stowy walked to the bar and started to pour a drink. "You don't mind, do you?"

"Help yourself."

"Want another one?"

"Sure, why not?" He put his glass on the counter. "My attorney is working on getting most of the evidence excluded, especially that tape. So, I'm good."

"And if he can't?"

"He says he has experts that can show that the tape's been edited. He says the jury will believe you set me up. I should've checked the damned tape. Hell. I should've destroyed it! She told me you'd been there and all about the interview. I had no idea she had a tape still recording when I arrived. Good thing I came in the back door, because what they have doesn't show my face, nor does it record my voice. So, since my face isn't on screen, I think the attorney can convince them it's you in disguise. Reasonable doubt, that's all I need. And with you the prolific killer you are, there will be plenty of doubt. No one will believe I'm guilty. No one."

"So, tell me. How did you do it?"

"What?" Hemp stopped pacing. "Why? Are you recording me? Don't tell me you're a stooge for the cops." Hemp laughed.

Stowy pulled his pockets out and opened his shirt. "See? No wires. I'm just curious. Believe me, I thought about doing her myself."

"If you must know, I parked away from the cabin and entered by the back door. Denise was in the shower and had started brewing a cup of tea, so I roofied the tea and waited." He smiled and downed a quick gulp of his drink. "I have to admit, the sex was better than when she participated. Then I dressed her in that stupid pageant gown with a sash, which I found in her old bedroom closet. The only hard part was slitting her throat. Harder than I thought it'd be, anyway."

"First cuts always are. I heard the nanny was going to be a witness against you."

"Money talks. Money always talks. Hell, I even offered to marry the girl, but all she wanted was cash. But the important thing is she's on the home team, so they've got no evidence of cheating." He touched his forehead lightly with his fingers, blinked several times, and gave his head a quick shake to clear it.

"Very clever. Your attorney may be right. Does that mean you don't want my help?"

"Thanks, but no thanks.

"A toast then." Stowy raised his glass. "To murder and getting away with it. Good luck, Mr. Hemp."

They drank. And Stowy set his glass down just in time to catch the falling Hemp. "You won't make it to trial because I've been elected judge, jury, and executioner."

CHAPTER SIXTY-THREE

The Sandman Uncovered

May 1st

Steven was in the desert overseeing the recovery of the women who'd disappeared from the streets of Phoenix when he got a phone call from Reed.

"Tyler Hemp's disappeared. Cut the ankle bracelet and ran off."

"Why am I not surprised? That guy's so full of himself, he genuinely believes he's above the law, but don't worry. He knows next to nothing about Alaska, so it shouldn't take long to find him. My recommendation is to put Cotton in charge of the search, and I'll be home as soon as I see things through here. They've already started excavations, so it shouldn't take long to wrap things up. Thanks for keeping me in the loop."

The bodies were loaded into the coroner's wagon, and Steven and Detective Archer followed it back to the morgue, where immediate autopsies were to be performed.

"First impressions, Doc?" Detective Archer asked once the bodies were laid out on the morgue's tables.

The coroner lifted the sheets from a few of the bodies. "First guess is exsanguination. On some, he cut the extremities without hitting any major arteries. That would ensure a slow bleed-out, but this girl was stabbed through the heart. This guy loves his torture, doesn't he? I'll check to see what drugs were used. They didn't go easy, most likely, and he probably wanted them aware before they succumbed."

"It's his MO," Steven said.

"I think a few of these women were buried alive," the coroner continued. "And their deaths were slow. If he stuck around for their final breaths, I couldn't tell you. Some of these others, well, what I can tell you is that it was brutal. I can also tell you that he used a lot of ammonia, on and around the body, and in the pit."

"He did the same in Alaska to keep the animals away."

"Not sure it worked. The vultures wouldn't have cared, but I also noticed when I was out there that he had other deterrents for the birds. For the most part, I'd say the only animal that bothered the bodies was Jenkins. What I believe to be his ejaculate was found on all of their heads."

"How long were they out there?"

"I believe the most recent one has been there for a few weeks, and we'll know more about the others after I call in a forensics expert and run a few other tests. Based on the varying amount of visible decomposition on all the bodies, though, I'd say he buried one or two women every week."

"I'd bet my bottom dollar the bastard buried the hookers on the outer circles and put the other missing women in the center. It'd be his twisted idea of a bouquet," Steven said.

The coroner shook his head. "Is this guy still in town?"

Before Steven could answer, a messenger arrived. "Detective Quaid, I was told this is of vital importance."

The package held polaroid pictures and a note: Time to let you in on the truth. While I admired Jack, gardening was my first love. But I must admit, it made for an exciting visit to the Grand Canyon State.

The polaroids showed each of his victims. Those in the gruesome garden, and the ones he'd butchered as the Ripper.

"HOLY SHIT!" Detective Archic said. "You were right all along, Quaid!"

"Well, you don't have to worry about him anymore, Detective. Jenkins is back in Alaska," Steven said, pointing to the Anchorage postmark. "Like I told you, he's got unfinished business there."

CHAPTER SIXTY-FOUR

Justice for Denise

May 2nd

When Hemp regained consciousness, he was naked and sitting on a toilet seat at least six feet above the ground. Strung up between two trees, the only thing holding him in place was a series of ropes and cables. He shivered as a cold gust of air caressed his balls.

"What the hell's going on?" he yelled groggily.

"I was wondering when you'd wake up. Thought you might freeze your ass off before the fun begins," Stowy said, crushing a beer can and tossing it aside.

"Jenkins?"

"Yes, Tyler."

"Shit! What have you done?"

"Me? Little old me? Mad killer extraordinaire?"

"Quit bullshitting. What's this all about?"

Stowy laughed. "I'm glad you asked. This delightful technique was used by our ancestors too many years ago to count, and I thought it'd be the appropriate way to end your sorry life. It's called impalement. I guess you could say it's a more imaginative type of colonoscopy." He opened another beer and took a swig. "You ever hear of Vlad the Impaler? No? Well, he's the inspiration behind Dracula. Anyway, this was Vlad's preferred means of torture, but I've improved on it."

"What the hell?" Now that Tyler's head had finally cleared, he frantically assessed his predicament. "What? Oh, no, no, no. Please, God, no. You can't do this! I'll confess. I'll do it on tape. I'll write it all down. Just please, don't do this!"

"Begging? That's so not like the arrogant Tyler Hemp we all know and hate. And here I thought I'd met a fellow psychopath. Begging is not the way a true killer goes out."

"Fuck you!" Hemp shrieked.

Stowy unclamped several cables. "I don't think so, Hemp, my boy. It's fuck YOU!"

The toilet seat began to lower, inching toward the hefty hand-carved spike awaiting below.

"No, no, no!" Hemp cried as his body crept closer to the spike.

"You realize the more you move, the worse it's going to be, but go ahead! Maybe you're more of a sadist than I am."

"Stop this! Dammit, you can't do this!"

"Oh, but I am. And for your comfort, I even added a lubricant to the stake. It'll only hurt a lot!"

"You're a fucking monster."

"Hey, what's with the name-calling? If you feel like screaming, go ahead. We're miles from civilization, so no one will hear you," Stowy said. "On second thought, it is hunting season." He stuffed Tyler's jockey shorts into his mouth. "We wouldn't want one of them to accidentally put you out of your misery before the real torture begins."

~***~

Steven was still talking with Detective Archer and the coroner when his phone pinged with a text message: Detective, I finished the job for you.

Then a picture of Tyler Hemp came on screen.

"Steve, are you all right?" Archer asked. "You don't look so good."

Steven held out his phone. "I've got to get home. The bastard has gone off the rails."

CHAPTER SIXTY-FIVE

Another Apology

May 15th

Tyler Kemp's horrific death made headlines, and while specific details were withheld from the public, rampant rumors and reports of the Snowman's return were more than enough to create a renewed atmosphere of terror throughout Anchorage. Amid spring's gloomy weather and rain, countless reports of Snowman sightings had the police running in circles again, and Captain Reed and his entire department felt the stress.

Because of a few close calls, Stowy decided a new letter to the editor was in order.

Dear Editor:

And to you, the good folks of Alaska. Yes, I did break my promise. I killed a man. A horrid man. He took from us, from all Alaskans, our beauty queen. I couldn't allow that injustice to go unpunished. So yes, I broke my promise. If you'll forgive me that one indiscretion, I promise not to kill again in Alaska. That poor girl in the cabin was not my doing! I was in Arizona. Ask Quaid. He knows the truth. I don't know if there's another copycat, but that killing was not mine!

You're all safe, at least from me — all the girls on Fourth Avenue, and the young women attending college, all of you.

I've stopped my vendetta. I swear. I'm home now, visiting my mother's grave and starting a new life. Breathe easy. The Snowman is done with the cold north.

You have my sincerest promise.

The Snowman

Stowy was pleased with the response his letter generated, especially when Captain Reed had to admit that the young girl in the cabin wasn't a Snowman victim. But he had no intention of leaving. At least, not yet. Knowing how difficult it would be to keep his promise not to kill, he came up with a back-up plan. He'd stock up on beautiful babes for his sadistic sexual desires, but first, he'd have to build cells to hold them.

For the next two weeks, he used concrete blocks to custom-build the cells in an abandoned building one of his former jail buddies had leased for him. Each sound-proofed room measured six feet by eight feet and contained a mattress and blanket, a small microwave and mini-fridge, and a water spigot and composting toilet. By adding the amenities, he could leave his ladies alone for several days at a time. He also installed hidden cameras, so he could keep an eye on them, no matter where he was.

Once the cells were finished, it was time to procure his occupants.

"Nancy, right?" Stowy asked the girl sitting in a booth at a downtown grill.

"Yes, sir," she said shyly. "I read your personal ad. Will I do?"

"I can only tell you that after we complete the interview," he said, taking the seat across from her. "Here's the application. Fill it out, and then we'll order lunch."

He watched her closely as she chewed her cheek and filled out the forms he'd produced on his computer. The application started with the usual employer/employee questions, and then it got more personal. There were questions about who to contact in case of emergency, closest living relative, goals, and dreams, followed by a section asking about her sexual likes, dislikes, and special skills. Without flinching at any of his questions. The young girl signed her name at the bottom of the sheet and slid it across the table to him.

He ordered lunch and then perused the papers while she ate.

"Thanks for lunch," she said, wiping her mouth. "The information sheet says you pay on a sixty/forty cut and that you cover room and board, food, and transportation. So, what comes next?"

He smiled. "The tryout. So far, I like what I see and what I read."

She smiled back at him. "Oh, I'm so glad."

"I see you're living at a flophouse on the south end. After you finish lunch, we'll test your skills, and if you pass, we'll go pick up your things. I have a large house, luxury like no other. You'll have your own room and a connecting bath. That is, assuming you can please me. All my girls have to serve me with willingness and enthusiasm."

"Believe me, I can blow your socks off," she said before downing her apple pie.

"Good. That's just what I'm looking for."

Stowy repeated the interview process six times, but only took four girls, and they all went with him willingly. That is until he stuck a needle in them, and they woke up in their custom-built cells.

Now that he had his own stable of sex slaves, the next thing he needed to do was find out where Quaid and his wife were hiding. According to the chatter around Anchorage, they were somewhere in the Brookes Range, but he didn't want to arouse suspicion by asking too many questions, so he explored, and he listened. After his first few unsuccessful trips, he used and abused the girls to quench his appetite when he got back, but as the weeks passed and his frustration grew, he stepped up the torture. Soon, bringing a woman to the brink of death wasn't enough for him. He had to kill. Once his desire for blood was satiated, he procured another girl to take her place and ventured back to the wilderness.

After he heard the Quaid's had a cabin in the mountains, he spent more time in the area, fishing in the river during the mornings, and fishing at the Coldfoot Station diner for information in the afternoons. One day, some FBI agents stopped in for lunch, and his perseverance finally paid off. While no names were ever mentioned, Stowy picked up more than enough clues to plan his next trip.

~~*~~

CHAPTER SIXTY-SIX

Watched

June 1st

The North Slope Haul road was pocked with ruts and rubble, but the RV Stowy had claimed from the newlyweds after they'd crossed the border was handling the bumpy trip admirably. As he drove north toward Steven's cabin, Stowy whistled along with his favorite tunes. The weather was clear, and the sun and his spirits were both high.

"I didn't even know this kind of place existed in Alaska. I should've built my chalet up here," Stowy said aloud as he drove the scenic highway. "No wonder he's not interested in coming back to Anchorage. This scenery, that woman, it must be heaven on earth. Oh hell, who am I kidding? I'd miss all my whores."

After a quick burst of laughter, he spotted a turn-off. "Looks like the perfect place to hide an RV." He veered into the overgrown side path and parked a hundred yards off the road. Then he turned off the engine and pulled out his map. "Now, let's see how far I have to walk to get a good look at this little haven of theirs."

He grabbed the dorky fishing hat from the seat beside him and put it on his head. Why anyone would willingly choose to wear a hat stuck with flies and hooks was beyond him, but if he wanted people to believe he was a fisherman, he had to look the part.

Once he double-checked the supplies in his backpack, he stepped out of the RV. Then with his pack strapped on and his fishing rod over his shoulder, he headed toward the river. "Time to put a little scare into the happy family."

~***~

Blood. Everywhere she looked, there was blood. She could hear her son crying, but she couldn't get to him. Steven seemed to be asleep, but she couldn't wake him. Blood, blood, and more blood, and it was coming from her. Her legs, her arms, eyes, and breasts. Her body was shedding its life force. She was dying.

Sarah woke up and immediately got out of bed. Sweat covered her body. In the bathroom, she rinsed her face in cold water and stared into the mirror. "I'll be ready. I promise I will

be ready." She went back to the bedroom, and tears filled her eyes as she watched the man she loved.

Sleep eluded her, so she stared out into the night that was bright as day, the light beyond the dark shades that brought nightfall to their bedroom. She looked at the sky above the trees and shivered, sensing evil. He was out there.

"Angel, are you all right?" Steven asked. "I can see you shivering from here." He got out of bed and draped a throw around her shoulders. "What is it?"

"I got this silly feeling that we were being watched. I know we have security everywhere, but for some reason…I'm sorry. It's just nerves."

~***~

Later that morning, Steven read another letter about Jenkins on the editorial page of the Anchorage Times. The writer opined that because the Snowman hadn't been heard from in a while and no new killings could be attributed to him, he was no longer in Alaska. He must be in West Virginia, like his last letter claimed.

Steven shook his head and crumpled up the paper. No way. The bastard was still here, biding his time, up to his old tricks, and hiding the bodies. Stowy Jenkins would not leave Alaska until his goal was achieved.

He frowned. Something's up. He dropped the crumpled paper into the garbage can so Sarah wouldn't read it and put his coffee cup in the sink. He needed to cut some more firewood to get rid of this tension.

Emma, cleaning the ashes from the fireplace, smiled up at him when he came into the living room. "Let me guess. Getting more wood?"

He smiled back at her. "You know me too well. Where's Sarah?"

"Still sleeping. I wish she would've eaten something before taking a nap," Emma fussed. "I think I'm going to take her some tea and make sure she's all right."

"I'm sure she's fine," Steven said. "She didn't sleep well last night, so she needs her rest."

"I know, but she needs nourishment, too. Was it another nightmare?"

Steven nodded. "She got rid of the headaches, but not the nightmares. I wish I could do more to help her."

"You're here, and for now, that's the best possible thing you can do for her. You're exactly where she needs you to be."

"Thanks, Emma. I hope you're right. Well, I'm going outside. Those logs aren't going to split themselves." And this stress wasn't going away by itself, either.

He had a sick feeling in the bottom of his gut, but no matter how many logs he split, the anxiety grew.

When Sky Quinn arrived several hours later, Steven was still working and covered in sweat. "Son, I've got some bad news," he said.

Steven's body stiffened, and he stacked another log before turning to greet his uncle. "What is it?"

"We've had a visitor." Sky pointed to a rise. "He's gone now, but he was right up there in those trees. Best as I can tell, he's been watching the house for at least two days."

"I thought we had the entire area covered."

"Claude and Andy were securing that section, but he got to them. The bastard slit their throats and left them to the animals. I've had men searching the entire area, but he's long gone."

"Shit." How does she always know? Steven looked toward the house. "Uncle, you should've told me as soon as you discovered them."

"Maybe, but I was worried about Sarah, and I knew you were with her. I thought that was the best option until I knew whether or not he was still on site."

Steven nodded. "I understand. But please, at least give me a heads up."

"I will."

"John needs to know, too, so he can check the surveillance cameras we set up on the haul road. If it's Jenkins, he'll be on camera, and so will his vehicle. We'll start there."

"We already know it was Jenkins. He left this for you." Sky handed him a note.

Steven carefully unfolded the paper. Detective, I see the pregnancy is proceeding well. I found it genuinely touching that you and the little lady still hold hands. Do you miss me, Detective? I broke my promise, but it's nice to see that you haven't. The Snowman

"Uncle, we have to change things."

"What are you thinking?"

"The best way to see the enemy coming is from high ground. We have to move this party to the cave."

Quinn patted him on the back. "Good thinking, son. Let's get the ball rolling."

~~*~~

CHAPTER SIXTY-SEVEN

Better Protection

June 10th

It took four days, but Steven and his men pulled it off. The cave-like cabin at the top of the mountain became their new home, and the second bedroom became a well-stocked birthing room, including a state-of-the-art incubator and a direct computer connection to Sarah's doctor. Although Dr. James made regular visits, she'd also be on 24-hour call the closer they got to the due date. If possible, they'd return to Anchorage for the delivery, but as a contingency plan, a local midwife was also on call.

He knew Sarah's nightmares were because of the constant threat Jenkins posed to their lives, and he did his best to ease those dreams, but every other night, she awoke with a new one. She did her best not to overreact, but he knew she was terrified. Thankful to be there for her, he held her close until she drifted back to sleep.

Despite the nightmares, there were moments when they forgot all about Jenkins and the danger lurking in the shadows, but as Sarah's August 21 due date rapidly approached, Steven's gut told him Jenkins was planning something big.

~***~

"I've got motion-detector cameras and men spread out all over this mountain, and they'll make sure no one crosses the safety net we've established. The only way that man can make it up here is if he's got wings," John Thomas said.

Steven huffed. "Don't put it past him. He's too quiet. We haven't heard a thing since that last note, and the tip lines have gone completely silent. I know the bastard is up to something, but what's he waiting for?" Even as Steven said the words, he already knew the answer. Jenkins wanted Sarah.

"How's Sarah holding up?" John asked.

"She refuses to leave. Maybe she's right."

"I can't see him getting up here."

Steven sighed and bowed his head. "This is torture, and I know that's all part of his plan, but she's been a real trooper." He walked to the rail on the deck. "God, I wish I hadn't married her."

He turned just in time to see Sarah in the doorway, and the look that passed between them was pure pain. She walked away.

"Oh, God," Steven mumbled. He looked at John. "I'll catch up with you later."

~***~

Steven found Sarah curled up on the bed, but he saw no sign of tears. How do you tell the woman you love more than life itself that the words she heard coming out of your mouth weren't meant the way they sounded?

He lay down behind her, curled his body around hers, and nuzzled her neck. "You do realize that you married an idiot."

She turned to face him. "I wouldn't say that. I'd say that I married a man who cares so much, he'd sacrifice everything for the ones he loves. Even his own happiness."

"I don't deserve you, and I know we've had this conversation before, but it's the truth."

"Shut up, handsome, and kiss me."

~~*~~

CHAPTER SIXTY-EIGHT

Found

July 25th

When Stowy made his second foray into the wilderness, he found the population to be restless and even more suspicious of strangers than before. Even though no one bothered him when he ventured closer to the Quaid's' cabin this time, he immediately sensed the game had changed. The security force didn't look particularly vigilant. In fact, they looked downright nonchalant. And lax.

He gazed at the cabin through powerful binoculars and cursed under his breath. The couple posing as Quaid and his wife didn't even look like them. He had half a mind to kill them anyway, just for pissing him off. "Fuck," he muttered. "Back to the drawing board."

Stowy returned to Anchorage to plan his next move. He was determined to get to them, but first, he had to figure out where they were. What if they left the state? Not too likely, but if they did, that wouldn't save them. Nothing was going to keep him from getting his hands on their little bastard. Nothing. If he had to, he'd forge a passport.

One night after a particularly satisfying murder, Stowy had the game-changing epiphany he needed. Gayln Southwick. Chances were that ex-con would know exactly where the elusive couple was hiding. The only man convicted in the kidnapping of Sarah Davis. Southwick only spent a few days in Seward, because his good buddy Steven Quaid pulled some strings and got him transferred. Instead of doing hard time, Southwick did a short stint in a medium-security joint. If anyone had a clue where his good buddy Detective Quaid might be, it'd be this man.

To contact him, Stowy used a common form of communication for most cons. He put a personal ad in the local newspaper, and before the month was out, he found his man.

~***~

Disguised as a pipeline worker, Stowy ambled into the dimly lit Nome saloon and looked around. As soon as he spotted Gayln Southwick sitting at the bar, he walked over and took the stool next to him. "Hey, buddy, how's it going?" he asked.

Gayln, nursing the only drink he could afford to buy, barely glanced at him. "What do you care?"

"Come on. Cheer up!" Stowy said, motioning to the bartender. "A bottle of your best whiskey and two glasses of your best draft." He touched Gayln's shoulder. "Come on, buddy, let's get good and drunk. I'm celebrating."

Gayln finished the last of his drink. "What are we celebrating?"

"I'm going to be a poppa soon. I just found out my girl's pregnant, and I'm on top of the world," Stowy said.

After the bartender brought their drinks, Stowy gave him a hefty tip. "Keep the drafts coming, my good man," he said. "We'll be sitting in one of the booths in the back."

They settled in the booth, and Gayln raised his glass of whiskey. "That's great news. Really. To new life." They clinked glasses. "Do I know you?"

Stowy laughed. "I'd like to say yes, but I guess not. I remember seeing you around at Goose Creek, but I don't think we ever spoke. I take it you got out on good behavior, too?"

"That, and friends in high places, but I'll be on probation forever."

"Sorry if I came on too familiar-like. It's just that I was in the mood to celebrate, and I didn't want to drink alone."

"No problem. I was feeling sorry for myself, so thanks. I appreciate the company…and drinks. What were you in lockup for?"

Stowy shrugged. "I got into a bar fight. It was my first offense, so they went easy on me. Been straight ever since and doing my best to earn some money for my girl and me." He smiled. "And our baby."

"Where is she?"

"In Oregon with her parents. I'm going to stay here and earn as much money as I can before the baby comes. I hope I can pull enough hours to make the sacrifice worth it. How about you? You got any kids?"

Gayln shook his head. "I'm never gonna have a family." He ran his fingers through his hair. "No woman wants a deadbeat like me to father her children."

"Bull. You're a strapping young man. You've got time."

"I am going to be an uncle, though. At least, I hope so. I'm trying to go straight, but I have this bad habit of spending cash faster than I earn it."

"Your brother or your sister?"

Gayln looked at him oddly. "What?"

"You said you were going to be an uncle. Which family member's expecting?"

Gayln laughed. "Neither. It's a friend, someone I've known since we were kids. We used to be like brothers, but my stint in the pokey changed all that. I haven't been in touch with him in ages, but I heard through the grapevine that his wife's expecting."

"You should go talk to him and try to mend your fences. That kind of friendship doesn't come around very often."

"Yeah, I guess." Gayln finished his beer and rose to leave. "Thanks, man. I appreciate the drink, but I'm going to call it a night."

Stowy stood and placed a hand on Gayln's shoulder. "Come on. Don't make me drink alone. Help me finish this bottle, and maybe when we're done, I can help you look up this guy, so you can make things right with him."

Gayln sat back down and accepted another shot. "I don't think that'd be possible right now, but I'll consider it once the baby's born."

Stowy held up his glass for another toast. "To family!"

Stowy was counting on the free-flowing alcohol to loosen Gayln's tongue, and he wasn't disappointed. The informative night came to an end at two in the morning, right after he slipped a sedative into Gayln's last beer. It would've been just as easy to slip something more deadly into his drink, but he decided against it. Why bother? The guy gave him everything he needed, and now that he knew where Quaid was hiding, all he had to do was get there. Besides, he had a much more satisfying kill in mind. Two of them, in fact.

After his last two remaining slaves fulfilled his sick sexual needs, he took great joy in making them fight to the death like a couple of gladiators. Even though they viciously went after each other with knives, neither of them turned on him. Which made him feel like an all-powerful puppet master, and slitting the victor's throat made him feel invincible.

He laid the victor's body on the mattress in her cell. "Thanks for being so accommodating. I told you if you performed perfectly, you'd win your release," he said as he locked the door. "Congratulations. Your spirit is now free."

~~*~~

CHAPTER SIXTY-NINE

Surprise Birthdays

August 9th

"Hurry up, Sarah! The chopper's going to be here any minute." Still carrying her suitcase, Steven hustled back through the cave to their bedroom, but the room was empty. "Sarah? Where are you?"

"In here! In the delivery room. My water broke. Our babies on the way!"

"Shit!" Steven mumbled as he rushed to her side. "Very funny! Come on. It's time to get you off this mountain and back to Anchorage. Dr. James is waiting for us at the cabin."

"Sorry, love, but I'm not kidding."

He dropped the suitcase and gaped at her.

"It's all right, Detective," Dr. James said. "See to your wife and send Elliott back to get me." The doctor smiled at him from the laptop screen. "Now, wash those hands and help your wife get ready to deliver this baby!"

Steven dropped his deer-in-the-headlights expression and started putting their plans into action. "Sorry, doc. I thought...I mean, she's not even due for three more weeks! And you said it'd probably be longer than that."

"That I did, but what can I say? Your wife's in labor now. It usually takes hours for the first baby to come, but with Sarah, we should never expect the expected." She laughed. "Happy birthday, by the way. Are you ready, Sarah?"

"Just about. Give me one more minute." Sarah finished getting situated in the delivery bed and then strapped the cardiotocograph machine's belt across her belly, just as Dr. James had taught her. "Okay. Ready."

Steven turned the machine on, and it immediately began recording and transmitting information about the fetal heartbeat and Sarah's contractions to the doctor. Sarah stuffed a pillow behind her back and took several deep breaths. With her eyes closed, she focused her mind and prepared for another contraction.

"That's it, Sarah. You're doing beautifully," the doctor said. "The baby's heart rate is perfect, but this next contraction is going to hurt, so stay focused."

Sarah whimpered through the contraction but refused to scream. She slowed her breathing and focused her mind on getting her child safely into the world, and the pain finally began to subside.

"Good job!" Dr. James said. "You're doing beautifully, Sarah. Looking at the strength of that contraction, I'd say you're going to be giving birth today. In fact, with the way you're progressing, I wouldn't be surprised to see you pushing soon, so you'd better tell Elliott to fly like the wind to get me there. Otherwise, you'll be on your own. Are you ready to deliver your son, Steven?" Dr. James smiled.

"Hi, Sarah, Steven. I hope you don't mind, but I just had to be here." Dr. Listten waved at them from the laptop. "Elliott left ten minutes ago and should be there any minute."

Sarah and Steven waved back at him. "That's good news. I'll send him back for you as soon as he gets here," Steven said, still looking a little shell-shocked. "But I'm confused. You told us earlier that Sarah was just having Braxton Hicks contractions, and they didn't mean anything. What happened?"

"Relax," Dr. James said. "What happened is your baby decided he was tired of waiting, but everything is going to be just fine. What I need you to do right now is check Sarah's cervix to see if she's fully dilated." She smiled at the expression on his face. "No need to panic. Don't worry. I'll walk you through it," she assured him.

They heard a noise from the other room and felt a sudden breeze. Steven smiled. "Sounds like Elliott's here," he said.

"It's about time!" Steven yelled, his back to the door as he smiled reassuringly at Sarah and pulled on a pair of surgical gloves. "Get your ass back on that chopper and go get the doc. Sarah's in labor!"

Sarah gasped, and her face contorted in abject horror. Before Steven could react, he felt a needle plunge into his neck.

"Sorry, Detective, but this delivery is all mine," Stowy said as Steven's body crumpled to the floor. "Mrs. Quaid, I presume?"

~~*~~

CHAPTER SEVENTY

Birth & Death

August 9th

Sarah reached for the gun she'd hidden beneath a towel on the table beside her, but Stowy was faster. He grabbed her arm and twisted it nearly to the breaking point. Then he laughed when she screamed. "That's much better. All women should scream during childbirth." He released her arm. "I know all about your skills as a sharpshooter, but they're not going to help you this time, sweetheart!"

Stowy tossed her gun to the other side of the room. "We won't be needing this. This is all I need," he said, holding up his razor-sharp hunting knife. "But these are cool, too. I've never used one of these." He selected a scalpel from the array of medical instruments that were lying on the table and examined it. "Think I should use this for the episiotomy?"

He grinned at the horrified expression on her face. "Surprised? Oh, believe me, I know all about how to do an episiotomy. When I found out you were pregnant, I studied everything I need to know about labor and delivery. And do you know why?" He grinned again, watching her face closely. "I've always wanted a son."

Sarah steeled her body and tried not to show the revulsion she was feeling. She refused to give him the satisfaction. And another contraction was starting. A big one.

"What's going on?" Dr. Listten yelled. "Are you okay, Sarah?" He and Dr. James stared at her from the computer screen.

Stowy turned toward the laptop. "Oh. I didn't realize we had company. Oh well. Mother and child are doing dandy. Thanks for asking, but we won't be needing your services today, after all." With a smirk, he slammed the laptop shut.

He was about to fling it across the room when he had a better idea. Why not record it? The revenge of the Snowman would make history, and his fans would love it.

He set the computer back down and switched it on to record. Then he clapped his hands together. "Hear ye! Hear ye! Ladies and gentlemen, it is now time for The Snowman's Show!" He ripped the belt from Sarah's stomach and gave the cardiotocograph a solid kick, crashing it to the floor. "And we won't be needing any of this crap, either. All we need is me and my trusty knife."

Sarah glared at him in silence while flexing her arm and trying to rub the soreness from her throbbing wrist. Then another contraction hit. With a slight gasp, she forced herself to relax and keep her breathing steady, in and out, in and out, as she rode out the pain.

Just as the contraction was ending, Stowy lifted Steven into the wheelchair next to the bed. "You know this will be a lot more fun if Papa's watching." He twisted Steven's head, so he was facing Sarah. "We wouldn't want to deprive him of seeing his son come into the world, now, would we? And as a special added attraction, he'll get to watch his beloved wife bleed to death." He laughed.

"Love this place, by the way," he said as he took in the room. He resituated the wheelchair to give the paralyzed, but still aware, Steven the best view. "It's not on Google maps, you know, and I bet it can't even be seen from a satellite, so great job with the camouflage! I couldn't have done it all without help. Elliott's help was priceless. If not for the Frenchman, I couldn't have found this place."

He grinned. "But don't blame him. He didn't know he was helping me. He thought I was with the FBI." He flashed his fake FBI ID. "Pretty good, huh? A new haircut, clean shave, and an Armani suit, good enough to fool anybody." He shoved the identification back into his pocket and smiled. "By the way, happy birthday, Detective. You're going to love your gifts. It's hard to beat a newborn baby and a dead wife. Don't you just love surprises?"

Stowy's attention snapped back to Sarah, who was quietly fighting through another contraction. "What the hell's the matter with you? Scream, dammit! Scream!" His eyes flashing with anger, he tossed her covers aside, grabbed the scalpel, and carved deep slices in both of her thighs.

Sarah screamed.

"Much better," Stowy said. "And look at all that blood. Your spawn will have the type of entry all children should…a warm pool of their mother's blood to greet them. Don't you agree, Detective?"

He walked to Steven's side. "Well, Detective, are you surprised? To see me, I mean. Remember your old boyhood pal Gayln Southwick? You can thank him for spilling the beans. The guy can't hold his liquor worth a damn." He laughed and then ran his fingers down the length of the scar on Steven's face. "You know, I like that scar. I really do. Maybe I should add a matching one on the other side."

"How did you know about the baby?" Sarah asked.

He turned to her. "Easy. I heard the rumors of your miscarriage last December, and then when I saw you two at the cabin, it was easy enough to guess the due date."

"But why? Why are you doing this? Why do you kill?" she asked.

He laughed. "Because."

"Because?" Sarah said, not understanding his answer.

"Just because," Stowy said. I do what I do just because I can."

Sarah wanted to keep him talking, but she was hit with another contraction. Stowy saw her stiffen. "Another contraction? Good. Unless you want me to do some more cutting, your next screams better bring the house down."

Sarah complied with some bone-chilling howls.

"Oh, my," Stowy said mockingly. "Is our big bad hero detective crying? Look, Mrs. Detective! Your warrior is weeping. The poor dear. What do you think he'll do when I cut his bastard out of your stomach?" He laughed. "I can tell you what he'll do. Not a damned thing! He'll just sit there watching it happen." He cut her nightgown from hem to collar, and then laid his hand on her round belly.

"Hmm, wonder where I should make the cut." He rubbed his chin, then laughed. "Does it matter? " He looked straight at Steven. "Do you think it'll bother me care if the bastard gets nicked?" He laughed harder. "Just imagining your internal reaction to what you're seeing is feeding my lust for her blood." He allowed his hand to circle Sarah's pregnant belly.

The ice-cold touch of his hand on her stomach had Sarah's skin-crawling, yet another contraction was building, and she knew she had to master her emotions. While taking careful breaths, she kept her eyes on the monster.

He grinned. "You can't fool me, little lady. I don't need any fancy machines to tell me you're having another contraction. And so soon, too. I think this little guy will be popping soon." He poked her in the stomach. "And I'd better hear your delight."

Sarah gave it all she had. She was surprised to find that her screams not only allowed her to liberate her emotions, but they also seemed to help alleviate some of the pain. Not in her legs, though. The contraction gradually eased, but the pain and bleeding from her legs were getting worse.

Stuff it inside Sarah, stuff it all inside. Your husband and son need you!

"Now that's what I'm talking about," Stowy crowed. "Keep that up, and we'll get along just fine."

He walked to the other side of the table, where the medical instruments were laid out and looked them over. "These may be fine for some people, but I think I prefer my own tools better." With his hunting knife in his hand, Stowy pointed to Sarah's burgeoning belly. "What do you think, Detective? Right down the middle?" Barely touching her, he lightly ran the tip of the knife down her abdomen.

"Don't worry," he said. "I'm not going to kill your son, but I am going to take him and raise him as my own. I'm sure rescue is on the way, so I'm afraid I'm going to have to speed things up. Then I'll be borrowing that lovely helicopter out there." He looked at Sarah. "As much fun at it'd be to let nature take its course, I'm going to have to take what I want. You'll bleed out oh so slowly, and your weepy warrior will be right here to see you take your last breath. Who knows, maybe the drug will wear off in time for him to kiss the last breath from you?" He turned his gaze back to Steven.

"You see, Detective, I want you to live. We aren't done. Not by a long shot. Our journey isn't over, and I'm having too much fun to end it now. I am curious, though. Where do you think you'll find me raising your son? What part of the world? And how old do you think he'll be when you finally track us down?"

Sarah felt the next contraction building, but this one was different. More intense, and it felt like every cell in her body was ordering her to push. To gain control, she began breathing in short huffs like Dr. James taught her.

Stowy noticed. "Looks like it's time, Detective!" He moved toward the end of the table and spread Sarah's legs. He stood and stared as though he thought the baby would come flying out. "Baby's trying to come the old-fashioned way, but I don't have time to wait." As he spoke, his eyes were on Steven, and his knife was pointed at Sarah's stomach. Then he quickly glanced at Sarah.

"Count your lucky stars, dear lady. If we had more time, I would've taken you. Fucked the very life out of you. Your blood and that perfect ass would've have been the icing on my cake. I've heard sex can bring on the birthing process, but look at you. Almost ready to pop the bastard out." He laughed and glanced Steven's way. "Our coupling would have been for the benefit of your dear husband. But believe me, sweet lady, it would've been the highlight of your day, too!"

"No, this is my highlight!" Sarah said.

Stowy laughed. "Exactly, no. I mean." He looked at her with the question unasked but written all over his face.

Sarah grinned and squeezed the trigger of her Glock.

The bullet hit him between the eyes. Jenkins dropped the knife, and for a few seconds, stood there with a bald expression of shock and disbelief on his face.

Then he crumpled to the floor.

"No, over YOUR dead body, asshole!"

Sarah set the gun on the counter and smiled at her husband. "See? I told you hiding guns all over the house would pay off. Although I will admit, the one behind my back was giving me fits with these contractions." She took a deep breath. "And here comes another one!"

After huffing through the contraction, Sarah grabbed a clean sheet off the counter by the bed and draped it over and between her legs, but it was soon drenched in her blood. "So much for giving her our son a nice clean place to land. So much for sterile." She shrugged, we'll have to do the best with what we have," she assured her husband.

She stuffed another pillow behind her back when the next contraction started. "Ahh, that's better. So much more comfortable without a gun shoved in it. " She said and winked at Steven. Dealing with the pain of birth and the evil threatening them while a weapon stabbed her in the back had been almost unbearable, yet strangely comforting.

Her entire body clenched, determined to push the baby out, with or without her help. She took a deep breath and pushed as hard as she could. After three more hard pushes, their son made his appearance.

And he came out crying. Sarah lifted him to her chest and kissed his forehead. After clearing his airway of mucus, she inspected his tiny body. "He is absolutely perfect," She told her husband. Then cooed words of love as she cleaned his little body. And with the skill of an expert, cut his umbilical cord.

Sarah smiled at Steven and saw the pride in his eyes. "Isn't he beautiful? I think the name we've chosen is perfect…Steven Tiama Quaid. Tiama means thunder, and I'd say he's had one thunderous entrance into the world." She put their son to her breast, and he immediately began to suckle. "I need to get the afterbirth to deliver, and this is supposed to help." She smiled again. "He's got your appetite."

She smiled down at their beautiful new baby boy, "So perfect. He looks just like you." She hoped the smile on her face and the love she held for them both showed clearly for her paralyzed husband. When a tear slipped down his cheek, she knew – Steven knew.

Twenty minutes later, Sarah was sitting in the rocking chair next to her still immobile husband and cradling their son when all hell broke loose in the heavens.

"Sounds like the Calvary's arrived," Sarah said.

She knew Steven was smiling because she could see it in his eyes, but his body still wasn't responding.

Men in uniform, guns drawn, stormed into the room and stopped short when they entered. It was quite a sight…a woman in white sitting in a rocking chair with a newborn baby, a man slumped in a wheelchair, a hospital gurney covered in blood, and a dead man lying at their feet with a bullet hole the middle of his forehead.

Dr. Grayson strolled in. A smile lit his face. "Saved him again, did you?" he said, kneeling in front of Sarah.

"Well, you know how it is. He saves the world, and it's my job to save him." She gave her old friend a weak smile.

"Just as God intended," Dr. Grayson said, standing to face his men. He pointed to Jenkins' body. "Get this garbage out of here." They jumped to comply.

Sarah touched Dr. Grayson's hand. "Please help, Steven. That creep gave him a paralyzing drug."

Grayson knelt again and opened his medical bag. "I most certainly will. We found your helicopter pilot with the same problem." He gave Steven a quick shot and patted him on the shoulder. "It'll just take a minute or two." Then he turned back to Sarah. "Now, young lady, how are you?"

She removed the blanket from her lap and whispered, "I tried, but I couldn't stop the bleeding."

Dr. Grayson yelled, "Clear that bed and get her in it. Now!"

He took the baby from Sarah's arms and said, "I've got him. Just let these men help you." The doctor carried the newborn to the incubator sitting in the corner. "You rest and stay warm right here, little man. I have to take care of that stubborn woman you'll call Mommy!"

~***~

That evening, the front-page headline announced IT'S A BOY! And featured a picture of the beaming mother, father, and their new son being escorted from the National Guard Transport when it landed in Anchorage.

On page two, the death of the Snowman was also announced, but with much less fanfare.

~~ THE END~~

Thank You!

Thank you for reading *Murder, Just Because*. If you enjoyed the story, please consider leaving a review. If you are interested in reading more about Detective Steven Quaid, you can learn more about the series detailing his most significant cases at Amazon.com

A Series Set in Alaska

Light is a fleeting moment in the frozen north that is Alaska. Although the sun shines brightly during the Summer Solstice. Detective Steven Quaid struggles to hold on to what he holds dear during life's darkest moments, his love for family, and professional achievement. Will a murderous stalker, a self-proclaimed Lucifer resurrected, or insidious obsession prove more powerful than this dedicated detective?

Several life-threatening situations. One determined man.

Find the entire series at Amazon.com
Murder, Madness & Love
Memories of Murder
Murder & Obsession
The Snowman
&
Murder, Just Because

Acknowledgments

If not for Susan Flett Swiderski, this book would not have seen the light of day. She spurred me on when I doubted it's worth. She was my beta reader turned editor turned proofreader, and she's excellent at each of those jobs. But more importantly, she was my personal cheerleader through more than just the writing of the book. Her dedication to me and the book came at a time when her own life was significant madness. She has no idea how much I value her friendship or her help with this book! Thank you, Susan, you are my hero, a Rockstar of serious magnitude and a friend I'll cherish always!

About the Author

Yolanda Renée

In my adventurous youth, Alaska called to me, and I answered. I learned to sleep under the midnight sun, survive in below zero temperatures, and hike the Mountain Ranges. I've traveled from Prudhoe Bay to Valdez, and the memories are some of my most valued. Despite my wandering spirit, I achieved my educational goals, married, and have two handsome sons.

Writing is now my focus, and my newest adventure was a recent move to Myrtle Beach, South Carolina.

Look for
A Passion for Murder
the 6th Detective Quaid novel

Please connect with me at:
Amazon Author Page:
http://tinyurl.com/j6wpqhz

Blog: Defending the Pen
http://yolandarenee.blogspot.com/

Facebook: Yolanda Renée
https://www.facebook.com/yolandarenee

Twitter: @yolandarenee
https://twitter.com/yolandarenee

Goodreads: Yolanda Renée
http://tinyurl.com/he2tjge

Pinterest: Yolanda Renée
https://www.pinterest.com/renee0240/

yolandarenee@hotmail.com

www.ingramcontent.com/pod-product-compliance
Lightning Source LLC
Chambersburg PA
CBHW070853180626
46817CB00003B/753